PRAISE FOR
UNIVERSITY OF DOOM

"A fun and zany mad science adventure."
— Richelle Mead, #1 International bestselling author

"Mario Acevedo's work is simply delightful, and UNIVERSITY OF DOOM is immediately engaging and wickedly twisted. Professor Moriarty, Dr. Frankenstein, and a kid trying to live up to his potential. What more could a reader want?"
— Kevin J. Anderson, *New York Times* bestselling author of the Dan Shamble, Zombie P.I. series

UNIVERSITY OF DOOM
Ludimus Deus

UNIVERSITY OF DOOM
A NOVEL OF THE PRE-APOCALYPSE

MARIO ACEVEDO

UNIVERSITY OF DOOM

Cover art by Kirk DouPonce
Cover design by Kirk DouPonce and Joshua Viola
University of Doom logo by Amy McKnight
Typesets and formatting by Dustin Carpenter

A Hex Publishers Book
Published & Distributed by Hex Publishers, LLC
PO BOX 298
Erie, CO 80516

www.HexPublishers.com
www.UniversityofDoom.com

Joshua Viola, Publisher

Print ISBN-10: 0-9964039-8-1
Print ISBN-13: 978-0-9964039-8-6
Ebook ISBN-10: 0-9964039-9-X
Ebook ISBN-13: 978-0-9964039-9-3
First Hex Edition: 2017
University of Doom previously published by Mario Acevedo June 2016

10 9 8 7 6 5 4 3 2 1

Printed in the U.S.A.

To my crazy artist friends.

ACKNOWLEDGEMENTS

Thanks much to Josh Viola and Hex Publishers for taking this project on. The best parts of this book are the handiwork of my critique group: Jeanne Stein, Warren Hammond, Angie Hodapp, Margie and Tom Lawson, Aaron Michael Ritchey, Tamra Monahan, and Terry Wright. I also have to give props to a bunch of other people, mostly writers, for their support and friendship: Mark Graham, Manuel Ramos, Rudy G., Quincy Allen, Eric Matelski, Jen Mosquera, Eric Jaenike, Lighthouse Writers Workshops, and Rocky Mountain Fiction Writers. And I can't forget my family: Alex, Emil, Sylvia, and Janet.

CHAPTER
ONE

A dead badger lay on Alfonso Frankenstein's lab table.

But the badger wouldn't stay dead for long.

Besides the standard electrodes attached to the creature's neck, Alfonso planned to juice the experiment by sliding a third electrode up the badger's butt.

He turned on the PortaBoy embalming machine and pumped the badger with Dipple's Oil—the fabled ingredient for reanimating the dead.

This was going to be an easy mid-term exam in Cadaver Recomposition at the Dr. Moreau Junior Academy, the school for aspiring mad scientists, the children of the evil geniuses at the University of Doom. Students and faculty alike, prided themselves in pushing science and engineering into the realm of the supernatural, beyond the limits of physics, chemistry, biology, and common sense.

Alfonso glanced to the university motto chiseled into the marble above the lab threshold.

LUDIMUS DEUS

We play God.

Everyone else in class had selected harmless creatures: chickens, bunnies, or small iguanas for their lab experiment. Alfonso had chosen a badger. Proof he was the best evil genius in the eighth grade. After all, as a Frankenstein, his family was the most famous of all revenant animators, notorious for playing God.

To pass the test, Alfonso's undead subject had to simply roll its eyes, curl its toes, maybe smack its jaws. This assignment was as easy as counting to ten.

The electrode gauge held steady at forty amperes. Alfonso was about to insert the third electrode when the badger's eyes popped open. They brightened from a dull pus white to danger yellow. Gray-green saliva frothed over razor-sharp teeth and dripped from the steel cage muzzling its snout.

The badger wasn't supposed to come to life so quickly. Or so mean. Alfonso's smugness melted into panic.

Matted, spiky fur bristled around the badger's neck like a collar of barbed wire. Long claws slashed the steel tabletop.

Nervous perspiration steamed Alfonso's safety glasses. Sweat puddled inside his rubber gloves. The third electrode slipped from his hand and it bounced, sparking, on the lab table.

Not only had he chosen the largest badger from the necropsy crypt, he had replaced his student-grade Dipple's Oil with industrial-strength from his father's lab.

And worse still, Alfonso had combined velociraptor DNA in the solution so God knows what vicious freak-of-nature he had created. The badger strained against the leather belts anchoring its paws to the table, and one-by-one, the rivets started to work loose.

Alfonso figured he had a minute—maybe—before the badger broke free and rampaged through class.

Something tapped his shoulder.

Alfonso jumped around, startled.

His best friend, Greg Kaminski, was at the next table, a rooster splayed on his reanimation tray. Greg was as tall as Alfonso, but with a thicker middle and a square head with a knobby chin. A shock of unruly hair stuck out from his scalp, the thick yellow strands resembling a frazzled cable of gold wires. A mechanical arm jutted from the tangle of servos and electric cords attached to a frame on Greg's back. Long steel fingers hovered over Alfonso. An ozone smell overpowered the odor of formaldehyde. Greg's face was marred with scratches and bruises, which always happened whenever he tried out a new mechanical gizmo.

He said, "Yo."

Alfonso swallowed his nervousness and answered with a nonchalant, "Hey."

The mechanical appendage wiggled its fingers. Greg smiled. "Need a hand, buddy?"

Alfonso reached behind his back and fumbled with the rheostat controlling the badger's electrodes. "Why do you ask? Everything is under control."

"Sure about that?"

"Positive. If there is anyone in class who knows anything about mad science, it's me."

"Of course," Greg rolled his eyes and his mechanical hand opened toward the ceiling. "Like the time *someone* borrowed his dad's genome replicator and installed the chromosome array configurator upside down. Ended up with a basement full of seven-inch roaches with heads growing out their backs. Jeez, can you say rookie mistake?"

"The replicator was more complicated than I thought."

"Kinda like your badger, huh?"

"Stick to your chicken, okay?"

The mechanical arm added emphasis to Greg's shrug as he turned away. "You need an assist, holler."

The zombie-badger whipped its head back-and-forth, growling, snarling, hissing like a bomb about to explode. Alfonso yanked on the electrode cables attached to the frenzied creature's neck.

Luckily, the instructor, Dr. Golem, wasn't in the lab. Alfonso couldn't risk the instructor helping him—or worse, the situation getting so bad that Alfonso had to hit the Panic Button—because that would mean he had lost control of the experiment.

His internal alarm screaming, Alfonso dropped the cables and grabbed his portal tablet. He dragged a thumb across its screen and tapped the side.

A second later, the university seal appeared, a pyramid enclosing an open left hand with an eye staring from the palm.

The invisible beam of an alpha-wave neural scanner massaged his brain as it surfed from his frontal lobe to the center of his gray matter.

He pulsed a thought to access his homework.

<lab notes>

The university seal dissolved, replaced by his lab notes. He rapid fired thoughts to flip through the pages to the emergency index.

All blank. *Figures.*

The zombie-badger tore one foreleg free. It ripped the muzzle off its face and flung it to the floor.

The badger snapped its head left and right and pulled the electrode cables loose. It chewed through the other leg restraints. The fiery-eyed mini-monster turned toward Alfonso and bared its slimy fangs.

Alfonso looped the electrode cables around the zombie-badger's neck and yanked hard. He pinned the berserk creature to the lab table where it snarled, spit gobs of saliva, twisted, and tangled itself in the cables.

"Having problems, Einstein?" taunted the girl from across the aisle, Lilith Vampira. Her bleached-corpse complexion gave a translucent glow. Safety goggles clung to her face. Thick eyelashes hooded large pastel green eyes that blinked from either side of a narrow nose. Lilith's tangles of shiny black hair hung past her thin shoulders and melted into her smoky-black lacey gown. She leaned close and jeered. "You screw up this lab and guess who'll get top honors?" She tapped a razor-tipped gold fingernail against her bony chest. "Everyone in this school knows I am the smartest evil genius in class."

"The second smartest," Alfonso replied, grunting and huffing to hold the badger down. "And the meanest, spider face."

The veins in Lilith's temple pulsed and turned a darker blue. Black widow spiders crept from her hair. They formed a crown across her bangs and reared menacingly on their hind legs.

Alfonso struggled to keep the crazed badger under control. If it escaped the campus, this could be the start of the zombie plague.

The zombie plague? The end of civilization. Imagine being the evil genius responsible for the Apocalypse. Major bragging points. Could mean extra credit.

The downside, he wouldn't live to see it.

"Lilith, I can't waste time arguing with you." Alfonso gasped with effort. The badger was really strong. "This thing gets loose, and things could get really *bad.*"

"Yeah, yeah. You don't have the I.Q." Her arachnid entourage shook their round bottoms at him. "For all I know, you injected the corpse with wonder-caffeine." Lilith gave him the stink eye—jungle-spider green—which looked way magnified and scary behind her goggles. "Like you haven't done that before." She returned her attention to the black bunny specimen on her table.

The zombie-badger gnawed through the last cable and sprang to the floor. Alfonso jumped up on his table. The undead fur bag circled him, growling and chomping on the table legs and his lab chair.

Lilith had been watching. Her face went so pale it made the whites of her eyes look sulfur yellow. The spiders tunneled into her hair. She retreated to the other side of her lab table, gliding as if on the backs on snakes and levitated to the top in a swirl of inky lace and curls of black hair.

Maybe it was time to hit the Panic Button. The teacup-sized button jutted from the front wall between a holographic poster of monster anatomy and a chart of the Periodic Table, showing all 122 elements, including the newest: Doomsdaysium and Annihilatium.

The badger stopped, sniffed, and pounced on Greg's table.

Greg staggered backwards, the fingers of his mechanical arm swiping through empty air.

The badger bit the rooster specimen and darted away, feathers clumped to its snout.

The rooster sat up, eyes dulled with zombie-ness, gray-green slime bubbling from its neck wound and beak. The zombie-rooster pecked at its restraints and broke loose. The bird fluttered to the next table, bit an iguana, infecting it.

The undead-iguana worked free and skittered away to attack the next table in a domino effect of zombie infestation.

Within a minute, the laboratory was overrun with revenant specimens darting and careening between the tables.

The other students had taken refuge atop their tables and fended off the zombie assault by pelting the creatures with lab equipment. Beakers and bottles shattered on the floor.

Alfonso bounded from table to table for the front of the room. Zombified iguanas and bunnies snapped at him.

His fingers were about to touch the Panic Button when his right leg was jerked from behind and he face-planted the table.

The zombie-badger had snagged Alfonso's boot, and it jerked his leg to keep him down.

He kicked with his other boot, smacking the badger on the nose. It let go and left a fang stuck in his heel.

Alfonso pushed up to his hands and knees, leapt forward, and punched the Panic Button.

CHAPTER
TWO

R ed alarm lights flashed.

Panels in the ceiling opened.

Yellow Civil Defense klaxons swung down and emitted wails so loud Alfonso covered his ears and gritted his teeth.

The lab door jerked open and Dr. Golem stomped into the room.

The alarm lights reflected off the top of his smooth bulb-shaped head. Intense blue-flame eyes peered through the circular lenses of his steel-rimmed spectacles. The high mandarin collar of his starched lab coat pushed up around his scrawny neck. His teeth were bared in a perpetual grimace, showing the lingering pain of a bio-alchemy accident. That accident had also left him with prosthetic steel claws for a right hand. A black rubber glove covered his left hand, which clutched an ice axe.

He flicked a wall switch with his claw hand. The sirens ground to a whisper, went silent, and retracted into the ceiling. The overhead panels snapped closed, but the alarm lights continued to flash.

The zombie-badger charged the doctor.

He raised the ice axe and whacked the badger, spiking it to the floor. "Never fails," he muttered, "happens every semester."

The remaining zombie creatures ducked under the tables and chairs.

Dr. Golem used his claws to whisk a kerchief from his coat's breast pocket. "Everybody, take a deep breath."

Alfonso and the other students gulped and pinched their nostrils. They were familiar with the drill: E.U.R.A.B.E.—Extermination of Unwanted Re-animated Biological Entities.

The doctor pressed the kerchief to his nose. With his left hand, he fished a key fob from his trousers and pressed the remote.

Vents along the floorboards beeped and clicked open. Thick orange mist jetted from the vents. *Poly-organic nuclear acid vapor.*

The acrid mist made Alfonso's eyes water. He watched in fascination from atop the table. The vapor poured over the floor like a ghostly syrup, swirled around the doctor's heavy rubber boots, and surrounded the zombie critters.

Black smoke hissed from the little miscreants, and their tiny mouths gaped in terror. Feathers and skin crinkled into ash and sloughed away, revealing flesh that glopped from skeletons toppling into the poisonous fog.

Dr. Golem glanced about to survey the annihilation. Nodding in satisfaction that all the re-animated specimens were accounted for, he again pressed the remote.

The alarm lights quit flashing. The orange mist got sucked into the vents.

Another mist, lilac blue, swept through the room and back to the vents. Piles of bones, polished white by the acid, and gleaming shards of broken glass littered the floor.

Alfonso and his fellow students relaxed. The room smelled April fresh.

The doctor lowered the kerchief. His mouth opened as if he was about to speak, but he stopped and looked to his left.

Lilith Vampira stood on her table, razor-tipped finger aimed at Alfonso, her crown of spiders also pointing with their spindly legs.

Dr. Golem turned to Alfonso and noticed him by the Panic Button. "Mr. Frankenstein, I'd be surprised if *you* weren't the one responsible for this disaster."

Alfonso slipped off the table. This incident was going to be expensive. Like the time he dropped a micro-fission cherry bomb in Ms. Igneous' coffee. He had to say he was sorry and worked all summer to buy her a new to-go cup. And desk.

He stepped around the bones and shattered glass.

The doctor stuffed the kerchief clumsily into his pocket with his prosthesis. "Class dismissed. We'll try the lab again tomorrow. Be careful as you gather your belongings." He waved his claws. "Remember, safety first."

Alfonso decided to call his father. Better that Dr. Frankenstein first hear about this disaster from him than the headmaster.

Whispered catcalls followed him. "Way to go, Alfonso. Now we gotta do this lab all over."

When he arrived at his table, something hard punched his shoulder.

Greg's mechanical arm pulled away, the steel fingers curled into a fist. His friend grinned. "Yo, that was awesome."

Alfonso returned a smile. *It was awesome.* He took off his goggles and gloves and dropped them on the table.

He picked up his portal tablet and projected a thought.

<message to Dr. Eugino Frankenstein>

Alfonso's full name appeared on the black screen, then morphed into the university seal which dissolved into glowing orange letters.

ACCESS DENIED

Alfonso frowned. How could he not have access to his dad? Child-to-parent communication was Tip-Top Two priority. Only a nuclear attack or the escape of tyrannosaurus clones was a higher priority.

What could be wrong? The university network was made to withstand a ten thousand tetra-joule electro-magnetic pulse, a magnitude eight hacker attack, even a type B42 hostile alien intrusion.

So why couldn't he, a middle-school student, log on?

Stupid network.

ACCESS DENIED? That only happened if you were considered a security risk. What thirteen-year-old, even he, could be such a risk?

Alfonso pulsed another thought.

Again. ACCESS DENIED

Followed by: SYSTEM QUARANTINE

The words disappeared, and his portal screen went gray with static. The university had shut him out.

Alfonso became light-headed with confusion. SYSTEM QUARANTINE meant the worst. Possible expulsion from the university campus. Expulsion meant banishment from the world of twisted academia and evil genius. For a future mad scientist, there was no worse fate.

His knees weakened as if the growing dread was a mountain of problems pressing down on his shoulders.

What had he done to deserve expulsion? Couldn't be because of the badger. He had done worse. Like the time he accidentally released a school of flying piranhas into the pterodactyl hatchery.

Maybe all his stunts had caught up to him.

"Mr. Frankenstein," Dr. Golem said in a grim tone. "Alfonso."

Alfonso looked to the front of the lab. He pointed to himself. "Me?"

Lilith sneered. "No, the other Alfonso Frankenstein."

Dr. Golem motioned with his glove.

Alfonso walked awkwardly from his table. He felt the gaze of every set of eyes in the room: from the students filing out of the lab; Dr. Golem's; plus those on the back shelves floating in the hyper-stasis jars.

"Mr. Kaminski," Dr. Golem said. "Could you please shut the door?"

Greg teetered through the doorway, unbalanced by the contraption on his back. His robotic arm groped for the doorknob, scratched the door and finally clicked it shut.

Dr. Golem pointed to the chair beside a front table. Alfonso sat.

The doctor's quivering left hand brought folded papers from inside his coat. "There is an inquiry into your father."

Inquiry. Your father. The words were hammer blows to Alfonso's heart. He had spent his entire life on this campus and knew that an inquiry was as feared as getting the Barsoomian Desert plague. This explained ACCESS DENIED and SYSTEM QUARANTINE.

Alfonso swallowed and forced a question around the dreaded word. "What kind of *inquiry?*"

Dr. Golem's complexion turned the dead color of gray swamp ice. "The university faculty board has convened an academic tribunal. The charges are very serious."

Charges?

The room seemed to tilt and Alfonso gripped the sides of his chair to steady himself. "How serious?"

"The complaint includes nine counts of playing God."

"Playing God?" The confusion in Alfonso's head formed a haze that grew thicker and murkier by the second. None of this made sense. "That's the university motto. *Ludimus Deus.*"

A darker gray tint flushed through Dr. Golem's face. "Your father will explain the specifics. Meanwhile, until the inquiry is completed and the outcome decided, you'll be reassigned to individual studies."

Alfonso could barely hear over the pounding in his ears. *Individual studies?* Only the worst of the students were assigned to individual studies. Why was this happening? Alfonso gasped for breath as if the room had been subjected to great pressure, unyielding as concrete.

He inhaled, his mouth gnawing at the air, and held his breath until his nerves calmed.

He at last exhaled and asked, "But why? What have I done?" Alfonso didn't want to say the next words, he felt like a traitor, but he blurted them out anyway. "The inquiry is about my father, not me."

"You are both Frankensteins. The rules are clear. Gather your things and report to the headmaster."

Alfonso looked to the lab door. "What about my friends?"

Dr. Golem's tone remained without emotion. "They will be instructed not to talk to you."

His father under investigation. For that, Alfonso was removed from class. His friends taken from him. How much more devastating could this get?

Tears collected in Alfonso's eyes and his vision blurred. His nose got moist. He didn't want to speak because that would unlock the last of his self-control and the tears and the snot and the blubbering would explode out of him.

The doctor's claws snapped over a box of shop towels on the table and plucked one.

Alfonso took the towel and blotted his eyes and nose. He fought to keep his voice even. "This is so unfair."

Dr. Golem's left hand trembled and the claws on his right clicked spastically. "Heed this lesson, young Mr. Frankenstein." The skin shrank tight around the bones of the doctor's face to show every grotesque detail of his misshapen skull. "I was once handsome as you. Tell me again that life is unfair. For you, this lesson is only the beginning."

CHAPTER
THREE

"Well son, this is home." Dr. Eugino Frankenstein pointed out their pickup truck's left window.

Alfonso felt too sick to look. This could never be home. The University of Doom was home.

The day his dad had told him that they were asked to leave the university—kicked out actually—Alfonso became delirious with shock. Then anger burned like fire ants stinging his heart.

His dad never gave a reason why he lost his job. He only said it was, "Politics. Being accused of playing God means the university turned against me. When you get older you'll understand."

Alfonso was practically fourteen. How much older would he have to be to understand?

In the weeks after the bad news, Alfonso wanted to tear up his room and yell at his dad about the injustice of it all. He even thought of running away. Maybe another family at the university would adopt him so he could stay where he belonged.

Alfonso could never forget the beautiful campus of the University of Doom with its pastoral and wooded grounds—surrounded by a perimeter guarded by man-eating Venus flytraps and scorpion-hyena mutations.

His heart sagged with homesickness. The university was supposed to last forever and never go away. Alfonso never guessed that it would be him going away instead.

The afternoon sun gave his dad's face a leathery patina. A scarred dent marked the bridge of his nose. His five o'clock shadow glinted like the ends of cut wire.

"We'll be okay." His dad turned from the house and gave one of his this-will-getter-better smiles. The ridge along his brow hooded his eyes.

Alfonso lowered his gaze. His dad would probably give one of those smiles even if they were getting sucked through a black hole in outer space. No, things weren't getting better at all.

"Cheer up, son. We're Frankensteins. Don't forget that."

How could Alfonso forget he was a Frankenstein? That was the reason they were outcasts.

Alfonso looked out the window of the pickup to what was to be their new home. The house was a split-level with a gabled roof of pistachio-green asphalt shingles. The color looked all wrong against the chocolate brown trim and the mustard yellow siding.

A rusted swamp cooler perched at an angle on the roof. Tire ruts crisscrossed the patchy lawn. The uneven driveway led to a doublewide garage door hanging crooked. Weeds sprouted around the porch and through cracks in the driveway and sidewalk. The house was even uglier than the others up and down the street.

This wasn't a home. It was a target for a ninety gigawatt blast from a neutrino disintegrator.

The harsh sunlight pressing at Alfonso through the windshield made him woozy. He closed his eyes and tried happy thoughts to make himself feel better. Chemistry beakers and embalming machines. Midnights helping at the reanimation tables. Monster fishing with electric harpoons in the Lake of Terror.

But those were memories from growing up at the University of Doom, dreamy images stolen from a time that no longer existed.

The queasiness became a deep sadness, deeper than he'd felt even when they left their concrete bunker home, 13 Nousferatu Lane, in campus family housing.

This just...this just...he couldn't think of the right word. Alfonso kept his head down to hide that he was wiping his eyes as he thought back to those final bleak days at the university.

After three weeks of secret deliberations, the academic tribunal issued its judgment. Dr. Frankenstein was dismissed as the head of the Doctoral Candidate Review Board and let go from his job teaching advanced gene splicing and apocalyptic eugenics.

Let go.

Terminated.

FIRED.

Accepting their fate was the hardest ordeal of this catastrophe. To see his dad humiliated by the faculty was like watching a bear getting nipped to death by wiener dogs.

Dr. Frankenstein leaned his muscular bulk against the driver's door. He sniffled. "There's tissue in the glove box, son. Hand me a couple."

Alfonso opened the glove box. A tangle of wire cadaver hookups spilled out. Rejuvenation neck bolts clattered to the floor. Alfonso sorted through a stack of papers and envelopes and found the small package of tissues. He took a couple for his dad and for himself.

His dad dabbed his eyes and blew his nose. "I didn't figure on the pollen count. Guess it got to you, too." He laid his big hand on Alfonso's head and mussed his hair.

Alfonso dried his tears and wiped his nose. "Yeah, it's pretty bad."

His father had explained the sacrifices they'd have to make. They sold most of their belongings. His dad bought this old Dodge pickup truck and told Alfonso not to expect a fancy home. That part he got right exactly.

If they were moving into this crummy house, they might as well be marooned on a desert island. No, wait. A desert island was surrounded by an ocean and full of fish and crabs. That would be cool.

The desert then. But wait. The desert had scorpions and poisonous snakes and Alfonso could make a solar still to recycle pee into drinking water. That was disgusting but a cool disgusting.

How about a desert planet? That would mean space travel and that's the coolest of all, recycled pee or not.

No, moving here wasn't at all cool. Not to this broken down house in suburbia.

Suburbia. Might as well have been Siberia except that at least frozen Russia had legends of awesome reanimation labs.

A semi-truck pulling a large moving trailer halted with a hiss beside them. The weight of even more sadness pressed upon Alfonso. Soon they'd be unpacking and planting themselves into this wretched neighborhood.

His dad popped the door and got out of the pickup. He guided the moving truck against the opposite curb. The driver presented a clipboard. The doctor whisked though a pad of forms and signed along the bottom.

Alfonso stepped out of the pickup and onto a lawn of the house across the street from his.

The neighborhood with its rows of cookie-cutter houses, cookie-cutter cars, and cookie-cutter gardens seemed so alien. He didn't belong here. *He didn't want to belong here.*

For once, the unknown scared him. How bad would it get?

"Hey, new guy."

The voice came from behind. Alfonso turned.

A girl stood on the sidewalk. She wore shorts and a colored T-shirt. Her hair fell in lazy curls past her shoulders and was the same brassy-blond color as Greg Kaminski's. She looked Alfonso's age and stared at him with curiosity like he'd just grown out of a giant Petri dish.

She tossed a buff-colored sphere the size of an orange in her right hand. "Hey neighbor, you play ball?"

Play ball? What did that mean? Alfonso was sure they'd all speak the same language—they were still in

America—but he had no idea what she meant. "You mean play a game with a ball?"

The girl rolled her eyes. "Yeah, that's what I said. Play ball. Show me your stuff." She gripped the ball in her hand, said, "Catch," and reared back to hurl the ball at Alfonso.

The ball shot at him in a blur. Alfonso put his hands up to protect his face but it was too late. The ball smacked his nose, the pain blinded him, and Alfonso crumpled to the ground.

CHAPTER
FOUR

Alfonso staggered up from the grass, his face pinched in agony.

The hard leather ball rolled between his feet. He closed his eyes and touched the bridge of his nose. Wherever his fingers pressed, it felt like fire.

"Alfonso, Alfonso," his father yelled and approached in a rush of stamping feet. His big arms scooped around Alfonso.

"I didn't mean it," the girl said. "I thought he would catch the ball. I didn't throw it hard. It was an easy pitch."

Alfonso squinted at the girl. He wanted her to shrivel into a leaf and blow away. Less than a half hour in the suburbs and already he had an enemy. *Great.*

The girl peered up at Dr. Frankenstein through the tops of her eyes. She rubbed her hands along the sides of her shorts. "Is there anything I can do to help?"

Alfonso's dad replied, "There's a cooler and a roll of paper towels behind the seat of my pickup. Bring them, please."

He yanked out his shirttail and dabbed Alfonso's nose. The pain was like that ball hitting him again. Alfonso winced then held still. His father pinched Alfonso's nostrils and pulled his hand away. There was a spot of blood on the cloth.

The girl carried a roll of paper towels and held the plastic handle of a gallon-sized metal cylinder. "You mean this cooler?" Vapor swirled from a crust of frost on the cylinder. The stenciled letters on the side read: Oakridge Weapons Lab. US Department of Energy.

His father pointed to a spot by his foot. "Set it there."

The girl put the cylinder down. She whisked a length of towels from the roll and ripped it loose. His father loosened the wing nuts along the rim of the cylinder's top. He opened the lid and reached inside. He pulled out two small bottles of orange juice and a baggie holding a frozen gerbil. He wrapped the baggie in the towels he took from the girl.

She leaned close. "What is that?"

Reanimation subject, what else?

"Fish bait," his father answered. He put the frozen mass in Alfonso's hand. "Hold this against your nose."

Alfonso did as his father told him. The cool wetness eased the pain.

The girl's eyes went from Alfonso to his father. She squinted one eye and tilted her head. "Why are you using fish bait? I can get ice."

Dr. Frankenstein replied, "This will do."

The girl turned her attention back to Alfonso. She was slender, with big eyes. Physically, she reminded Alfonso of Lilith Vampira. They had similar builds but this girl had purple-gray eyes and a tanned skin with a red stripe of peeling sunburn across her cheeks and the bridge of her nose. Plus this girl gave Alfonso an expression he had never seen on Lilith: compassion.

"It looks really swollen," she said. "Might want to take him to a doctor."

His father replied, "I am a doctor. He'll be all right."

The girl straightened. Her brow creased in puzzlement. "You're a doctor?" She pointed at the house. "And you live there?" As in, *that dump.*

"Things happen."

The girl gave an understanding nod. "You got laid off, huh?"

"Why would you say that?"

"My dad's been laid off three times and that's how he explains it to our relatives. 'Things happen.'" The girl scoped out their pickup and the moving truck. "Where are you guys from?"

Alfonso watched his father to see how he would answer. Those outside the world of mad science were the *la mano destre,* Italian for "the right hand." It was a play on the joke that the right hand did not know what the left hand was doing. Those in the world of mad science were *la mano sinistra,* the sinister or left hand. The truth about mad science and especially the University of Doom had to be kept from *la mano destre.*

"We come from upstate."

Alfonso smiled. *Clever answer, Dad.*

"Upstate?" The girl made air quotes. "Around here, when we say upstate we mean the state prison. You're not..."

His father's cheeks reddened. "I'm no convict. I *am* a doctor. I worked at a small college."

"No need to explain." She waved a hand and struggled to keep a polite face. Braided strings dangled from her wrist. "I had an uncle who did time. Things happen."

"Nothing like that happened."

The girl stared at Alfonso's dad and blinked. She gave a tight smile.

His father offered orange juice to the girl. She said no thanks. Alfonso didn't want one either. He adjusted the frozen gerbil against his nose to keep pressure on the tender spots. His father put the bottles of juice back in the cylinder, tightened the wing nuts, and grasped the handle. He stood and beckoned that the girl hand him the roll of paper towels. "Your name?"

"Sarah. I live around the corner that way." She pointed north.

"Thank you, Sarah. You're a lovely girl."

"Really?" Sarah brightened. "You don't think I'm going to be an early bloomer, do you? My mom hopes not."

What did that mean? Alfonso stared at Sarah. Was her sister some kind of a flowering plant? A vega-human mutation? Out here in the suburbs? For some reason Alfonso's father cleared his throat.

"My older sister was an early bloomer. She's always getting grounded 'cause she stays out late with boys riding motorcycles."

His father cleared his throat again. "I'm sure your mother knows what she's doing."

Sarah lowered her voice. "She's worried my sister's gonna get pregnant."

Pregnant? Because she's riding motorcycles? Alfonso shook his head in disbelief. *Doesn't Sarah know anything about procreation?*

This time his father didn't clear his throat. Instead he whistled softly and made for the pickup. He opened the door and put the cylinder and towels inside.

Sarah followed him. "We're officially neighbors now. So what's your name?"

His father shut the door. "Frankenstein."

Her eyes popped wide. "You're Doctor Frankenstein? No kidding?"

"No kidding. Dr. Eugino Frankenstein. This is my son, Alfonso."

Alfonso raised his free hand and squeaked, "Hi."

"Like Dr. Frankenstein and the terrible monster?"

Alfonso and his father looked at each other. *Terrible monster?*

Dr. Frankenstein turned to Sarah. "There's another side to that story."

The driver of the moving truck called to Alfonso's father. "Hey doc, better unlock the house. Gotta start unloading."

Dr. Frankenstein pulled Alfonso's hand away from his face. "The swelling's stopped. But give it a few more minutes." He nudged Alfonso's hand back into place and gave an encouraging smile. Dr. Frankenstein jangled keys in his pocket and approached the house.

The gerbil began to thaw. Cold fluid leaked from the baggie and dripped down Alfonso's nose to his jaw and neck. *Yuck, gerbil juice.* He wiped his face.

Sarah glanced to the pickup. "Where's your mom?"

Alfonso had heard that question for years and it always opened a hole in his heart. "My parents are divorced."

He was six when they broke up. Those memories lashed at him like a whip. The loud fights. His mom shrieking and using dinner plates as ammunition. Her many sudden vacations and her final return as the passenger in a red Mercedes convertible—with her boyfriend at the wheel, an agent from the CIA's Office of Extraterrestrial Hospitality.

Alfonso noticed Sarah's eyes studying his. "What's the matter?"

"You got real quiet," she said. "Do you miss her?"

"I miss not having a mom." When his mother left for the last time, she acted like she couldn't get away fast enough from Dr. Frankenstein. And their son.

"What was the problem?"

"I guess my mom discovered she'd married the wrong kind of doctor." The barbed memory pricked Alfonso.

"What do you mean?" Sarah asked.

"She wanted diamonds and country club parties. But my dad didn't get into medicine for the money."

Sarah looked at the truck and the house. "Yeah, I can tell."

Alfonso's father unlocked the front door and went in. A minute later the garage door stuttered open. The door kept sliding back down until he propped it up with a length of two by four.

A long white car appeared at the far end of the street. Alfonso immediately recognized the white Bentley limousine. *Not him. Please.*

Sarah said something but Alfonso was too distracted to reply. He wanted to shout a warning to his father and decided against it. The last thing he needed was his father to come charging into the street. Alfonso felt the weight of every breath. His nose no longer hurt and he lowered the gerbil.

The limousine looked as sleek and imposing as a space shuttle. Points of sparkling light tripped along the chrome grill and the spoked wheels. A rainbow of colors flashed from the iridescent parking sticker on the front bumper: Faculty Administration.

The Bentley skimmed alongside Alfonso and Sarah. Their faces reflected across the dark windows. It glided to a halt beside his father's Dodge. Compared to the gleaming Bentley, the red pickup seemed a faded, dirty pink.

To Alfonso, the tension was like watching a reduction flask of liquid plutonium go critical before exploding. The rear door window scrolled down. Chilled air wafted out. A man's face, shiny and pink as a lump of raw greasy hamburger, hovered in the gloom of the Bentley's interior. His black clothes blended into the shadow and black upholstery surrounding him. A small European turkey buzzard rested in his lap.

He was one man Alfonso never wanted to see, ever. Alive anyway. The Provost Marshal of the University of Doom and the head of the academic tribunal that had stripped his father of his tenure and job.

Professor Moriarty. The nemesis of the family Frankenstein.

The man who humiliated his father.

The man who destroyed their lives.

The man who had robbed Alfonso of his future.

CHAPTER
FIVE

Professor Moriarty showed a crescent of silvery-white teeth. His lips were twin rinds of flesh, looking swollen and unnatural.

There was evil genius, evil as in:

A) reckless,

B) prone to court disaster,

C) dismissive of good judgment,

D) and drawn to the dark side of knowledge.

And there was Moriarty with his EVIL genius:

A) sneaky mean,

B) cruel,

C) got his jollies hurting others.

Alfonso's hand cupped the baggie holding the thawing gerbil. Cool slimy water leaked from the baggie and pooled between his fingers.

Moriarty nodded a greeting, the way a reptile might upon meeting its prey. "Alfonso, it's so good to see you.

Please summon your father." The refrigerated air spilling from the limousine got colder as Moriarty spoke.

Years ago, for his fifth-grade mad science project, Alfonso and his father had created a mutant talking garter snake. The snake sounded like a miniature Professor Moriarty and was the hit of the fair. Everyone laughed, even the professor except that his chuckling sounded uncomfortable and forced. On the morning before judging, Alfonso discovered that the wire top of the snake's locked cage had been snipped open. Remains of the little snake lay outside under the tree where Beelzebub, the professor's turkey vulture, liked to roost.

The professor said it was a tragedy but nature must take its course. *Especially when nature used a pair of wire cutters.*

Now, instead of dread, Alfonso was overcome with contempt. Moriarty deserved a loogie.

Sarah stepped closer to the Bentley.

Moriarty's gaze slid to her. "I see you've been accepted by *these* people."

Alfonso's hands trembled and he kept them still. He wanted to yell—scream—at the professor and say how much he hated him for ruining their lives. But all that came out was a muted and bitter, "I don't like you."

Sarah joined in. "Yeah, *these* people don't like you either."

Moriarty's eyes swiveled back to Sarah. He grimaced and resumed flashing his insincere smile. "You're supposed to respect your elders. Weren't you taught any manners?"

"I was taught plenty, don't you worry. About manners and about how to smell a rat." She pinched her nose. "P. U."

Moriarty tried to keep his smile but Sarah's words had cracked that shell of fakeness. His thick lips wormed into a sneer.

He turned his eyes to Alfonso and glared like the boy was an insect that needed to be squashed. Alfonso felt a shiver of fear until he realized, *We're not at the university anymore. You're in our neighborhood now, buster. New rules.* He returned the glare.

The seconds passed. Moriarty's face grew redder and redder. His forehead became shiny with perspiration. Beelzebub squawked uncomfortably. All that air conditioning in his fancy car wasn't helping them.

A shadow fell across Alfonso and he recognized the tall, broad silhouette gaining on them. His father approached and Alfonso felt relief. Reinforcements had arrived.

Moriarty raised his eyes from Alfonso. The big phony smile inflated his expression. "Doctor Frankenstein... Eugino...it's good to see you."

Alfonso's dad halted behind his son and Sarah. He put a hand, heavy and reassuring, on each of their shoulders. Alfonso reached across his chest to grasp his father's thick fingers.

"What's the matter, Moriarty," his father growled, "are you short a knife and figured you left one in my back?"

"Doctor, please," Moriarty replied, "I came to clear away any lingering misunderstandings." He extended an arm out the window of the Bentley. His pale hand had the look of a crab that had recently molted. He motioned with his fingers: *Take them in friendship.*

Sarah whispered, "This guy is so creepy I bet even flies stay away from him."

Moriarty's eyes tightened into mean little slits. His lips bunched into a lemon-sour pucker.

Alfonso giggled. Dr. Frankenstein patted Alfonso's shoulder. *Quiet. I'll handle this.*

"After what you've done to us, Moriarty, the only way I'd take your hand is if you bite it off first."

Alfonso would like to see that, Moriarty biting off his own hand. Might make it worth moving to these suburbs.

Moriarty scowled. He withdrew his hand, and his arm retracted like the tentacle of an octopus.

"What brought you here, Professor?"

"You are a brilliant scientist and your absence represents an enormous loss to the university."

Dr. Frankenstein chuffed. "If you really believed that I wouldn't have these boot prints on my pants where you guys kicked me out."

Moriarty closed his eyes and exhaled a long, soft breath. The buzzard rubbed its bald leathery head against his chin. The professor's wrinkled eyelids twitched and the gloss of sweat on his forehead dulled as if by magic. When he opened his eyes and exhaled, he appeared refreshed and relaxed. "You've mistaken me completely. I came to express my condolences about your dismissal. It was a painful experience."

"Let's trade places and then we'll see who's in the greater pain."

"I've also come to see how you're doing. The success of the university's alumni reflects on its image." Moriarty's gaze shifted from Dr. Frankenstein to the dilapidated house. "Or lack of success."

"It's home. And until a moment ago, far from you."

"But never far enough." The gloating behind Moriarty's smile cut like broken glass. "We'll keep in touch, Dr. Frankenstein."

Alfonso's dad breathed heavily. He kneaded Alfonso's shoulder. Alfonso patted his father's fingers, it was his turn to do the reassuring.

Moriarty motioned to his driver. The Bentley started to roll forward.

Dr. Frankenstein called out. "Moriarty. One more thing."

Moriarty signaled his driver and the limousine halted.

"How's your doctoral dissertation coming along, *Professor*? The board passed on your project again, even with me gone. Not a good way to remain provost even for a sponge like you."

Moriarty scowled like everything in his stomach had turned into battery acid. He dismissed the insult with a curt wave. The limousine rolled off again and his window scrolled upward.

Alfonso remembered that his father had chaired the Doctoral Candidate Review Board. He would've voted against Moriarty, whose failed experiments sputtered like wet matches. His dad losing his job was purely about revenge. Moriarty was lower than the poop in the bottom of a tapeworm breeding vat.

"This professor needs a lesson in manners." Sarah took the baggie from Alfonso's grasp. She cocked her arm, leaned back, and hurled.

The baggie spun through the air and burst against the center of the Bentley's rear window. The slime splattered across the black glass. The limousine lurched to a halt. The gerbil stayed in place for an instant, then slid down the window and left a gooey trail.

Alfonso couldn't believe Sarah's nerve. He clenched his fists and shook them in delight.

Moriarty's window lowered. The driver's outside mirror buzzed and searched for Sarah.

She bared her teeth and made her hands into claws. *Grrr.*

The window on the Bentley scrolled up again, and the big white car motored away. The gerbil remained stuck along the bottom of the rear window.

Alfonso wished he had a second gerbil to throw himself. He laughed. His dad joined in. Maybe things were going to get better.

Sarah punched Alfonso's arm. Hard, and it hurt.

"That was a good one, huh?"

Dr. Frankenstein patted their shoulders. "Very nice, Sarah. You have a career throwing things with great accuracy. I hear there's money in it. Now we have to get back to work moving into the house."

Alfonso stared up the street to where the Bentley had turned the corner and disappeared. He was sure Professor Moriarty had another reason why he'd come by. Something sinister remained in the air like a foul stink of more trouble.

CHAPTER
SIX

Sarah swished her hands across her shorts to wipe off the gerbil juice. Alfonso wanted to clean his hands with a paper towel but if this was how kids did things in the neighborhood, then he better start to blend in. He rubbed his hands along the sides of his pants and left stains.

His dad started for the house. "Alfonso, I need you to bring what's in the pickup."

Sarah went to the back of the Dodge and lowered the tailgate.

Alfonso said, "You don't need to help."

"Course I don't need to." She loosened a knot securing the tarp over the pickup's bed. "I want to."

"Why?"

She stopped working the knot. "Cause we're friends. Aren't we?"

Coming to this neighborhood was like an experiment where everything went wrong from the beginning.

And now, surprise, something good happened. "Yes, we are friends."

Sarah folded the tarp back. "Now that we got that cleared up, let's get to work."

They pulled out plastic crates filled with lamps, extension cords, and lots of books.

"You and your dad sure read a bunch."

Her comment surprised Alfonso. "You don't?"

"Naw. It's too much like schoolwork."

"What do you do for fun?"

"Not read, that's for sure. I like to play outside."

"And inside?"

"Watch T.V. Play games and stuff."

Dr. Frankenstein asked them to start putting things in the garage. Alfonso and Sarah detoured through the house to see what the place looked like inside. As rundown as the outside, unfortunately. The interior smelled of musty carpet. Their steps and voices echoed against the bare walls and old linoleum.

The movers brought in heavy coffin-sized crates made of thick plywood. They stacked the crates in the garage.

Sarah looked the crates over. "Where's your furniture?"

Alfonso didn't anticipate that question. "Uh...it's in the crates, where else?"

Two men carried a crate stenciled: aquarium, but it contained a nucleolus manipulator.

"No furniture in that crate of course." Alfonso stepped aside for the men. When he turned around, Sarah was gone.

Where to?

"Look at this," she said from behind a stack of crates.

Alfonso rushed to see what she'd found.

Sarah crouched beside a large canvas bag. "Awesome. I love tools." The bag had a stencil of a skull superimposed over crossed arrows, the insignia of the U.S. Army Special Forces future combat program. She reached inside the bag and pulled out a prototype military plasma blaster.

She held the blaster by the pistol grip. "What's this? A cordless drill? What brand?"

Sarah's fingers danced on the buttons. The arming sequence lights flashed on, blinking from yellow to green.

The breath caught in Alfonso's throat.

She put the blaster to one ear. "It's making a funny noise. Like a hum."

That's the blaster's electric mega-capacitor. One touch on the trigger would unleash the power of a thunderbolt.

"Is it supposed to make this noise?" Sarah stood and aimed the barrel at Alfonso.

In that instant he thought he was going to pee in his pants. That blaster was about to tear his body into molecules. Alfonso very calmly and quietly said, "Please put that down. It's dangerous."

Sarah lowered the barrel. "Is this a nail gun? Those *are* dangerous. My uncle Charlie accidentally nailed both feet to his roof. He spent all of Labor Day weekend alone on top of his house. Serves him right for drinking and messing with power tools."

Alfonso took the blaster and pressed the switch on top of the power housing. The lights went out and the humming stopped. He rested the blaster inside the canvas bag and zipped it shut.

"That was so cool looking," Sarah said. "Like something from the movies. I can't wait to tell the other kids about it."

"Please don't say anything."

"Why not?"

As much as he was growing fond of Sarah, she was still one of *la mano destre*. She couldn't know the truth. Not the entire truth. "We're not supposed to have it."

Sarah nodded. "Ah." She cocked a finger at the bag. "Your father stole it."

"He didn't steal it."

Her finger moved to Alfonso. "You stole it."

"I didn't steal it. You see..."

Sarah covered her ears. "Say no more. I know the deal. My dad was in the National Guard and his garage is full of tools and army stuff he didn't steal."

Alfonso decided to put Sarah to work. She was like a puppy that kept sticking her nose into everything. That would keep her from poking around where she didn't belong. He took her to the kitchen. Together they unboxed dishes and glasses and placed them along the sink.

Sarah unwrapped beakers, flasks, and retorts. "These are fancy dishes. Your dad must be a gourmet cook."

"He does okay." Actually, his dad was a good cook.

"Mind if I ask a question?"

Apparently she was going to ask anyway. Alfonso shrugged. "Go ahead."

"What's it like being a Frankenstein? It's a weird name."

Thankfully, the question wasn't about the plasma blaster. "It's not weird in my family."

"Wasn't there a book about the first Frankenstein?"

Thanks to Mary Shelly and her account of Alfonso's distant uncle Victor, the world would forever associate the Frankenstein name with the twisted genius of a mad scientist.

"He wasn't the first Frankenstein," Alfonso explained, "we go back generations before him."

"So where is your family from?"

"Mexico."

"I thought Frankenstein was German or something like that."

"It is German. Some of my ancestors got in trouble and they left Europe."

"Why?"

Alfonso shrugged. If he didn't say anything, he wouldn't have to lie.

"What about all that bringing the dead to life and making monsters? Was that made up? I've seen the movies."

Alfonso fought to keep from blurting the truth. It happened. The movies were close. The scandal still haunted the University of Doom: who revealed secrets of *la mano sinistre* to Hollywood?

Alfonso let his denial bubble into a chuckle. "The dead back to life? It's not scientifically possible." Not with normal science, anyway.

"Too bad," Sarah said. "Being a mad scientist would be so cool."

Yes, being a mad scientist is very cool.

Sarah opened another box. She pulled out a picture frame wrapped in paper. "What's this?"

Alfonso reached to take the picture from her hands but too late. She turned her back to him and hurriedly tore off the paper. "Hmmm," she said, interested.

The frame held a sepia photograph of fierce-looking men: thick mustaches, someberos, bandoliers, canvas leggings and spurs—Mexican revolutionaries armed with Colt revolvers and Mauser rifles—standing under a tree and posing for the camera.

"Who are they?"

"After my family settled in Mexico, one of my great great grand uncles, Javíer Frankenstein, was in Pancho Villa's army as a technical advisor." Alfonso pointed to the man in the middle of the group.

Sarah squinted. "That's your uncle?"

"No, this is him." Alfonso moved his finger to the top of the photo. "See that?" It was a pair of legs jutting downward from the tree. "Those belonged to my uncle. Pancho Villa hired him to invent something." A steam-powered robot airplane that had gone out of control, chased the bandit general, then crashed into his house and burned it down. "Let's just say it didn't quite work right so they hanged him."

"Tough audience." Sarah grimaced and handed the photo to Alfonso, who put it back in the box.

Then there are times when being a mad scientist can be very not-so-cool.

Dr. Frankenstein and the movers settled business in the front room. The movers went out. They banged shut the back doors of their truck and drove off.

Dr. Frankenstein studied the wooden crates crowding the room. "Let's start unpacking. Alfonso, have you seen my bag of tools?"

"They're in the garage," Sarah said. "I wanna help. I know all about tools. Ask your son."

Alfonso gave his dad an I-don't-know-what-she's-talking-about expression.

Dr. Frankenstein read his wristwatch. "It's getting close to dinner time. You better get home. Alfonso and I can handle this."

Sarah hooked a lock of hair behind her ears. "Oh. Sure." She glanced at the crates and grinned. "I bet you guys have lots of neat stuff."

Dr. Frankenstein held the door open for her.

"Later, gator." Sarah punched Alfonso on the arm and ran out.

His father locked the door and lowered the blinds. "We'll see how much we can get done before you have to go to bed. You've got another busy day tomorrow."

Alfonso didn't want to be reminded. Tomorrow would be bad, even worse than seeing Professor Moriarty again.

Tomorrow would be his first day in public school. What ugly surprises would he find there?

CHAPTER
SEVEN

The move and the long hours helping his dad uncrate the lab equipment wore Alfonso out, and he should've gone right to sleep. But he lay restless on a blanket folded over a foam pad; his bed was still packed away. He missed the university and all of his friends there, especially Greg Kaminski. Alfonso wished he could talk to him.

He lay on his back and stared at the ceiling, thinking, "Greg, I hope you're never this sad."

Alfonso woke up when his father pulled at his foot. He yawned and rubbed the sleep from his eyes. As he became conscious of his bedroom, overrun with opened and unopened crates, the dread of going to his new school settled onto him like cold dew. Alfonso sat up and closed his eyes for a moment to think.

Please, let me get through the day without any new problems.

He stumbled over coils of electrical cables and blood transfusion tubing on his way to the bathroom. After getting dressed, he went to the kitchen. His father cooked eggs and chorizo in a surgical autoclave marked Centers for Disease Control. He wore a suede-leather shop apron to protect his suit and tie as he warmed tortillas over a Bunsen burner. His face was a mask of sullen resignation; he was starting his first day of work. Alfonso appreciated that his father didn't dump a load of false cheeriness on him. The gloomy mood fit.

After breakfast, his father gave him a large manila envelope. "Here's the paperwork the school sent for your transfer."

Alfonso tucked the envelope into a cheap nylon backpack. He'd rather carry his leather satchel. But the satchel was embossed with *Dr. Moreau Junior Academy* so it remained hidden with his other University of Doom supplies. Anything with his old school's name or crest was to be kept hidden from *la mano destre*.

"If you need me," his father reminded, "you have my work number?"

"I wrote it down." Without a portal tablet, he had to rely on paper and pen. They might as well be back in ancient Greece writing on sheepskin. He slipped his arms through the straps of the backpack and followed his father to their pickup.

On the ride to school, Alfonso carefully zipped open the backpack and slipped his hand inside. Despite what his father had told him about packing anything that could tie him to the University of Doom, Alfonso brought something special: his "tricks kit," a leather pen pouch given to every fourth-grade student on the first day of class at Henry Jekyll Grammar School. The pouches were decorated with an ibis superimposed over a moon to symbolize Toth, the Egyptian god of writing and learning.

Alfonso's pen pouch was made from the iridescent hide of a volcanic cephalopod harpooned in the Lake of Terror. These deadly creatures were the offspring of giant squids whose DNA had been contaminated with the genes of a fire-breathing Gila Monster. "It's only a matter of time," his father had warned, "before these things learn how to walk on dry land and hunt *us*."

Besides a fountain pen—another prized gift—a glass vial of ink, a divider, ballpoint and pencils, Alfonso had stored in the tricks kit small implements of the evil genius trade.

His fingers stroked the pebble-grained leather. This squid hide had a special property. If Alfonso shook the pouch, the movement would activate the bioluminescence in the skin cells. The hide would mimic the surface beneath it and blend in for a few minutes.

Alfonso caught sight of his new school and a cold, rancid taste soured his mouth. He withdrew his hand from the backpack and closed the zipper.

Ty Cobb Middle School was a collection of brick rectangles, like cardboard boxes pushed together. Scrawny juniper hedges bordered the yellowed grass. The large windows were all dark. Despite the cars in the parking lot, the grounds looked deserted. The school had the dismal charm of an abandoned shed.

Dr. Frankenstein reached across the bench seat and tweaked Alfonso's shoulder. "You sure you can manage enrolling by yourself?"

Alfonso didn't want to manage anything except staying away from this school. But he had to reassure his dad that he could take care of himself. "I'll be all right. You know the evil genius creed. *Efficere debes quis efficere debes.*"

Dr. Frankenstein nodded. "You gotta do what you gotta do. Remember, that doesn't change as you grow older."

They continued onto the parking lot. A sign read: Teachers and Staff. The cars crowded together were either rusted barges with wheels—one was a Ford Fairlane with clear shipping tape holding the taillights in place—or miniscule sedans that looked like eggs on roller skates.

As they drove closer to the main building they passed a shiny Porsche SUV surrounded by empty spaces. This sign read: Executive Administration Only! Violators will be ticketed and towed!

This side of the main building was a windowless brick wall, which framed an enormous plywood cutout of a cartoon mascot: a snarling man wearing a striped uniform, a sports cap, and wielding a smooth club. Written in an unfurled scroll across the bottom was: *Hey ump, are you blind?*

Alfonso wasn't sure what that meant. What was an ump? And why was that man so angry? Was he Ty Cobb? What did he have against the blind?

Their pickup stopped against the curb in front of the building. At Dr. Moreau, whenever a new student arrived in the middle of the school year, he or she would have to run through the Gauntlet of Welcome, where fellow homeroom students would pelt the newcomer with exploding cupcakes filled with tickle confetti.

Here at Ty Cobb, nothing. Just that ugly mascot on the wall.

His father said, "Try to make friends."

What kind of friends would Alfonso have here? "I will, Dad." He shut the door. The Dodge rumbled out of the parking lot.

Alfonso tried not to feel like he'd been stranded. He read his watch and noted the school day had already started. He studied the entrance. A plain slab of concrete bordered by asphalt. Two doors with chicken wire sandwiched between the glass panels. No moat. No gargoyles. No arched entryway overgrown with ivy and bougainvillea.

He pulled open one of the front doors and went inside. The office was to the left, where an older, heavy-set woman stared at a computer monitor on a counter.

A computer? The school wasn't so backward after all. Until now, Alfonso would've suspected they used manual typewriters and the telegraph.

The woman wore thick glasses as big as safety goggles. The nameplate on the edge of the counter read: Ms. Banard. She looked like a weather-beaten rock and her green dress was the color of lichen. Apparently, at Ty Cobb the gargoyles were on the inside.

A tall girl in baggy cargo pants and a red top sorted envelopes into rows of tiny cubbies along the wall behind the counter. She acted like a typical older student—they were the same everywhere—displaying a conceit like she was doing the school a favor by being here. Still, Alfonso found himself wanting to be close to her because she was so pretty.

Ms. Banard swiveled her chair toward Alfonso.

In that instant, with that big wrinkled face looming before him, Ms. Banard had gone from looking like a gargoyle to looking like an ogre.

CHAPTER
EIGHT

Ms. Banard kept her ogre face focused on Alfonso. Her spectacles magnified her eyes so that her irises looked like balls of algae floating inside twin fishbowls. "May I see your hall pass?"

"My what?"

She rapped a pen against her nameplate. "My name is not what," she snapped at Alfonso. "Where is your hall pass?"

He took a step back.

"You're not supposed to be in the halls when class is in session unless you have a pass." Ms. Banard paused to screw her lips together in disapproval. "Who is your homeroom teacher?"

"I...I'm new here. I don't have a homeroom yet." Alfonso opened his backpack and withdrew the manila packet. "Here's the paperwork my dad filled out. I'm a transfer student."

"And where is your father?"

"He had to start work today."

"And your mother?"

"She doesn't live with us."

Ms. Banard raised an eyebrow and took the packet. She sorted through the forms and documents. Her eyebrow remained lifted in suspicion.

She turned to her computer and tapped the keyboard. Her eyebrow lowered and she frowned at the monitor. "You can't be a transfer student. The district policy is that every transferring student must give sixty days notice."

"We didn't have sixty days. My father contacted you as soon as we found out we were moving here."

Ms. Banard huffed. "Sixty days is sixty days. It's policy."

"Then what do I do?"

"Your father must take this form," Ms. Banard fumbled under the counter and shoved a paper in front of Alfonso, "and explain why the district should consider an exemption."

This made no sense to Alfonso. He was here. What did Ms. Banard want? That he not attend school?

Alfonso reached over the counter for his paperwork and removed one form. "This explains why we moved." He handed the form to Ms. Banard.

She dropped the form on the stack and crossed her arms. Her eyebrow flattened and her wrinkled, hairy lips curled like dying centipedes. "This won't do. It's a form 407A. I need a form 407B."

Alfonso rolled his eyes. "A, B, what is the difference?"

She fussed with a shelf and slapped a sheaf of papers on the counter. "Young man, I've had enough of your questions. I don't know where you came from but in this district we respect authority and obey the rules."

The cover sheet had the title: *District Policy on Respecting Authority and Obeying the Rules*. Her pen stabbed the sheet to emphasize her point. "School is about obeying the rules, not asking questions. The sooner you understand that, the sooner you will adjust to life as a student in this district."

Alfonso's jaw slackened in disbelief. This wasn't a school, this was an institution of lower learning.

Ms. Banard flipped to the last page in the sheaf and ran her pen along a line at the bottom. "Sign here that you understand the policy."

The policy was twelve pages long. "Shouldn't I read this first?"

She growled. "Again with the questions." Ms. Banard looked like she was going to lunge over the counter and bite him. She was scarier than anything at Dr. Moreau, in or out of a cage. "You either sign this or I'll call the police and have them pick you up for being truant."

"Don't I have to be enrolled in a school before I can be considered truant?"

Her face reddened like it was about to pop. "No more questions." She jabbed at the line.

He was about to ask that if he signed this, would she enroll him but realized that was a question. Alfonso took a ballpoint from his shirt pocket and signed his name.

Ms. Banard smoothed the papers with a triumphant flourish and took them back. She inhaled deeply, as if preparing herself for an acrobatic jump. The crease in the center of her brow deepened. "What I can do is file a temporary exemption. It requires that I submit a form 407C."

A. B. C. Did this process involve the entire alphabet?

She moved her mouse and tapped twice on the keyboard. "There. Done." Seconds later, the ink jet printer on the counter whirred and out scrolled a paper. She handed the paper to him. "This is your temporary schedule. Don't lose it. I don't want to print another one. Remember, paper doesn't grow on trees."

Actually it grows from trees, though Alfonso knew Ms. Banard wouldn't appreciate being corrected.

"Your homeroom is 143. Biology with Ms. Humboldt."

Biology? Finally, good news. Alfonso loved biology. He couldn't wait to show these kids at Ty Cobb how much smarter the students were from Dr. Moreau Junior Academy.

Ms. Barnard told the girl sorting the envelopes to show the new temporary student the way to Room 143. Since there was a map of the school on the wall, Alfonso could've figured how to find it himself. He had led snorkeling expeditions through the coral labyrinth in the Lake of Terror so finding his class would've been a snap.

The girl put the envelopes down and without a word, walked into the hall. Alfonso stepped behind her.

Once out of the office, the girl looked over both shoulders, then dug into a side pocket and pulled out a pink cell phone. Alfonso gazed in wonder. None of the students at Dr. Moreau could own a cell phone.

The rule prevented inadvertently revealing secrets to the outside world.

The girl walked absently while her fingers danced over the screen. *Manual input. How primitive.* Maybe these kids were too dumb to focus their thoughts.

Alfonso walked in step beside her, becoming amazed by the nimbleness of her fingers. She seemed to type as fast as she thought. The girl gave him the elbow and he dropped back.

Alfonso marched behind her, at first resentful and then losing interest. He veered to admire the trophies and metallic plaques set inside glass displays along the wall. Eager to discover what scholarly achievements deserved such glittering prizes, he paused to read the inscriptions. Incredibly, none of the awards was for academic excellence, only for sports. Weren't the students here smart enough to win anything in nano-robotics, subatomic chemistry, or exoskeleton bionics?

Alfonso turned from the trophies and quickened his pace to catch up with the girl. They passed rows of battered lockers stretching down the quiet halls.

At Dr. Moreau, the halls hummed from the force fields surrounding the mutant creature pens. Smoke alarms went off regularly whenever lab assignments went awry.

"Without risk," Dr. Gefährliche the chemistry teacher would explain as they ran out of a burning classroom, "there can be no gain."

Ty Cobb seemed inertly silent and without risk. Obviously there would be no gain. Maybe the only challenge here was surviving the day without getting scolded.

The girl moved like she was under control of the cell phone. They turned down one corridor, past closed doors and more lockers, until she stopped outside a door with 143 written in black marker across the top of the frame.

The girl motioned to the door. She spun around and kept tapping on her cell phone while starting back to the office.

Alfonso stared at the room number. He was now officially a student at Ty Cobb Middle School. His shoulders clenched until they hurt and his face tightened in discomfort.

Voices murmured from behind the door. Should he knock? What were the rules? Do the wrong thing and they might act like he'd deliberately let loose a swarm of invisible octo-bats.

The seconds ticked from his wristwatch. Rather than stand here all morning, he decided to knock.

A woman answered. She invited him in, her voice unexpectedly pleasant.

Alfonso turned the knob and swung the door open.

Sunlight flooded the room through the expanse of windows along the opposite wall. He blinked uncomfortably at the harsh light.

A glorious smell astounded him. Formaldehyde. He thought he'd never smell it again and here the odor rolled over him.

Kids his age sat in pairs beside tables. Every one of their eyes fixed upon Alfonso as if asking the same question: *Who are you and what are you doing here?*

CHAPTER NINE

Alfonso cleared his throat and tried not to feel like he was the weirdest creature that had ever walked on Earth.

He again became aware of the formaldehyde odor. He noticed the steel dissecting trays resting in the center of every table. On each tray lay the pale forms of embalmed hamsters, the tiny corpses splayed on their backs and pinned to pale green dissecting mats. The abdomens and torsos were split open and the organs arranged along the edges of the trays.

His gaze tripped along the trays and dissecting tools. Probes. Forceps. Scalpels.

To his right, at the front of the class, stood a woman in a white laboratory smock—a smock like those worn by the professors at Dr. Moreau.

Alfonso's heartbeat jumped. He felt as if he was back at the University of Doom and on the road again to becoming a mad scientist.

The woman dropped a marker into the trough along the bottom of a white board. Her large eyes reflected the welcome of her smile and as he drew close, he could see that her irises sparkled like aquamarine gemstones.

Alfonso stammered, "Uh, uh," and blushed, feeling suddenly awkward and off balance. He held out his schedule. "I'm a new student."

She took his schedule. "Welcome to my class. I'm Ms. Venus Humboldt."

Delicately arched eyebrows emphasized the elegant lines of her face. She wore her wavy brown hair in a ponytail. Her tanned complexion and trim build told him she probably liked to do a lot of fun things outside.

Ms. Humboldt paused to read the schedule. A curl of hair escaped from behind her ear and dangled beside one cheek. She glanced at Alfonso, her expression amused.

Why the smirk?

She addressed the students, "Class, this is our newest student," and pronounced his name with great formality, "Alfonso Frankenstein."

Mocking laughter rippled through the class. "Frankenstein?"

What was so funny? The chuckling jabbed at his pride and he wanted to slink out the door.

"You'll take that seat for now." Ms. Humboldt pointed to an empty place at the end of the second row.

Alfonso slid the backpack off his shoulders and walked to the chair. Eyes lingered on him and as he crossed the room, the laughter ebbed and he felt that everything different about him—his heavy black shoes, the backpack, his face—had been spray painted in neon colors. He sat and pushed his backpack into the wire basket under his seat.

At his left sat a pair of students with smooth round heads like parakeets who stared at him like he was an intruder in their cage. Alfonso said hello and the two inched their chairs away from him.

Directly behind Alfonso sat another student with a physique too stocky for an ordinary thirteen year-old. He reminded Alfonso of a young rottweiler, way past puppy, not yet adult, though aware of his growing strength. Acne and freckles dotted his face and blond whiskers dusted his upper lip and chin. He wore a brush-like flattop. The boy's eyes blazed amused scorn. He tipped his head toward his partner and whispered loud enough for Alfonso to hear. "Frankenstein? More like Franken-stupid."

Alfonso narrowed his eyes. He'd like to drop a lamprey-roach down this ugly kid's pants.

"Jerry," Ms. Humboldt asked, her tone disapproving, "you have something to share?"

Jerry shook his head and crossed his arms. "No ma'am." His eyes accused Alfonso of bringing the teacher's wrath.

Alfonso didn't care. If he didn't like that kind of attention, Jerry had no one to blame but himself.

Alfonso inspected the room. Every bit of wall that wasn't window or white board was decorated with science posters. Sinks and cabinets lined the back of the class. Padlocks secured the cabinets which hinted at experiments requiring powerful and dangerous chemicals. Maybe they used the new hydrogen mitosis catalysts, highly reactive and toxic but the best stuff for accelerated cloning.

Ms. Humboldt resumed the lesson. "We were discussing how we can apply what we've learned today to the taxonomy of zoology."

The words snagged Alfonso's attention. *Taxonomy? Zoology?* He sat up straight and waited for her questions. *Now these kids will see a superior mind in action.*

"Protists," Ms. Humboldt asked, "fungi, plants, and animals are members of what domain?"

Alfonso's arm shot up.

Ms. Humboldt nodded. "Alfonso."

"Eukaryote."

She smiled, pleased.

A girl in the front row twisted around and gave Alfonso a glare through the lenses of her glasses as if his answer had violated yet another rule. Her pudgy face tightened around a pout and her lower lip jutted angrily at him.

When Ms. Humboldt started the next question. "Eukaryote are characterized by..."

The girl turned around and snapped her arm upward. Her fingers fluttered like a pinwheel.

"Candace?"

"They have a cytoskeleton and membranes."

Ms. Humboldt rewarded her with an appreciative nod.

Candace turned around and smirked.

Alfonso grinned. *So she got one.* These were easy questions.

"In taxonomy, Mammalia is an example of...?"

Alfonso lifted his arm. "Phylum." As soon as he spoke the word, he clenched his teeth in regret.

Ms. Humboldt's eyes continued past Candace's outstretched arm to settle on another student, a big kid with a milk chocolate complexion. He slouched in his chair and doodled in a spiral notebook. He swatted the air with his large hand and blurted. "Mammalia is an example of class. The phylum would be Chordata."

"Exactly right, Reginald," Ms. Humboldt said.

Alfonso felt his face darken with embarrassment.

"Geez," Jerry snickered, "you really are Franken-stupid."

Alfonso sulked. He wanted to impress Ms. Humboldt and instead gave that doofus Jerry a reason to ridicule him.

Whack. Something wet stung the back of Alfonso's neck. He swiped at his collar and scooped a gum-sized wad of gooey flesh. It reeked of formaldehyde. *Who threw this?* He turned around and looked for the culprit.

Jerry parodied Alfonso's reaction and gave a what-are-you-going-to-do-about-it snicker.

Alfonso dropped the wad into the tray beside him. *Jerry wants to make me a chump, I'll make him the chump.*

"We have a few minutes before the period ends," Ms. Humboldt said. She recited the procedure to clean up and dispose of the hamsters.

In a bustle of activity, the students gathered lab equipment and cleaned their tables. Meanwhile Jerry and his lab partner chatted with the girls at the table next to theirs, all of them ignoring Ms. Humboldt's instructions.

Alfonso reached under his chair and opened his backpack. He didn't have the plasma blaster, but he had something just as good. Stealthily, he pulled out his tricks kit.

Alfonso wished he had on a white lab coat so he could rub his hands together and give the infamous maniacal laugh of a mad scientist while lightning crashed in the background. "Mwua-ha-ha-ha."

CHAPTER
TEN

Alfonso shook the tricks kit. The bioluminescence in the squid hide shimmered. He slid his thighs apart and rested the kit on the chair. The hide mimicked the pale blue color of the plastic seat and disappeared. Working by touch, he snapped open the leather flap, and retrieved a small atomizer. Bubbles in the glass barrel rolled through the reanimation fluid—made using the original recipe for Dippel's Oil.

Candace went to each table and collected the dissecting tools. Other students congregated at the back of the classroom and upended their lab trays over a cardboard box labeled biohazard.

Alfonso palmed the atomizer in his left hand, turned in his chair, reached to the lab tray on Jerry's table, and spritzed the hamster carcass. Alfonso capped the atomizer and put it back in the tricks kit.

The reanimation fluid would take a minute to soak in. Alfonso pulled the pocket neural stimulator from the kit. The stimulator was the size of a marker pen with two knobs forking from one end. He rotated the power adjustment switch on the opposite end and pressed the trigger button mounted midway down the length. A spark cackled between the silver electrode contacts on the knobs.

Alfonso hunched over to muffle the sound and lowered the power setting. The stimulator had plenty of electric juice, but considering the embalmed state of Jerry's hamster, Alfonso debated if this would work. All he needed was for the carcass to reanimate for several seconds, long enough to scare the heck out of Jerry.

He checked to see if anyone noticed. Everybody was busy cleaning up or chatting. Jerry and his lab partner were still at the girls' table.

Alfonso spread the hamster's ribcage and pressed the knobs of the neural stimulator against the top of the tiny spinal column. He pushed the trigger button. The electrodes went *zzzt*. The charge tingled his hand.

The hamster did nothing.

Alfonso added more power and repositioned the electrodes. He pressed the trigger again.

Another *zzzt* and a feather of smoke curled from inside the ribcage. The shock numbed his fingers.

But the hamster did nothing.

Disappointed, Alfonso turned the power off on the neural stimulator. He put the stimulator in the tricks kit which he dropped into his backpack. Something wasn't working. Maybe the carcass was too far gone. Maybe the reanimation fluid didn't have enough time to soak in. Maybe a lot of things. He would have to wait another day to give Jerry what he deserved.

Alfonso glanced back at Jerry's hamster. It twitched.

It's alive!

The hamster's clouded eyes became shiny as glass and rolled in their sockets. The tiny mouth opened and closed.

Alfonso pumped his fists in triumph.

The hamster pulled its left foreleg free. The pin dropped from the paw.

Alfonso glanced around the room. He didn't want anyone to see the dead hamster moving. Not yet.

The hamster lifted its right foreleg and sat up on the green plastic pad.

No, not yet. Alfonso snatched a paper towel from his table to cover the hamster.

He looked back at Jerry's table. The tray was empty.

The hamster was gone.

Where did it go?

He searched under the table. No hamster.

He scanned the table again. He peeked inside Jerry's open backpack. No hamster.

Alfonso's heart drummed so loud he was sure everyone in the class would hear it. Was the hamster in Jerry's notebook binder?

Jerry and his lab partner rose from the girls' table. Jerry frowned at Alfonso. "What are you looking at, Franken loser?"

Alfonso ignored him and scanned around their chairs. No hamster.

Jerry screamed.

Hamster.

Jerry dropped his notebook binder and staggered from his table. The pale carcass of the hamster clung to a lock of hair on his forehead. He stared cross-eyed and in horror at the reanimated rodent.

The other students shrieked, retreated a couple of steps from Jerry, and gave a collective, "E-yew."

Formaldehyde trickled from the hamster and down Jerry's face. His hands clawed the air as if afraid to touch the embalmed rodent. He screamed, "Get it off me."

Jerry's lab partner stared, mouth gaping. The color washed from his face. He closed his mouth and groped toward their lab table. "Hold still. I'll get it." He whisked the lab tray off the table and swatted Jerry across the head.

Jerry stumbled into a girl rinsing trays in a sink. She jumped and her trays clattered to the floor. Jerry slipped on the puddled water, and the hamster plopped to the floor. Jerry sat up and toed the tiny, lifeless body.

Ms. Humboldt shouted, "Jerry, Spike, stop horsing around."

Laughing and clutching his sides, Alfonso left his chair and approached Jerry. This turned out better than expected. "Who's stupid now?"

Jerry's eyes glowed like the ends of hot pokers. He launched himself from the floor, moving at a speed that astonished Alfonso. Jerry seized Alfonso's shirt and yanked him close.

Alfonso's throat choked with fear. Jerry cocked his right arm. The fear compressed into panic. Jerry's knuckles looked as menacing as a battering ram. Alfonso brought his hand up to block the punch.

Jerry let go of the shirt and sucker-slapped Alfonso hard across the cheek with his left hand. Alfonso's eyes watered. His knees buckled. But he wasn't going down alone. As he fell, Alfonso swept his right leg across Jerry's ankles.

Jerry tumbled to the floor. The two boys scrambled to their feet. The other students formed a circle around them. Jerry glared at Alfonso and curled his fists.

Despite his size, Jerry moved quick as a scorpion. Alfonso wasn't a fighter and couldn't outrun or out punch him. Rule one of the mad scientist code: Expect the unexpected. Rule two: Always have an escape plan.

The unexpected had happened. Now what about the escape?

Ms. Humboldt marched between them, her rage strong enough to make the other students step back. Her nostrils flared, and the only sound in the room was her heavy breathing and the nervous shifting of feet.

Spike broke the silence. "Alfonso started it." Spike pointed to the hamster on the floor. "He threw *that* at Jerry."

Ms. Humboldt stared at the hamster, the trays littering the floor, and the spilled water. Her eyes settled on Alfonso and the anger in them softened into a disappointment he could feel inside his skin.

Alfonso's eyes watered again, not from pain but shame. "I didn't throw the hamster, Ms. Humboldt. Believe me, I didn't."

"Oh yeah," Spike insisted, "then how did it get on Jerry? Did that dead hamster come to life all of a sudden? Some sort of zombie rodent?"

Alfonso panned across the dozens of eyes fixed upon him. *Well, yeah.* But he was forced to shrug. "I don't know, Ms. Humboldt."

She snapped the latex gloves from her hands. "We don't tolerate fighting. Both of you, report to the principal's office."

Principal's office? Alfonso knew he was in serious trouble. And this was only day one at Ty Cobb Middle School.

An electronic bell sounded, the exact alarm at Dr. Moreau used to mean a mutant species was loose in the halls. Alfonso stiffened with fright. What were the defense plans here?

None of the kids panicked. They collected their belongings and filed out the door. Alfonso realized the bell signaled the end of the class period. Aside from Jerry, there were no loose monsters in this school.

"Alfonso," Ms. Humboldt said. "Are you okay?"

No, he wasn't okay. He felt distant from everything. The rules here served only to confuse and humiliate him. "I'm all right, Ms. Humboldt."

Her eyes remained stern. "I'm impressed that you like science so much. As your homeroom teacher, it's my responsibility to see that you get settled in. Right now you're off to a rough start. See me at the end of the day. In the meantime..."

He slung his backpack over one shoulder. "Yeah, I know. Report to the principal's office." So far this day was a disaster. The bright spot was that it couldn't get any worse.

He stepped into the hall, now crowded and noisy with loud conversation and the slamming of lockers.

Jerry and Spike waited for him, eyes hooded with bad intentions.

Alfonso approached, his steps light in case he had to run.

Jerry and Spike parted enough to let him pass between them.

Alfonso's swiveled his eyes to Jerry, then to Spike. When he started to walk clear, certain that they had only wanted to intimidate him, a sharp blow knocked Alfonso to the floor. His left ear burned in pain and all he could do was curl on the floor and clasp the side of his head.

Jerry towered over him, flexing the fingers of his right hand.

"Ms. Humboldt isn't around to protect you here, Franken-sissy." He crouched close. "Listen good, you little twerp, this is my school. I'm going to do my best to get rid of you."

CHAPTER
ELEVEN

The sun shone like a brilliant white ball over the University of Doom. Professor Moriarty stood atop Judgment Knoll, the highest point on campus. He had tread across rectangles of fresh sod, recently planted to cover the crater from someone else's disaster. Down the slope, the Lake of Terror glinted, mirror-like. Volcanic cephalopods basked on the surface the way they do after a good meal, burping flames out their siphon tubes, long tentacles extended and relaxed. The charred remains of raptor-walruses and grizzly-sharks bumped against the shore. To the east, the Tesla coils on the spires of the Dr. Moreau Junior Academy building cackled softly.

The members of the Doctoral Candidate Review Board—Drs. Gefährliche, Thiên Tai, and Golem—floated on hover chairs behind a table on the crest of the knoll. All three doctors wore starched white smocks embroidered above the left pocket with *University of*

Doom Faculty. In contrast, Moriarty wore a white lab smock with Doctoral Candidate stenciled over the breast pocket and across the back.

Dr. Gefährliche occupied the left-most chair, stiff, like he was made out of Pyrex. He said, "Will the candidate step forward."

Professor Moriarty advanced two paces and halted before the table. His shoes sank in the damp sod.

He smiled, a warm lamp of confidence on the outside, though inside his nerves simmered in frustration. How humiliating that he had to prove himself to the faculty, these geeky, self-important clowns, just to have them stamp *approved* on his dissertation.

He was the university provost, and usually they answered to him. Plus...and more importantly...he was a Moriarty. Because of his great-grandfather's reputation alone, the university should've awarded him a doctorate long ago.

But no. For a bunch of super-intellects, the faculty was painfully small-minded and bossy; a mob of spoiled kids keen on protecting their little corner of the playground.

As head of the board, Thiên Tai sat in the center. A carbon-fiber wig hung straight past her shoulders. Her eyebrows were woven of similar material; all the hair on her head having been burned off during last week's symposium on Recreational Incendiary Devices.

Golem was on the right, his lipless mouth flattened into a thin oval inside a perpetual grimace, his blue eyes centered within circular spectacles, his bare bulbous head as reddish-pink as the skin under a scab. The steel fingers of his right hand clacked together like the claws of a metallic crab.

A monitor at the left of the table was turned toward the committee and Moriarty. The monitor was future-state-of-the-art using 3-D analog trans-locomotive-luminescence (reverse-engineered from the Roswell UFO), which in Earth digital technology would've equaled a resolution of one gazillion dots per inch. Duct-taped cardboard ran around the monitor to shade the screen. As advanced as the aliens were, they hadn't thought of everything.

The monitor was connected by an EMP-pulse-hardened cable to a small black box—the Identity Confirmer—resting before Dr. Thiên Tai. Sadly, it wasn't beneath evil geniuses to send imposters to these proceedings. Not that a candidate couldn't handle the board, but these demonstrations were notorious for going *ka-boom!* And what's the point of getting the title "Doctor" if they had to scrape you off the ground with a spatula?

A blast tarp of ballistic nylon cloth and titanium steel chain mail was draped over the table. A red Panic Button rested in the middle. Standard protocol for all demonstrations—just in case. And hopefully there would be a "just-in-case." Nothing stimulated faculty gossip like an experiment gone terribly wrong. Gore and flying body parts were a big plus.

"State your full name." Dr. Thiên Tai readied the Identity Confirmer.

"James Moriarty the Fourth," he declared and added, "Great-grandson of James Moriarty." Moriarty waited for the doctors to acknowledge his legacy with an *ooh* and an *ahh*. After all, the first James Moriarty was the man, legend had it, *who had killed Sherlock Holmes*, and forever put the evil genius feather in the Moriarty family hat.

Gefährliche, Thiên Tai, and Golem stared back with the listless boredom of cows chewing their cuds.

"And James Moriarty the Second?" Thiên Tai raised an eyebrow. It got unstuck and swung over her eye.

Moriarty felt like a hand squeezed the back of his neck. She would have to mention his grandfather. In an ignored footnote in aerospace history, for his doctoral dissertation, Moriarty the Second had been the first man in orbit. Unfortunately, eighty years later, he was still in orbit, his corpse anyway.

"This is not the time nor place to dwell on my family history," Moriarty replied.

"You're the one who brought it up." Thiên Tai adjusted her eyebrow. "And James Moriarty the Third?"

Oh jeez, twist that scalpel a little more, you witch. At least Moriarty's father wasn't dead. Wasn't quite alive, either. He had been close to perfecting teleportation. But before presenting his doctoral dissertation, he forgot to plug in the matter re-atomizer and so, his atoms remained disintegrated into electromagnetic waves.

"Well," Moriarty answered, "he's still around." True, James Moriarty the Third existed somewhere around 1190 kiloHertz on the AM radio band.

Thiên Tai pressed a button on the Confirmer. The monitor said: *Voice Pattern OK*

Still, what was to prevent an evil genius from grafting a voice modulator into a minion's throat?

Thiên Tai rotated the function switch to *Chromosome Read* and pressed the *Go* button. The lid of the Confirmer snapped open. A chrome tube extended on scissor joints and rotated toward Moriarty.

He suppressed a nervous gulp. He hoped Thiên Tai had entered the correct function. Mad scientists were notoriously absent-minded, and how many doctoral candidates had been lost because someone had dialed *Obliterate* by mistake?

A thin blue ray shot from the tube and centered on Moriarty's sternum. His heart hitched. The beam widened and traced up and down Moriarty's silhouette. He sighed, *whew*. Iridescent waves surged through the beam, sorting through the nuclei of his cells, reading his DNA and tickling him at the molecular level. He wanted to giggle but a true mad scientist didn't giggle—he chortled.

The beam went dim, the tickling stopped, and the cylinder retracted into the Identity Confirmer. The lid snapped closed, and the monitor flashed: *Identity Confirmed!*

Thiên Tai said, "Professor Moriarty, now you may begin."

He turned about and waved. From down the slope, a forklift rumbled toward them. It carried a steel cube, two meters along each side. At last, after three generations, he would break the family curse and become the first modern *Doctor Moriarty!* "My dissertation, Bio-Heuristic Automatonic Force Multipliers—"

"Translation?" Gefährliche interrupted.

"Robotic warriors," Moriarty explained. "It's a military project, and the more obtuse the title, the larger the funding."

"And the 'bio?'" Thiên Tai asked.

"Let me get to that." Moriarty tingled with anticipation. Evil geniuses loved to rant about their projects before a captive audience.

The forklift's wheels dug ruts in the sod. The driver wore a plastic helmet, safety glasses, and the forest green overalls of a university groundskeeper. An immense ring of keys dangled from her belt. The forklift lowered the cube and backed away, alarm pinging.

"We've tried robotic warriors before," Moriarty said, "but even our most advanced computers leave much to be desired when it comes to self-learning, i.e., heuristic programming. What I've created is a completely autonomous robotic warrior. A fighting machine that learns as it goes and is capable of improvising tactics."

"This is your third attempt, isn't it?" Golem sounded dismissive.

Moriarty squared his shoulders. "Nothing prepares a man like failure."

"Failures," corrected Gefährliche.

Moriarty shifted weight from foot to foot. "Yes, well...the previous robotic warrior was the victim of an unfortunate typo. When I entered 'heuristic' the software autocorrected and substituted 'hedonistic.'"

Gefährliche put his terminal portal on the table and read. "According to the report submitted by Dr. Eugino Frankenstein—"

Frankenstein! Moriarty got an immediate brain freeze. He had rid the university of Frankenstein yet the name still tormented him. Moriarty's neck hardened, and he felt his head twist to the side.

Gefährliche continued, "Upon activation, your prototype ran off campus, hocked its Mark 626 blaster for cash and an airline ticket, and spent a long weekend in France contaminating its circuit boards with wine, and, indulging in other, ahem—," the doctor made air quotes, "'activities.' Which I thought would've been outside the mission parameters."

Moriarty gritted his teeth and willed himself to relax. He stepped toward the steel cube, all fresh smiles and contentment. "My updated prototype has solved the problem of self-learning artificial intelligence." He pulled a remote from his smock. "What I've done is replace the digital processor with the brain of a baboon, an adult male African Olive baboon. *Papio anubis*. A particularly large and aggressive species."

"A baboon?" asked Golem. "Why?"

"Of all the apes and monkeys, baboons have the qualities most desirable in soldiers. They are intelligent. Social. Aggressive. And quite adaptive."

Thiên Tai stroked her chin. "This is a cyborg?"

Moriarty stabbed the air with an index finger. "Not just a cyborg, but a Moriarty cyborg."

"I thought it's a baboon cyborg," she said.

"Same difference," whispered Gefährliche.

Moriarty pretended he hadn't heard the comment and aimed the remote at the cube. "Prepare to be impressed."

Drs. Gefährliche, Thiên Tai, and Golem reached under the table. They donned Kevlar helmets with bullet-resistant face shields.

Moriarty projected a thought to the remote. <open>

The front of the cube popped open and revealed a gloomy void. Two yellow lights burned in the darkness. Servos hummed. The cyborg emerged, a mechanical beast made of stainless steel so highly polished it gleamed with a blue tint. It looked like a cross between a mechanical baboon and a robotic football linebacker.

<threat scan> The machine growled, slit its yellow eyes, and opened its mouth, revealing dagger-like canines. The three doctors leaned back.

Moriarty gloated. "It senses your hostility."

"What mission did you program it with?" asked Golem.

Moriarty paused. *Hmmm.* Actually, he hadn't programmed it with a mission. "It's acting on baboon instincts."

"The instincts of an adult male baboon?" If Golem had eyebrows, they would've popped over the tops of his spectacles. "Which are?"

Moriarty spoke as he wondered. "Scratch its butt? Throw poop? An immediate attack on hostile intruders?"

The cyborg hunched forward. A grenade launcher popped out its back.

Thiên Tai slapped the Panic Button. The hover chairs dropped to the ground, and the three doctors disappeared behind the table and the blast tarp.

Grenades spewed from the discharger and exploded against the tarp. The blasts knocked Moriarty off his feet and peppered him with pieces of torn chain mail. Spent grenade cartridges ejected from the launcher rained on the grass. Poop would have been much better.

The volcanic cephalopods in the Lake of Terror awoke and complained by slapping their tentacles against the water.

The cyborg's head rotated toward the giant squids. The grenade launcher pivoted and adjusted elevation. A fresh volley arced toward the cephalopods.

Exploding grenades bracketed one of the squids. A shell penetrated the cephalopod's mantle and detonated its combustible fluid bladder. The hide blew apart, and a fireball *whooshed* into the sky.

The cyborg turned to the committee, grasped the blast tarp, and ripped it from its anchor bolts. Drs. Gefährliche, Thiên Tai, and Golem remained in the hover chairs resting on the sod.

Gefährliche gazed through his face shield at Moriarty. "Well?"

Moriarty scrambled to his feet. If the cyborg killed the Doctoral Board, how long would it take to overcome that disgrace? Shouting, "I got it," he pressed the self-destruct button on the remote.

The cyborg straightened and turned toward Moriarty. Did the machine actually grin?

It reached to its chest, opened the center breast panel, and withdrew the self-destruct module, the detonating wires dangling useless. Apparently, this cyborg was too adaptive.

With the module in its immense steel paw, the cyborg advanced on Moriarty. He backed away and kept mashing the self-destruct button.

A rectangular shadow grew around the machine. The shadow grew wider and darker with each second.

The cyborg halted, apparently confused, aware that something was wrong.

In one instant, the cyborg was there. In the next, *wham!* a giant anvil smashed it into a wad of crumpled metal.

"They never expect that," Gefährliche said.

The three doctors levitated on their hover chairs.

Moriarty studied the crushed junk wreathed around the bottom of the anvil, the tattered remnants of the blast tarp, and gazed down to the Lake of Terror. The smoldering remains of the dead cephalopod floated on the water. A cloud of black smoke dissolved into the sky. The air smelled of failure and burned calamari.

Dr. Thiên Tai recited the words every doctoral candidate loathed to hear: "Back to the drawing board." She added, "Better luck next time, *Professor.*"

The doctors rotated in unison and glided on their hover chairs down the knoll.

The forklift rumbled up the slope. It lowered a sweeper attachment to the grass and circled to gather cyborg debris. One of the cyborg eyes gazed at Moriarty. He kicked the eye into the path of the sweeper as it crept down the hill.

The roar of the bronze dragon in RJ Gatling Plaza echoed from the direction of Dr. Moreau Junior Academy. Time for recess. Lines of school children snaked out the doors.

Moriarty propped a hand against the ten-ton anvil and drummed his fingers. He wondered what laughs the faculty would be sharing at his expense.

Laughs.

Like the ones he was hearing.

He became aware of the distant laughter and catcalls of the school kids. Moriarty pushed away from the anvil and watched the clumps of blue uniforms.

The evil genius light bulb clicked on.

Bio-heuristic programming was sound. Only he needed smarter brains. Like those belonging to children.

CHAPTER
TWELVE

Alfonso shambled to the principal's office like a zombie. On the outside he might have looked okay, but inside he was rotting in sorrow. Dozens of school kids flowed around him, chatting, slamming wall lockers, but stepping clear as if he was blanketed in a stinky cloud of shame.

Who was responsible for this heartache?

First of all, Jerry what's-his-name. If it wasn't for that stupid bully, Alfonso wouldn't be in all this trouble.

And Professor Moriarty. Where was that snake in human skin? Probably about to get his evil genius doctoral degree, laughing *Mwua-ha-ha-ha* while Alfonso and his dad were drowning in misery.

Needles of pain pressed against the back of Alfonso's eyes, hurting worse than the lingering burn where Jerry had punched him on the ear. It was bad enough Alfonso had been marked as a troublemaker; he couldn't let anyone see him cry.

He turned the corner of the hallway. Sarah was busy arranging books in a locker. She wore a faded blue dress and a ponytail, which surprised him by how girly she looked.

She faced him and her eyes shined with a happy greeting. "Hey, buddy. How's the first day of class?"

At last, a friendly face. Her cheeriness eased his pain, and he tried to smile. "So-kay."

She tipped her head to one side. "*So-kay?* You look like my mom after she's wrecked the car. What's going on?"

He mumbled, "Gotta see the principal."

"What for?"

"Fighting."

"*Fighting?*" Sarah shook her head. "No offense, Alfonso, but you don't seem the type. My friend Polecat on the other hand, first day of school, it took him until third period before he got busted for fighting. And you, it's not even second period. A new record. Congratulations."

The bell rang.

Sarah cried, "Ack, I'm late," grabbed a spiral notebook and slammed the locker closed. She gave the padlock tumbler a quick spin and got ready to dash down the hall. "What lunch period you got?"

He pawed at his backpack, having not bothered to look at his schedule. "Dunno."

"If it's first, look for me in the cafeteria. If not, catch you on the way home." She slugged his arm, "Later, gator," and sprinted away.

Sarah disappeared through a classroom door catty-corner from him. A woman teacher leaned into the hall, gave him the stink-eye, and closed the door.

Alfonso was alone in the deserted hallway, the fluorescent lights flickering overhead, like they were dying, much like his hopes for happiness.

Maybe none of this was real. Maybe he and his dad were in a crazy experiment where they got sucked through a wormhole to a Bizarro-land way beyond Earth's orbit.

But if someone had gone through the trouble of shooting dad and me across space, they would've sent us to someplace awesome. The Tar Tarkas Temple on Mars. The forbidden alien palace on the moon Io. The lair of Cthulu.

Unfortunately, the dull odor of disinfectant and the rows of beat-up lockers reminded him that he was still on Earth and still at Ty Cobb Middle School.

He followed a sign pointing right, toward the front office. With every step, his mouth got drier and drier. Ms. Banard sat behind the counter—waiting, smiling— her eyes magnified inside goggle-like spectacles. In this light she no longer looked like an ogre but resembled an enormous pink-skinned frog guarding her lily pad.

And he was a fly.

Alfonso halted before the counter and worked spit into his mouth until he could say, "I'm here to see the principal."

She draped a fleshy hand over the counter telephone. "Ms. Humboldt told me all about your troublemaking and rule-not-following." Ms. Banard's smile spread wide. Wider. So wide he expected her face to split in half and roll out a huge tongue to suck him into her gullet.

Goose bumps pimpled Alfonso's skin.

"And you're here for fighting? *Tsk-tsk.*" She glanced to the wall clock and then blinked at him through her frog-face eyeglasses. "It's not even ten. A new record."

"So I've heard," he mumbled.

She pointed a meaty arm to a door at the far end of the room. "Principal Mulligan is waiting."

Alfonso side-stepped the counter. He passed six chairs along the wall, all occupied. An older student, a girl, slumped in an end chair. She was chewing a fingernail, then stopped to glower at Alfonso through mascara-caked eyes that said, *Whatcha lookin' at?*

The other five kids were boys. All of them shared an expression Alfonso had once seen in a movie of prisoners waiting for the chain gang. The look of the punished. The forsaken. *The damned.*

Alfonso stopped at the door and studied the polished brass nameplate: *Dolph Mulligan, Principal.* He knocked.

"Come in," a man answered.

In the brief moment between Alfonso opening the door and stepping over the threshold, he imagined a ghastly medieval torture chamber waiting for him. Shackles. A rack. An iron maiden. Steel tongs heating in a brazier. A hunchback torturer ready to flay him.

But there were no shackles. No rack. No iron maiden. Only bookcases jammed with notebooks and stacks of paper.

No tongs or smoking brazier. Only a desk and a filing cabinet overflowing with more papers. Rows of gilded trophies crowded every horizontal surface.

And no hunchback torturer. Only a very ordinary-looking man sitting in a big black chair behind the desk. Stocky build. Apple-shaped face with eyes so wide apart it appeared he could look in opposite directions at once. A peach-colored shirt and a striped necktie. Plus a billed cap, dark blue with a red letter B embroidered on the front. His gaze was down and focused at a magazine, the *Sporting News*.

Alfonso advanced. *Relax. You're no stranger to trouble. At Dr. Moreau Junior Academy, you've been to the head-master's office so often, they kept a chair reserved for you.*

But that was different. Back there, he had bent the rules a little bit. *Make that a lot.* Like that rainy night when he had welded Air Force-surplus rocket boosters to the statue of Dr. Faustus and hydroplaned the German geezer across the campus mall.

At least then, Alfonso deserved a scolding.

But now?

Tangled by rules he didn't understand.

"Principal Mulligan?" Alfonso squeaked.

The principal slapped the magazine flat on the desk and his eyes snapped to Alfonso. "So you're our newest troublemaker, Mr"—-he opened a red folder on his desk—"Frankenstein?"

"No sir," Alfonso replied.

Mulligan mashed his lips and wormed them for a moment. "You're not Alfonso Frankenstein?"

"Yes, sir. I am."

"Then why did you just say, no?"

"You had asked me if I was the newest troublemaker. I'm not"—Alfonso gulped—"sir."

"Not what?"

"A troublemaker...sir. There's been a mis-understanding."

The principal raised his hands. They were compact and yellow with calluses. "There's no misunderstanding." His hands returned to the folder. "Says here that Alfonso Frankenstein was caught fighting in Ms. Humboldt's class." His gaze drilled him. "Maybe there is another Alfonso Frankenstein. Hmmm?"

"No, sir. That would be me."

"The troublemaker?"

"I guess so."

Mulligan nodded, triumphant. "Now we're getting someplace." He pointed to the empty chair in front of his desk.

Alfonso's eyes swiveled left and right, and he absorbed the surrounding details. The walls were decorated with photographs of groups of smiling boys and young men in identical strange getups. Billed caps, striped or solid-color uniforms with weird lettering on the front, pants bunched at mid-calf to show off socks the same color as the caps. Other photographs showed men in similar clothes, arms cocked back to hurl something or posing with a smooth club resting on one shoulder.

Alfonso sat and noticed a round ball resting in the palm of a clumsy-looking glove—with thick fingers and made of bronze—front and center on the desk. This ball looked similar to the one Sarah had used to hit him, only this ball was a brilliant white with a pattern of red stitches and a confusion of signatures. Sarah's ball had been plain dirty beige.

Mulligan shook the red folder. The front had a white label scrawled with a thick black marker: *Alfonso Frankunstiene Frankenstein*

"This is your permanent record. The information here will follow you for life. Your grades, marked in here. Your deportment, right here. Go on to high school, apply for a job at Walmart or Taco Bell, this is where they'll check your references." He shook the folder again. "Should you decide on a higher education, people will look in this to see if you're community college material."

He flipped pages in the folder. "Says you transferred from Upstate Middle School. Never heard of it. Probably because they never made it to division playoffs." He put the folder down, reached forward, and snatched the ball from the glove.

Alfonso flinched and closed his eyes, thinking Mulligan was going to throw the ball at him. When he cracked them open, he saw Mulligan holding the ball up for inspection.

"You know what this is?"

"A...a...ball?"

Mulligan's face went *Duh!* "What else could it be?" He raised the ball like it was a talisman. "This is a baseball, man's most perfect creation. Made more perfect as it's signed by the 2007 World Series Champions. The Boston Red Sox."

Who? Alfonso was about to argue that the most perfect creation might have to be the perpetual motion machine but decided against it.

Mulligan presented the ball. "Baseball is life; everything else is just details." He cocked an eyebrow and squinted with the other eye. "You get what I mean?"

The word *No* echoed in Alfonso's mind, but after his experience so far, he knew that he better go along.

"Sorta..."

"Sorta?" Mulligan leaned back in his chair. "Let me put this in a way you can understand. This trouble you were in today? Strike one."

Strike? One?

Mulligan cocked his eyebrow again.

Alfonso had to ask, "That's not good, is it...sir?"

"Of course not. Especially considering your batting average in my school." Mulligan curled the fingers of his free hand against the tip of the thumb. "Which is zero."

Batting average. Zero. This had to do with statistics, that much Alfonso comprehended.

"Do I get any more strikes?"

Mulligan's eyebrows flattened, then pressed together to bunch the skin at the center of his forehead. "You're not following me, are you?"

Alfonso gave his head a meek shake.

Mulligan placed the ball back in the glove. He propped an elbow on the desk and raised his hand. He extended three fingers. "You get three strikes," he folded his hand and jerked a thumb over his shoulder, "then you're out."

Alfonso's shoulders drooped. Kicked out of the University of Doom and now expelled from this dump? He may as well be spiraling down a drain.

"What about Jerry? He started the fight by picking on me."

Mulligan sat straight and broke eye contact. "That's your side of the story. I'm sure Jerry Tremont has another version." Mulligan ran his fingertips along the edge of his desk. "Granted the kid is a handful but what an outstanding ball player. Wouldn't be surprised if he made all-state his freshman year."

Mulligan rapped the desk. "But I can't condone fighting, so I'm going to suspend you both for the rest of the day. Let me call your parents and have them pick you up."

He read from the folder and made a call on his desk phone. No one answered, and he left a message for Eugino Frankenstein in lawyerly-sounding words that meant Alfonso was in big, big trouble.

Mulligan hung up. "Got a number for your mom?"

"My parents are divorced. She doesn't live in town."

The principal lifted his cap, ran a hand through his hair, and scrunched the cap back into place. "Unless a guardian gets you, I can't send you home until the end of the day. Guess that means, in-school suspension." He scribbled on a blue note pad. "Report to the librarian. You're confined to the library until the final bell. You keep to yourself. You don't talk to anybody. And you stay"—Mulligan wagged his pen—"*Out. Of. Trouble.*" He plucked the note and handed it across the desk.

Alfonso took the note.

"A word of caution, Alfonso Frankenstein. Learn to respect authority and follow the rules. Remember, at Ty Cobb Middle School, there are no do-overs." Mulligan reached for the *Sporting News*. "Now go and keep your eye on the ball."

What ball? What did that have to do with following the rules? Alfonso stood and did another zombie-shamble out the door. The kids in the chairs didn't meet his eyes but they stared at the blue note in his hand like it was something evil.

Ms. Banard was missing from her perch. Good. He didn't need her lashing him with a bullfrog stare.

Spend the day in the library? That wouldn't be so bad. Books didn't pick fights. Books were his friends.

Someone walked behind him. "If it isn't Franken-stupid."

Alfonso whirled and was face-to-chest with Jerry Tremont.

Jerry looked down at him and was hitching the strap of a gym bag slung his shoulder. "Cuz of you, I know I'm gonna get suspended for the day and miss practice. Thanks a lot, you little creep."

The oaf was crowding him but Alfonso didn't budge. "What about me? This is my first day, and I'm close to getting kicked out."

Jerry pretended to cry. "Well, boo-hoo-hoo. Who cares?" He abruptly cocked his hand back.

Alfonso winced.

Jerry's mouth twisted into a cruel grin. The zits on his face turned fire-alarm red.

Alfonso's guts shriveled into a ball of confusion and fear. He'd made enemies before but never with anyone as monster-scary as Jerry. "Why are you doing this?"

"Cuz I don't like you. That's reason enough."

Alfonso gulped. The tension was like standing next to the cage of an allosaurus clone and watching the bars slowly rise. "What do you want from me?"

"Stay out of my face. Otherwise"—Jerry brandished his fists—"I'm going to pound your smelly Franken-butt."

CHAPTER
THIRTEEN

Jerry Tremont and Alfonso glared at one another like a couple of tomcats in an alley, ears flattened, tails twitching back and forth, claws at the ready.

A vein throbbed on Jerry's left temple and air whistled through his nostrils.

Alfonso gulped. He didn't want to fight. He'd lose and was already in enough trouble. *But if I back down, Jerry will keep pushing me, keep bullying me.*

"What's going on?" The booming voice was like a spray of cold water and Alfonso was relieved to feel the tension go slack. The voice boomed again, "Jerry, step back."

Jerry whispered, "I'll get you, Franken-stupid," and retreated.

A large man approached, so large he made Jerry look puny. His torso was as big as an oil barrel with two giant arms attached and a head and neck made from one imposing clump of muscle. His skin was so purple-black it caused his teeth and the whites of his eyes to glow. "Tremont, what are you doing in my hall?"

Jerry answered, "I'm on my way to see Principle Mulligan."

"You're not there yet, so keep walking."

Grumbling, Jerry ducked into the front office.

An ID badge dangled from the man's neck lanyard: Otis Carroll. His dark complexion and lively eyes reminded Alfonso of Dr. Umpetha HooDoo, the head of the revenant department at the University of Doom. Not only was Dr. HooDoo the master re-animator, he could also make his creations dance and play instruments. Except that tone-deaf zombies sounded terrible, especially on the trumpets and trombones.

Mr. Carroll turned to Alfonso. "And what's your story?"

Alfonso offered the blue note Mulligan had given him.

Carroll took and read it. "Then you're looking for me. I'm the librarian." Biceps ballooned against the cuffs of his short-sleeved shirt, muscles almost as enormous as Alfonso's father's.

But Mr. Carroll wasn't just beefy, he projected an authority that told Alfonso there was someone powerful and caring between him and Jerry and any other bullies at this school. Alfonso let his anxiety cool.

Until he noticed the three-inch scar on the outside of Mr. Carroll's arm. A burn scar of wrinkled flesh in the shape of the Greek letter Omega.

An Omega!

Alfonso's nerves sizzled into the red zone.

He'd heard of them. Omegas were alien enforcers—intergalactic assassins—the feared Order of Black Knights who traveled to this solar system through the Neptune portal. Alfonso thought Omegas were fables meant to scare nursery kids back at the University of Doom daycare. *But there was an Omega right here! In Ty Cobb Middle School. Who else would have that scar?*

Terror creepy-crawled up Alfonso's neck to the top of his head.

Carroll folded the note into his shirt pocket and squinted. "What's with you?"

Alfonso pointed a trembling finger at the scar.

Carroll flexed his arm and stared at the mark. "Oh that. Omega Psi Phi. My college fraternity."

"But it's a burn scar. From a brand." It could only be a souvenir from an Omega's gruesome initiation ritual into the Black Knights.

"Kids today aren't the only ones who can be young and stupid." Mr. Carroll laid a heavy paw-like hand on Alfonso's shoulder. "Forget the scar. That's my business." He nudged Alfonso down the hall. "Your business is that way. The library."

Omegas didn't exist, did they? And if they did, what would one be doing in this dead-end school?

Alfonso and Mr. Carroll walked side-by-side down the hall.

Carroll asked, "You're new, right?" His tone was friendly and open, not at all what Alfonso expected from an extraterrestrial killer.

An extraterrestrial killer? Get real, Alfonso snorted before answering, "It's my first day."

"And already in trouble? With Jerry Tremont, too. Between you and me," Mr. Carroll lowered his voice, "that kid is a punk. A gifted athlete but a punk. Do your best not to antagonize him."

"But he antagonized me. Got me in all this trouble."

"I'll talk to him," Carroll said. "In the meantime, go with the flow."

"What if the flow is taking me in a direction I don't want?"

Mr. Carroll halted. His eyes crinkled. "Good point. Then get used to being in trouble. Life is not fair."

Alfonso jammed his hands into his pants pockets. "Tell me about it."

He arrived at the library halfway down the hall. Mr. Carroll propped the door open.

Alfonso entered, surprised by the large size of the library, spacious as two regular classrooms. Neat rows of books lined the wall. An island of computer workstations sat in the middle of the floor between the bookshelves.

Carroll gave Alfonso a two-second tour.

"There are the books. Here are the computers."

Alfonso could keep himself busy—what kid wouldn't love to be stranded in a library, with computers no less?—but wished he had the chance to meet his other teachers and get on with his studies. After all, he was a future evil genius.

He was pulling a chair back from the closest workstation when Carroll told him: "Sorry, Alfonso. Those have been reserved for a class."

Figures.

Carroll pointed to a table and chair in the far corner, tucked between a bookcase and a wall of outside windows.

Alfonso shuffled away. He shrugged the backpack off his shoulders and placed it on the table.

The cackle of giggles and conversations pulled his attention to the library entrance.

Ms. Humboldt shepherded noisy, younger students—probably sixth-graders—though the door. She had taken off her lab smock and looked extra pretty in a tan dress covered with colorful swirls.

She caught sight of Alfonso, and her eyes flickered in a double-take. He sensed her friendliness and empathy and added a wave to his smile. He really wanted her to like him. She smiled in return—his heart warmed—then turned away to gather her mob around the computers.

Alfonso didn't resent her for sending him to the principal's office. Her job was to keep the peace and yes, enforce the rules. Once Alfonso settled into the routine of school—and learned the rules, whatever they all were—he'd make a heroic effort to prove he was the best student she ever had.

He plopped into the chair and gazed out the windows to his right. The view overlooked a ragged hedge onto the asphalt front lot, the street, and a neighborhood of older ranch houses and crooked telephone poles.

A big red SUV turned off the street, circled across the lot, and halted in front of the school entrance. The SUV shined like jewelry, unlike the Frankenstein's dented and faded Dodge pickup. From the left, Jerry loped from the school toward the SUV, frisky as a pony.

He was thumbing a cell phone and his grin was the expression of someone expecting ice cream and cookies.

Jerry opened the front passenger door, threw in his gym bag, and climbed aboard. The SUV drove off, Jerry cruising into freedom and sunshine while Alfonso imagined himself locked inside a jail. No ice cream for him. No cookies. Not even a computer to play on. Nerves prickling, he kicked his feet and felt his right shoe thump against cardboard.

Alfonso tipped his head to investigate.

There was a cardboard box next to the table, a box two-foot square on each side with the top flaps interlocked. One flap was scrawled with *Lost N Found*

He hooked his foot around the corner of the box and pulled it closer. Reaching down, he opened the flaps and saw a collection of junk. *Interesting.* He sorted through the pile. A green hoodie. A red glove. A blue mitten. Parts of a radio. Assorted broken toys, mostly plastic military vehicles. And at the bottom? His pulse quickened. *What was this treasure?*

A taxidermied alligator head!

Alfonso grasped the head. It was as long as his forearm but disappointingly light, like it was made of paper mâché. He examined the chipped scales, the pinky-sized yellowed teeth, and the lifeless glass eyes.

Nope, this was real, some poor reptile captured, killed, and stuffed. Now decapitated. He turned the head around and studied the hollow circle of the neck stump.

He spied one of the toy army tanks in the box and set it on the table. The turret was missing its cannon but no matter. Alfonso's gaze ping-ponged from the alligator head to the tank. Both were about the same size. He fit the head over the tank's turret and worked it back-and-forth until the lower jaw lay flush against the armored hull.

Alfonso pulled his hands away and admired his creation. The green reptile head with all those sharp teeth looked positively ferocious atop the caterpillar treads. This would make an awesome project for a re-animation class.

He zipped open his backpack and rummaged for his tricks kit. He placed the glass atomizer of Dippel's Oil and the neural stimulator next to the alligator-tank. He could try...

His conscience went *twang!* He heard Principle Mulligan's voice ring in his memory. *Stay. Out. Of. Trouble.*

And he had to guard the secrets of *la mano sinistre*.

Alfonso stared at the alligator-tank. Maybe this was as close as he'd get to becoming a mad scientist. His yearning and regret melded into sad pain. He placed the alligator-tank in the box, slouched, and crossed his arms, brooding in frustration.

Then he got the suspicion of being watched.

Alfonso looked over his shoulder. Ms. Humboldt circled the computer workstations and kept her students on task. Mr. Carroll sat behind a desk by the door, inserting a thumb drive into a laptop. If anyone was watching, must have been one of Ms. Humboldt's students.

Alfonso reached for his junior re-animator implements. Better put them away.

But that feeling remained. Eyes watching.

Something brushed against the shelves above and behind him. A delicate rustle like cloth. Or feathers.

His nerves tingled from the heebie-jeebies. Slowly, he rotated his head and looked up.

A pair of eyes big as quarters stared from the top shelf. Shiny black eyes in a red wrinkled head. The ugly head of a miniature turkey vulture.

A pendant hung from a collar around the bird's ruffled neck. A pendant with the seal of the University of Doom. He recognized the bird and the pendant. It was Professor's Moriarty's pet buzzard, Beelzebub.

The vulture blinked, tensed, and launched from the shelf in a blur of feathers and talons.

Alfonso mouthed a scream and barely had the time to grab his backpack. He swatted the vulture and sent it crashing against a bookshelf.

Alfonso backed away. Beelzebub bounced against the books, sending them tumbling to the floor, but continued flying toward the ceiling.

Mr. Carroll bolted from his desk, eyes brimmed, big arms flailing. The vulture circled above and behind him, then dive bombed the laptop and sprang upward.

Ms. Humboldt and the students cried out. She spread her arms and gathered the kids like a mother hen.

Alfonso jumped in front of the vulture and swung at it with his backpack. Beelzebub hovered and slashed with its claws.

The kids shouted. "Awesome."

Carroll bounded toward Alfonso and the vulture, a broom in hand.

Sharp talons snagged the backpack and yanked it from Alfonso's grasp. He staggered against a post and knocked against a fire extinguisher.

Beelzebub shook the backpack loose from its claws and something else, something small and gray, fell to the carpet. The vulture shrieked, a cry so electric with rage the hairs rose on Alfonso's arms. This bird was going to shred him to ribbons.

Alfonso needed a weapon.

The fire extinguisher!

He lifted it off the hook and aimed the nozzle at Beelzebub. He yanked the safety ring and squeezed the trigger, spraying the vulture with a plume of white powder. Beelzebub spun backwards—coughing—and tumbled over the table to fall into the cardboard box.

No one moved.

Alfonso heart thumped *rat-a-tat-tat* and breath rasped though his mouth.

No noise from the box. He rested the fire extinguisher on the floor.

Ms. Humboldt and her students panned the scene, their eyes saucered in wonder.

Mr. Carroll advanced with the broom like it was a pole ax. "Where did that buzzard come from?"

Alfonso knew exactly where it came from, but thought it best to lie. He shook his head. "I don't know."

Something rustled in the box, followed by a series of clicks, a rattle, and a grinding noise. Beelzebub rose from the box, moving in a steady, mechanical fashion. Fire extinguisher powder dusted the bird and made him look like a ghost. The side of the box flexed, bowed, and the box tipped over. Beelzebub stood on the head of the alligator-tank as it crawled into the open. The reptile's glass eyes burned with life, and its mouth snapped open and closed.

The kids screamed as one. "Super awesome."

Alfonso glanced to the table. The Dippel's Oil and the neural stimulator had spilled into the box and somehow reanimated the alligator head, fusing it to the toy army tank, creating a *cyborg!* Why had he been so careless?

Beelzebub steered the alligator-tank with left-right clenches of its talons until the cyborg was aimed at Alfonso. Then the bird and alligator-tank zoomed across the carpet.

The sixth graders scattered, some jumping on the chairs, others on the computer tables, all screeching in delight.

Alfonso spun about and sprinted between the bookcases, flinging thick volumes off the shelves, in the hopes of burying the alligator-tank and its buzzard commander under an avalanche of encyclopedias.

Beelzebub squawked, making the vulture equivalent of "Heh, heh, heh," as it chased Alfonso. Alligator teeth nipped the back of his ankles.

When Alfonso ran past the end of the bookcases, Beelzebub sprang from the cyborg. A broom swung at the bird from around the corner and missed. Mr. Carroll leapt into view and stomped his boot on the alligator-tank, smashing it to pieces.

Beelzebub circled the room, shrieking. Carroll swiped at it with the broom.

Alfonso picked up the fire extinguisher and heaved it at the vulture. Beelzebub juked to the side. The fire extinguisher arced into a window and crashed through the glass.

Beelzebub darted through the rectangle of broken shards and disappeared.

CHAPTER
FOURTEEN

Principal Mulligan rushed into the library, red-faced like he had spilled hot coffee down his pants. He circled the computer tables and stood in front of Mr. Carroll, Ms. Humboldt, and her mob of students.

Eyebrows cinching, Mulligan seemed to catalog the destruction: alligator-tank debris on the carpet, strewn books, the plume of white powder, and glass from the shattered window.

He leveled a hard gaze on Alfonso. "I was told you were attacked by a vulture."

"And an alligator-tank," one of Ms. Humboldt's students piped in. "It was so cool."

Mulligan took off his cap, rubbed a hand through his hair, and replaced the cap. "Young Mr. Frankenstein, I don't know how it happens, but trouble follows you like a shadow. Maybe Ty Cobb Midddle School isn't the place for you."

Alfonso toed the floor. *No kidding.*

Carroll crouched to collect the largest alligator and tank pieces. "Probably a prank running on remote control. I'll get the janitor to clean up the rest of this mess." He paused and raised the small gray object that had fallen from Beelzebub's claws. It was a thumb drive.

Carroll glanced back to his laptop.

"Is that yours, Mr. Carroll?" Alfonso pointed to the thumb drive.

Carroll clasped the thumb drive in his meaty hand and shoved it into his pocket.

"What was on it?" Alfonso asked.

"Test scores. Grades."

The deep wrinkles appearing on Carroll's dark brow looked like furrows in brown clay. "Why did the vulture want it?"

Alfonso backed away, replying, "I have no idea," but his mind said *Moriarty is behind this. He must be.*

Ms. Humboldt's students scampered about the library like kid goats escaped from a pen. She chased after them, getting them to quiet down and return to their workstations.

Mulligan said, "Your dad still hasn't called me back, so you'll have to remain here, unfortunately." He addressed Mr. Carroll. "Otis, any other weirdness, and I'm holding you responsible."

Mr. Carroll swiveled his big face to Alfonso. "We're going to behave, aren't we?"

Alfonso let his head hang. He started back to his table and mumbled, "Good thing I'm here so you have someone to blame."

He got on his hands and knees to pick up the scattered items from the Lost-N-Found box and search for the neural stimulator and the vial of Dippel's Oil. When he found them, he hurriedly stuck them in their case and into his backpack.

Mr. Carroll brought a stack of thick books and dropped them on the table. "Keep your nose in these and out of trouble."

Alfonso sighed. Some education this was. He spent the rest of the morning leafing through color photographs of snakes, sharks, and arachnids. Not long ago, he got to experiment on these creatures. Now he just looked at their pictures.

For lunch, Ms. Banard escorted Alfonso to the cafeteria. The last of the other students wandered out the doors. A squad of lunch-ladies in hairnets and pastel aprons wiped the tabletops and mopped the floor.

Banard sat at the opposite end of their table and ate from her tray. Alfonso squinted at the cover of the book she was reading—about a serial killer—then averted his eyes when she glanced up and poked him with a serial-killer glare of her own.

Afterwards, Ms. Banard followed him back to the library, keeping close, like he was attached to a short leash.

Alfonso returned to his corner table and slumped into the chair, already bored. He flipped through the pages of the books. The hour and minute hands on the wall clock seemed glued in place. The second hand made slow, hypnotic circles that made him sleepy. So sleepy.

He woke with a start.

Mr. Carroll was tapping his shoulder. "The last bell was fifteen minutes ago."

Alfonso panned a drowsy gaze across the table. He made sure the tricks kit was secure in his backpack and stood.

"How about a ride home?" Carroll asked.

Alfonso yawned and replied with a nod. He waited in the hall while Mr. Carroll did a final check of the library and locked the doors.

Carroll led him to the teachers' parking lot and to a gleaming burgundy coupe. Up close, Alfonso read the brand and model. Cadillac Eldorado.

The door locks clicked open. "Don't get used to this," Carroll said. "Figured you could use a break to make up for your very bad day."

"Thanks, Mr. Carroll." Alfonso slid onto the front passenger's seat and buckled up. The interior was white leather, as immaculate as the exterior. Dozens of switches and gizmos covered the instrument panel, clearly after-market additions. Now this was a ride worthy of a mad scientist.

As big as the Eldorado was, Mr. Carrol had to wedge his muscular bulk between the steering wheel and the driver's seat.

The Cadillac started with a purr and glided out of the parking lot. Alfonso gave directions to his home. They drove past strip malls and parking lots. School kids wandered in groups of twos and threes. Everything looked so plain and dull. So alien.

They reached his neighborhood and rounded the corner onto Ennuyeux Lane.

Alfonso pointed to his house, an embarrassing rectangular heap surrounded by weeds and yellowed grass. The family pickup was in the driveway.

Alfonso chirped, "My dad's home," though he wondered why his father hadn't replied to the principal's messages.

Mr. Carroll parked along the curb. He eyed the Frankenstein's abode. "Interesting place..." his voice trailed off, "...has lots of potential."

Potential, Alfonso thought. *Meaning: right now it's a crappy dump.*

Carroll presented his hand, a huge mitt of dark leathery skin. "Tomorrow is a new day. A fresh start."

They shook hands. Alfonso stole a glance at the Omega scar on Carroll's immense arm. Nobody this nice could possibly be an intergalactic assassin.

He climbed out and started for the front porch. Carroll's Eldorado motored away.

"Hey ya, Alfonso." Sarah trotted up the sidewalk and joined him. She was still in her yellow school dress. "Heard you got into big time crazy trouble. A fight with Jerry Tremont. Then you got attacked by a buzzard in the library. And a remote-control tank. How cool is that?"

"Not cool at all."

"Didn't mean the fight. That wasn't cool. But the buzzard and the tank. How did that happen?"

Alfonso shrugged.

The front door was unlocked. He opened it and caught a burned smell.

Sarah sniffed. "What's that? Smells like clothes that caught fire." She crowded behind him and sniffed again. "And hair?"

He left the door open, and they tiptoed into the front room. Disasters at the Dr. Moreau Junior Academy had taught him to be ready to scram. They halted at the threshold of the kitchen. An ice tray and his father's bottle of rye whiskey rested on the counter.

Sarah whispered, "I didn't know your dad was a boozer."

"He's not," Alfonso replied. His father drank only occasionally, and only to celebrate or commiserate.

Please let it be celebrate. I've had enough bad news for one day. For the week. The month!

Maybe the University of Doom had contacted his dad about returning. Alfonso's mind grasped at hopeful images. Decanting hydroflouroxide fireworks propellant. Chasing winged thoats on hover bikes. Reuniting with Greg Kaminski. Yes, he'd even be glad to see Lilith Vampira.

Please be good news. But what was that burnt smell?

He entered the kitchen. *Please be good news.*

His father sat at the breakfast table. A melted and blackened ID badge hung from a lanyard draped across the front of his scorched shirt. Smoke wisped from his hair, singed at the ends and plastered into grimy spikes. A raccoon-mask of clean skin outlined his eyes where safety goggles had rested. He stared glumly at a half-empty glass on the table.

Not good news. In fact, very bad news.

Dr. Frankenstein raised his eyes and asked in a hoarse voice, "And how was your day, Alfonso?"

"About the same as yours, Dad."

"That bad," his father quipped.

Alfonso wrung his hands. "The school was calling you, Dad."

Dr. Frankenstein reached deep into one trouser pocket. He pulled out his hand and dumped a broken cell phone on the table.

"What happened?" Sarah asked.

"First day on the job. I noticed the benzene-ring defibrillator could use some tweaking. That design should've been robust enough to accept an increase of power to one hundred megawatts."

Alfonso's father reached for the glass. "For a company that brags about cutting-edge technology, they sure don't have much of a sense of adventure." He gulped the whiskey. "Or a sense of humor."

He took the glass from the table and set it in the sink. He stripped off his shirt and draped it over a chair. His smudged undershirt bulged with muscles. After wetting a clean shop rag, he squeezed it and dabbed his face and neck. The rag left splotches of clean skin ringed in dirty gray.

"Uh, Dad," Alfonso began as he launched into his story about the fight with Jerry Tremont and getting suspended. He didn't add details that he'd reanimated Jerry's hamster or had accidentally created a cyborg.

His father's heavy sigh knifed into Alfonso.

Sarah blurted. "Professor Moriarty was back."

"At your school?" Dr. Frankenstein turned from the sink and ricocheted an angry look from Alfonso to Sarah. "You saw him?"

She retreated a step. "No. But I remember he was that creep in the fancy white limousine...didn't he have a buzzard?"

"Couldn't be the same bird," Alfonso made his reply sound as casual as possible.

Sarah added, "Tell your dad about the remote-control tank with the alligator head."

His father ricocheted another angry glare.

"Dad, I'll tell you the details later." Alfonso motioned with his head toward Sarah to signal he had to reveal mad scientist secrets. Sarah might not like school or books but she sure knew how to collect pesky details with her magnetic brain.

He changed the subject. "I hate that school. The only way I'll fit in is if I learn about this stupid game called baseball. That's all Principal Mulligan cares about."

His father's eyes focused on something distant and unseen. His anger sloughed off, replaced by a wistful expression.

"What is it, Dad?"

He tossed the shop rag into the sink. "Now you're digging at my secrets."

"Secrets?" Sarah's gaze locked on Dr. Frankenstein. She groped for a chair and sat.

He shook his head and pointed to the door.

Sarah pouted. "These had better be some awesome secrets you're keeping." She stood and waved at Alfonso. "Tomorrow. Maybe."

He wanted her to punch his arm and say, "Later, gator," like she always had. But she didn't and that made him feel a little bit lonely.

His father remained still until they heard Sarah exit the front room and close the door.

Satisfied she was gone, Dr. Frankenstein stood straight. "Son, once upon a time, the University of Doom had a baseball team."

He towered over Alfonso and flexed his arms, his biceps swelling huge and round, like a pair of artillery shells. "And I was their champion outfielder."

CHAPTER
FIFTEEN

His father—a Frankenstein—had played baseball? Alfonso didn't know much about baseball other than he hated whatever baseball was.

And his father had once been a baseball champion? This was beyond crazy. Now the world had popped inside-out. Alfonso braced his hand against the breakfast table to remain steady against a swirl of dizziness.

"C'mon," Dr. Frankenstein walked across the kitchen. He flicked on the basement light switch and opened the door.

Alfonso followed his father down the rickety steps. Descending into a dank basement usually promised scientific adventure and mayhem.

The basement floor was a maze of crates and boxes from where the movers had left them. Dust sifted from the ceiling.

His father pushed aside heavy crates and carefully moved a metal box containing amphoras of Dippel's

Oil. He bumped against an upright crate, tipped it over, and out clattered a skeleton.

Dr. Frankenstein grasped a familiar, battered footlocker by the end handle and hauled it to the middle of the floor, directly under the overhead bulb.

A rusted iron padlock secured the footlocker.

Like any other kid curious about what was in his home, Alfonso had tried for years to pick this lock, without success.

His father crouched beside the locker, swiveled the padlock close to his mouth, and whispered, "Open channel F."

A white light glowed in the keyhole.

Voice recognition! Clever, dad.

The glow extended over the padlock. The rust seemed to melt away and the surface became shiny steel. The padlock snapped open.

Alfonso knelt beside his father, anxious to see what secrets had been locked up. But surprisingly, Dr. Frankenstein didn't move. He gazed at the footlocker, brooding, as if wrestling with second thoughts.

Maybe this was another Pandora's Box (the original was in the Los Alamos Atomic Museum), and the instant his dad cracked the lid, *Armageddon!*

His father creaked the lid open, and Alfonso winced, closing his eyes.

He kept them closed and listened.

Nada.

Awfully quiet Armageddon.

He peeled his right eye open.

The padlock in hand, Dr. Frankenstein remained still and stared into the footlocker.

Alfonso peeled his left eye open and craned his neck to see what mesmerized his father.

Dr. Frankenstein reached in and lifted a gray cloth shirt that he let unfold. A word was embroidered in red across the chest in the same curvy script as those weird costumes in the photos in Principal Mulligan's office.

"This was my jersey," his father said, "when I played for the University of Doom *Actinides*."

A shirt? Not too mysterious. Alfonso studied the letters. At least the team name was cool. *The Actinides.* Dangerous radioactive elements that included uranium and plutonium.

His father handed the jersey to Alfonso. The material was heavy cotton, coarse and cool to the touch.

Dr. Frankenstein slid his hand under a pair of pants that matched the shirt and rummaged in the footlocker.

"What are you looking for, dad?"

"A bat."

Alfonso leaned forward to see. A live bat? Couldn't be. Maybe a dormant zombie bat.

His father withdrew a wooden "baseball" club, and Alfonso frowned, disappointed.

The skinny end of the "bat" was wrapped in dingy cloth tape. His eyes sparkling with growing excitement, Dr. Frankenstein cinched his fingers around the tape. He stood and swung the bat slowly in front of him like it was an enchanted sword.

But Alfonso didn't see anything magical. The bat. The jersey. The footlocker. There had to be more. "So what is baseball?"

"Son, in a perfect world, baseball is life, everything else—"

"...is just details. Yeah, I've already heard that from Principal Mulligan. So baseball is a game?"

His dad swung the bat in slow, deliberate arcs and explained the game. Alfonso followed along as best he could and got completely lost when his father recited some bizarre, convoluted thing called the "infield fly rule."

Alfonso unbuttoned the jersey and slipped it over his shoulders. It billowed over his thin frame like a sack.

Now that he wore the jersey, Alfonso had to admit he enjoyed its weight and the way the uniform implied that he belonged to something bigger than himself. A team of *champions!*

"The Actinides were feared," his father commented proudly with another measured swing of the bat. "Our team dominated our collegiate league."

"You guys must have trampled the competition with all your mad scientist tricks." Alfonso wanted to hear the schemes.

His father shook his head. "No, son. We played a clean game. Otherwise it wouldn't have been a contest of the better baseball players. We had plenty of other opportunities to trounce our evil genius competitors."

"What happened to the team?"

"Our athletic program was terminated in mid-season during a home game against the Havana *Colegio de Locura Scientifico.*" Dr. Frankenstein halted his swing and caressed the thick end of the bat. "Their bats had been juiced with kinetic kryptonite."

He bent over the footlocker and picked up a large, clumsy-looking leather glove. It was splotched with stains and so worn and creased it flopped closed like a clamshell. Maybe this glove was used to handle samples of actinides. His father opened the glove to reveal a fist-sized hole scorched through the pocket. "Those cheating Cubans were pounding the ball at Mach-plus speeds."

Alfonso studied the burned void in the glove. His father had tried to catch a supersonic ball?

Before Alfonso could ask if his father had been hurt, Dr. Frankenstein tossed the glove back into the footlocker.

"The game was called after a foul ball blasted through a patron's luxury box. An admiral and two generals were decapitated. Damn near cost us our military funding until someone pointed out that the Pentagon might be able to weaponize kinetic kryptonite."

Dr. Frankenstein lowered the bat. "But the Cubans weren't acting alone. Turned out it was someone from the University of Doom who had corked the bats."

"Who?"

"Who else? James Moriarty."

"*The* Professor Moriarty?"

"He wasn't a professor then, just a teacher's aid in the Alchemy Department. And already a treacherous pain-in-the-butt know-it-all."

"Why did he want the Actinides to lose?"

"Because of a girl."

"A girl? Who was she? His accomplice?" Every good story had a femme fatale—the undoing of many a mad scientist's perfect plan.

Dr. Frankenstein crouched and slid his hand back into the footlocker. He withdrew a green vinyl note-book, which he handed to Alfonso.

He took the binder and set it on his lap. His father reached over one shoulder and flipped the cover open, then whisked through photographs in plastic sleeves.

Alfonso caught glimpses of his father as an undergraduate—youthfully lean yet still muscular, mustachioed, with sideburns, an Actinides ball cap perched on his head. Heroic.

His father stopped at one color photograph.

Alfonso's heart jammed on its brakes.

A slender, pretty woman stood beside his father. Veronica Galvan.

Alfonso whispered, "Mom."

Shoulder-length brunette hair. Delicately arched eyebrows. Her left hand was draped over his father's big, sinewy forearm. Alfonso wanted muscles like his dad but had inherited her litheness and brunette hair. And her eyebrows.

Alfonso zeroed in on something he had seldom seen on her in the last months before she had left the Frankenstein household—a pleasant, guileless smile.

She looked so young and beautiful, not at all like the bitter woman who slammed the front door when she raced away from her husband and her son Alfonso.

Dr. Frankenstein's expression surrendered to a darkening pain. The picture was merely an image on paper tinted with inks. But that was the magic of photography. A memory captured long before Alfonso was born now tore at Dr. Frankenstein with regrets sharp as hooks.

Alfonso asked, "Mom and Moriarty were evil pals?"

"No," his father replied. "That photo was taken the day I proposed to your mother. Moriarty thought if he could humiliate me on the ball field, he could somehow win Veronica's affection. Didn't work. What saved him from getting booted from the university was his family name."

Dr. Frankenstein closed the binder and took it and the jersey from Alfonso. He placed the notebook and the jersey back in the footlocker, closed the lid, and secured the padlock.

Alfonso kept the bat. It felt clumsy and heavy. But as he swung the bat to-and-fro, he sensed its wizardry, its power to both lift hearts and crush them. Alfonso couldn't do anything about his lingering Mom pain, but he could act against someone else who tormented him.

Alfonso tapped the bat against the floor. "Dad, will you teach me to play?"

His father gazed at him with eyes shadowed by the overhead light. "Why?"

"Playing baseball might help me fit in with the other kids."

But that was not the whole truth. His father wouldn't have used mad science to win at baseball. But Alfonso would. He'd combine baseball and evil genius to humiliate that bully Jerry Tremont. Get revenge.

Mwua-ha-ha-ha.

CHAPTER
SIXTEEN

Professor James Moriarty walked beside his office desk, an enormous plateau of oak and mahogany, a family heirloom, complete with blood stains, burn marks, and bullet holes—souvenirs of betrayal, treachery, and doing-what-it-takes-to-get-ahead.

Moriarty paced to-and-fro with his hands clasped behind his back and tried to ignore the anxiety scouring his belly. Dr. Gefährliche was due at any moment to discuss the professor's dissertation and his string of failures.

Something scratched the office window. Moriarty turned and saw Beelzebub perched on the windowsill, clawing at the glass.

The professor undid the window latch. "Welcome back. What did you bring me?"

The little vulture sneezed a cloud of white powder.

Moriarty backed away. He brushed the powder from his lapel and wrinkled his nose at the smell.

Potassium bicarbonate? Who had shot a fire extinguisher at his poor bird?

He scowled. *Who else? Alfonso Frankenstein.* The professor examined the buzzard's torn feathers and the bumps on its bald leathery head. Seems whatever had happened, Beelzebub got the worst of it. *Curse those Frankensteins.*

Moriarty gestured into the room. The bird hopped through the window and fluttered clumsily to the mantle.

"So you came back empty-handed, or should I say, empty-clawed. Don't worry, Beelzebub, I've got other ways to get what I need."

The professor slid his hand under the lid of the aquarium on his office credenza and plucked a newt stuck to the inside of the glass. He offered the squirming amphibian to Beelzebub and caressed the vulture's featherless noggin as it munched the hapless creature.

The professor went to close the window when the laughter and chatter of children made him pause. He panned the grounds of the adjacent Dr. Moreau Junior Academy, watching school kids clustered under the trees or following their teachers across the lawn.

Moriarty's gaze skipped from student to student as he imagined studying their young brains under an x-ray. So many magnificent specimens. Their gray matter would be perfect bio-computers for his next series of cyborgs. He shook his head with regret, knowing from experience that parents—even evil genius parents— could be fiercely protective and narrow-mindedly selfish about their innocent spawn.

Really, what mad scientist wouldn't want his or her child immortalized as a cyborg? *A Moriarty cyborg!* With a sturdy carbon-fiber frame instead of a soft adolescent body. A flawless exterior of chromium stainless steel, no zits of course. Attachable tools to complement hands. Adjustable volume in the voice module. You could bypass the theatrics of puberty with a quick software upgrade. And best of all: an On/Off switch! What parent wouldn't love that option on their precious meat-bag progeny?

Moriarty swung the window closed. *Why was life so unfair?* In a better world, he could pick through the faculty litter and their parents would shower him with gratitude.

A knock on the door interrupted his musings. It had to be Dr. Gefährliche. Moriarty gave himself the once-over. Socks matched. Shoes tied. No toilet paper stuck to his heel. Zipper up. Necktie not flipped around. He finger-buffed the lapel pin identifying him as the university provost and announced, "Enter."

The door clicked open. Dr. Gefährliche stepped through the doorway, a leather satchel in his hand. His starched white faculty smock fit him like a carapace, making his torso match his demeanor: steady, rigid, and inflexible.

Moriarty welcomed him and pointed to the empty chair in front of his desk.

Gefährliche nodded thanks. He glanced at Beelzebub and sat. He placed the satchel on the floor and unsnapped the latches. The doctor withdrew a stack of bound papers, the edges scorched and brittle.

"I'm sure we're in agreement that the demonstration for your latest dissertation could've gone better."

"We learn most from our mistakes," Moriarty replied as he took his chair behind the desk.

"Then I'm sure you must've learned quite a bit." Gefährliche dumped the stack of papers into Moriarty's in-box. The hefty tome settled in a puff of ash that drifted across the desktop and dusted the professor's portal tablet.

"There is another matter," the doctor added. "The university is going to bill you for the additional expenses incurred during your demonstration. Re-levitating a ten-ton anvil won't be cheap."

Moriarty swallowed his groan and replied with as much acceptance as he could fake. "Understandable."

Gefährliche rested his hands on the chair's arms. The scars on his gnarled fingers and knuckles matched those on his chin and throat. "I trust you'll take a break before your next attempt?"

"Not at all." Moriarty pointed to the red binder on the edge of the desk. "My new proposal."

Gefährliche squinted at the binder. "Why the rush?"

Revenge, thought Moriarty, but he answered in a virtuous tone. "It's an excellent opportun—"

"The question was rhetorical," Gefährliche interrupted.

Moriarty shrank back into his chair and smiled though he wanted to snarl.

The doctor took the binder and blew ash off the cover. He laid it on his lap and flipped it open. A holographic carousel of schematics and photos sprang up and hovered over the binder. He flicked at the hologram, making it spin. He extended a fingertip to stop the spinning and furrowed his brow. He flicked to another image, studied it, his brow still furrowed, and flicked to another image.

He asked, "A video game?"

"Not just a video game," Moriarty straightened in his chair, "but a research tool. It's a 3D masterpiece I created called *Undead Siege*. Kids are crazy about shoot-em-up games featuring zombies and the Apocalypse. And what better authority about the undead and world destruction than someone from the University of Doom?" The professor tapped his chest. "In this case, me."

He extended an index finger and pointed dramatically to the ceiling. "*Unum passus.*" Step one. Using Latin made any scheme sound so much more scholarly. "Deploy the game over the Internet. Gather data on the reactions and skills of the players."

Another dramatic gesture to the ceiling, this time with two fingers. "*Duae passus.* Use that data as a template to program my new cyborgs."

A final dramatic flourish with three fingers. "*Tres passus.* Demonstrate the cyborgs."

He smiled triumphantly, like he already had M.D. appended to his name. What Moriarty didn't share was that he intended to target Alfonso Frankenstein and his schoolmates. He'd use the game to lure those brats where he could steal their brains for his cyborgs. And he had already figured out how to snag Alfonso. Use his best friend here at the university, that bumbling Greg Kaminski, to gain his confidence.

How deliciously evil.

So deliciously evil that Moriarty drooled. He wiped his mouth and suppressed a demented snicker.

What will Eugino Frankenstein think when he learns I have his son's brain in my cyborg, ready to do my bidding? Actually, I'd be doing Alfonso a favor. He'd be released from his humdrum existence to serve me. What an honor.

Even if this dissertation didn't pan out, getting revenge on the Frankensteins would be a tasty treat.

Blinking, Moriarty came out of his trance and waited for Gefährliche to congratulate him on the video game proposal.

The doctor closed the binder, and the hologram crumpled and disappeared inside the cover. "You may have to adjust your schedule." Gefährliche put the binder on the desk.

"Why?"

"Igor Bartul, your minion, starts his sabbatical next week."

Frustration nipped at Moriarty. This masterful plan had been disrupted by his assistant's sabbatical? First, he'd been forced to give that deadbeat over-time pay. Then health benefits. Paid vacation. Now Igor was entitled to a sabbatical? Since when did minions get tenure?

Maybe it was just as well Moriarty didn't have a dedicated assistant. His plan to steal the children's brains was a dangerous secret, and Igor might figure the details. Minions were notorious gossip mongers. If Moriarty needed help, he'd requisition part-time lackeys or trained tech-apes from the minion pool.

The doctor added an indifferent, "Besides, the Internet is flooded with video games of this sort."

"No one can compete with what I'm offering." Moriarty reached beside his desk and lifted a silver quilted nylon bag containing something the size of a basketball.

Moriarty set the bag on his desk, unzipped it and revealed an astronaut helmet of gray and beige camouflage with a mirrored-gold visor. "The helmet includes a heads-up display to allow a full-body 3D interface with my game. What kid could resist?"

The doctor folded his arms. "How will your test subjects get these helmets?"

"From the university. Through a bogus online company to hide our identity."

"So you're now in the helmet manufacturing business?"

"Not at all. I'm using surplus hardware left over from the lunar war maneuvers and—"

A frown cracked through Gefährliche's stone-cold expression. He put his hand up to silence the professor and remind him that the debacle of the top-secret lunar military games had been shunted to the Department of Denial. No one was to ever again mention Operation Harebrain.

"Look at it this way," Moriarty quipped, "at least I'm getting rid of the evidence."

Gefährliche allowed a trace of a smile. He reached for the helmet. "It does look cool."

"Go ahead. Try it," Moriarty insisted.

The doctor grasped the helmet. He warily lifted it and studied the inside. With a boyish grin, he slipped the helmet over his head and twisted it into place.

Moriarty picked up his portal tablet and pulsed a thought to activate *Undead Siege.*

Gefährliche rose from the chair, a tall white giant with a domed head. Hands raised, he rotated left and right. "This is amazing. Like I'm there." His muffled voice was echoed by his tinny words coming from the portal tablet. "Kudos to you, professor."

"Total visual and auditory immersion," Moriarty declared proudly. "Plus tactile feedback."

"Are those zombies shooting arrows?" Gefährliche leaned forward. Suddenly, he jumped around and clutched at his backside. "Ow. Ow. Ow."

"Sorry," Moriarty blurted. "Let me reduce the sensitivity."

Gefährliche relaxed and groped for his chair. "Okay, I'm convinced."

"Wait, there's more. An upgrade to include Smell-O-Rama!" He pulsed a thought to the tablet. <chili bean burritos>

Gefährliche yelped, "Ahhhhh! What is that horrible stink?"

"Boys love fart jokes."

The doctor grasped the helmet with both hands and bent over, wrestling to take it off. "Help! Help! The stench is killing me."

"Lift the visor."

"You fool, I'm trying. It's stuck."

Moriarty pulsed another thought at his tablet but the game controls were frozen.

Gefährliche fell to the floor, kicking his legs and twitching like a suffocating cockroach.

Moriarty dropped his tablet and scrambled around the desk to help the doctor. The professor grasped the rim of the helmet and planted his right foot on Gefährliche's shoulder.

"Oh God," he moaned, "it's like I'm trapped head first in a bus station toilet."

Moriarty yanked as hard as he could and stamped his foot on the doctor's shoulder. The helmet squeaked, then popped loose.

An intense dog poop odor made Moriarty wince and his eyes water. Beelzebub perked up and squawked, *Yum!*

Gefährliche staggered to the aquarium, where he tore the lid off and splashed water over his face.

The doctor returned to his chair and plopped into the seat. His eyes were shiny red welts and his mouth swollen and pink. Water stains covered his wrinkled smock and a dirty shoeprint decorated his left shoulder.

Moriarty picked the helmet off the floor. "At least we know what doesn't work. What else could go wrong?"

CHAPTER
SEVENTEEN

Alfonso centered himself over home plate and readied his bat.

Reginald faced him from the pitcher's mound, the tip of his dark nose shining with sweat, his hooded eyes glinting under the shadow of his cap.

They were practicing in a weedy softball field six blocks from Alfonso's home, where the railroad tracks ran close to the ditch. Sarah took shortstop. Her friend Polecat, a quick, strong kid with loads of twitchy energy, was at first base. A couple of other kids played center field and catcher. Candace had brought empty pizza boxes they used as bases. She didn't play, but watched from behind the chain link fence and snacked on tiny chocolate doughnuts she plucked from her purse.

Sarah crouched and rocked back and forth, holding her fielder's glove in front of her mouth and snapping the glove like a set of hungry jaws. She shouted, "Feed me. Feed me."

Reginald nodded at Alfonso. "Relax. Follow the ball as it comes toward you."

Alfonso inhaled and raised the aluminum bat off his shoulder. He so wanted to capture his father's spirit as a feared slugger. But as with all other evil genius activities, reality remained his worst enemy. At first, hitting the ball seemed impossible and made him feel like a super clumsy dork. After a week of practice he could hit most pitches. Now Reginald was getting fancy and throwing curves, sliders, and heat.

Reginald cocked back for the pitch. Way back. Then he uncoiled and the ball zoomed at meteor speed.

Alfonso tracked the ball, a blurry white smear tearing at him. He snapped the bat forward and connected with a satisfying *ping!* that stung his hands. The ball arced past Reginald and to the right of Sarah.

Polecat yelled, "Don't look at the ball, Alfonso. Run!"

Alfonso launched into a sprint.

Another voice yelled, "Drop the bat!"

Oh yeah. Alfonso let the bat clatter to the ground as he raced along. Polecat waited at first base, one foot on the cardboard square, glove stretched toward Sarah.

Alfonso followed the ball out the corner of his eye. No way could she make that catch.

She catapulted upward, her body springing into an exclamation mark. Her glove snagged the ball with a loud *Thwap!* She dove into the dirt, rolled to a sitting position, glove held high, the ball tucked in the pocket.

Alfonso gasped in disbelief. His legs churned to a halt.

Polecat popped a thumb over one shoulder. "You're out, buddy."

Sarah jumped to her feet, ponytail swaying behind her cap. "That's me. Quick as lightning and twice as dangerous."

Against anyone else, that line drive would've been a double. Alfonso turned to pick up the bat where it laid on the baseline. "One more pitch."

Reginald tucked his glove under one arm and headed toward the corner of the backstop. "That's it for today. Gotta go home. I want to get some time playing this new awesome video game."

Now that Reginald wasn't pitching, the other kids wandered off the field.

Alfonso trotted to him. "What game?"

"Undead Siege. It's brand new." Reginald motioned that he follow. "Wanna play?"

"Sure. What about Sarah?"

Reginald shrugged. "Ask her."

Alfonso shouted if she wanted to join them.

"Sure you want me to play?" She sloughed dust from her jeans and t-shirt. "I'd kick both of your butts." Her voice flattened. "But I gotta go home and help Mom clean the carpet. We got company coming and our cat's been coughing up hairballs like it's an Olympic sport." She turned away and dragged her feet through the dirt.

Reginald called to Candace. "How about you?"

"Can't." She wiped chocolate frosting from her lips. "Have to get home for dinner. Shrimp scampi." She grinned like she was already tasting the meal.

Alfonso and Reginald walked side-by-side through the neighborhood, a rambling collection of ranch and split-level homes. Reginald chatted about musicians and songs Alfonso had never heard of.

But he didn't mind. This was the first time since moving here that Alfonso had been invited to another home. He felt the circle of his new friends grow a little tighter and a little warmer.

A bizarre thing about Ty Cobb Middle School was that most students acted embarrassed to talk about schoolwork, as if being smart was wrong. Reginald and Candace weren't like that. They kept a seat for him at lunch in the cafeteria and happily discussed what they'd learned in Ms. Humboldt's biology class.

Sarah usually walked him home and pestered him—in a friendly way—with nosey questions. Especially about the vulture attack.

Alfonso pretended he didn't know anything. But of course he did. That vulture belonged to Professor Moriarty. Alfonso was bound to keep secret all knowledge of *la mano sinistra*. This wall between himself and his new friends made him uncomfortable. Why did acting normal and fitting in mean he had to be a liar?

School here was so boring that he'd quit caring about learning anything. As a future evil genius, Alfonso used to look forward to school. Too bad that even his labs were so simple and dull. Dissecting little critters and physics experiments involving ping-pong balls and string didn't compare with zombiefication or anti-matter alchemy.

Nothing at Ty Cobb Middle School matched the excitement and danger of the University of Doom.

They turned the corner. Jerry Tremont cruised toward them on a bicycle, a big freckled lump of trouble. Alfonso's heart groaned and went plunk. Speaking of danger.

Jerry halted at the curb. "Oh jeez. No wonder I was getting an upset stomach. It's Franken-pest."

Reginald stepped between them. "Lay off, Jerry."

Reginald was not only taller than Jerry but he also played on the school baseball team. Alfonso was sure there would not be a hassle.

But he had to fight his own battles, so he nudged past his friend. "Jerry, stay away from me."

Jerry rolled his eyes. "When did you grow a spine? Reggie won't always be around to protect you."

"I can protect myself."

Jerry laughed. "Don't kid yourself, loser. I don't pound your ugly little head for two reasons. One, it'll be me who gets in trouble and your smelly butt isn't worth it. And two," Jerry waved his fingers, "I don't want to dirty myself with your Franken-funk." He snickered and glanced around as if he had an audience of fellow creeps.

"Oh yeah," Alfonso replied, "if you did get dirty, it would give you another excuse to lick yourself like a dog."

Jerry's freckles darkened to the color of blood. He clasped the rubber grips of his bicycle, squeezing until his man-sized hands got red as his freckles and the knuckles blanched white. "I am so looking forward to the day," he spoke slowly and deliberately like he was slicing the words, "I can drop-kick your skinny tail out of my life."

His eyes cut to Reginald's glove. A grin formed on his mouth. "Heard you've been practicing ball. What for? You probably suck at that like you do everything else. I doubt anyone in your Franken-sissy family is man enough to play baseball."

The comment nailed Alfonso. No way could this moron Jerry know Dr. Frankenstein had once been a champion baseball player. Still, the insult was more than a jab at Alfonso, it was rotten dig against his father.

Alfonso knew the wise move was to keep silent and let this meathead ramble on until he went away. But defending his family's honor made him reply, "We Frankenstein's don't suck at baseball."

Big mistake. Jerry's grin deepened into a leer, and Alfonso knew he'd walked into a trap.

Jerry puffed up and crossed his arms. "Then prove it, Franken-clown. With a 'friendly'..." he used air quotes, "game of ball. Your team versus mine." He cocked his head at Reginald and raised his eyebrows in a question.

Reginald draped his arm over Alfonso's shoulder. "I'll play on his team."

Jerry shook his head. "You wanna hang with those losers, your choice." He started to pedal away. "Next Saturday afternoon. Unless you chicken out."

"I'll be there." Alfonso stared at the ground and grew quiet as the weight of the future smothered him. The game was another chance for Jerry to humiliate him. This time in front of a crowd.

He couldn't beat Jerry at baseball—Alfonso's mind sparked in all directions in search of a solution until it focused on what he knew best: mad science. "I'm going to get him."

Reginald patted his shoulder. "Forget it. Jerry's being his usual jerk-self. Let's go play Undead Siege."

Reginald lived two blocks from Alfonso, in a house with an identical floor plan but in much better condition and painted in colors that didn't hurt the eyes. He led Alfonso to his bedroom, in the same place as Alfonso's would be. The boys stepped through shoes and clothes littering the floor.

A flat screen television hung from the wall, surrounded by posters of athletes, musicians, and action movies. A braid of cables connected the screen to a laptop sitting on a small crowded desk.

Reginald used a remote to click on the television. The program was already queued to the splash page of *Undead Siege*. The image was of a war-ravaged castle smudged by smoke from fires on the hills below. Zombies shambled through the ruin. *Join the skirmish in progress*, scrolled across the screen.

"How did you find out about this game?"

"Email. Said I was one of the few selected for a free Beta trial. At first I thought it was a scam. You know, like those free money offers and pills that'll make you happier and stronger. But I'm glad I signed on." Reginald grasped a controller and worked the buttons. "Prepare to be amazed."

The image went black. Suddenly, shrieks blared from the speakers, shrieks so horrifying the hairs rose on Alfonso's arms, a teaser for the next thrill.

A gaggle of zombies rose from the rubble and advanced. Alfonso wasn't just looking at the screen but deep into it.

A zombie swiped at a broken wall and hurled a loose brick.

Alfonso ducked.

The 3D effect was mesmerizing. No special glasses or goggles needed. This was good. University of Doom good.

Reginald's avatar—a muscled ghostly high-tech soldier grasping an assault rifle—materialized life-size between the boys and the screen.

Again, Alfonso had never seen anything like this.

Reginald started shooting. The muzzle blast from the avatar's rifle stung Alfonso's ears. Empty cartridge cases whirled from the gun and rattled across the floor before dissolving into nothingness.

Zombies crumpled in chunks of rotting flesh and gobs of blackened blood. What fun!

"Whatever you do," Reginald said, "don't ever play against Electro101." He motioned with the controller to the player menu along the right side of the screen. "He's not just deadly, but super deadly. Of course he's got the advantage of using one of those special helmets."

"What helmets?"

Reginald pounced left and right, the avatar mimicking his movements. "Special helmets that give him an advantage, like being right in the battle. Complete peripheral vision. Surround-sound. Tactile feedback. Shoot a gun and you can feel it jump in your hands. Talk about rock-n-roll!"

"How can you get a helmet?"

"Score enough points and the Undead Siege people send you one for free."

"Who is Electro101?"

"Some kid like us, I guess. Wanna talk to him?"

"Sure."

Reginald clicked buttons. A disembodied helmet appeared to their left, hovering at face height. It looked like an astronaut's, with a gold-mirrored visor and in gray and beige camouflage, the same colors as a moon rock. "Yo."

I know that the voice. "Can he see me?"

Reginald replied, "Not unless you're playing the game."

Alfonso asked, "Who is this?"

"Chief Petty Officer Electro101."

The voice definitely sounded familiar. Could it be... "Greg Kaminski?"

"Alfonso?" the voice answered. "That you?"

"It is." Alfonso wanted to do a happy dance. He could almost smell the University of Doom. This video game was one step closer to getting back where he belonged.

CHAPTER
EIGHTEEN

A soft *putt-a-putt* nudged Alfonso awake. Blinking, he sat up in his bed and focused on the noise, not sure what it was but certain it came from inside the house.

He yawned and stretched, still weary from last night's marathon of *Undead Siege* at Reginald's home. What a surprise to learn that Electro101 was Greg Kaminski. They didn't talk much considering the priority at the time had been to kill zombies. Plus, they had to be careful chatting around Reginald or else they could've revealed the existence of the University of Doom.

It was a wonder the university's Internet firewall had allowed him and Greg to connect. Now they could stay in touch using the game's online chat room, that was until the security breach would be discovered and slammed shut.

The *putt-a-putt* continued. Alfonso slid out of bed and shuffled in his pj's to the bedroom door. He cracked it open and peeked out. The noise came from the bedroom across the hall.

He tiptoed to the door and listened. The *putt-a-putt* sounded familiar but he couldn't place it.

He knocked. "Dad?"

His father answered, "Come in."

Alfonso opened the door and stepped over chunks of drywall piled on the carpet. Dr. Frankenstein sat facing him in a tall executive chair behind a chest-high workbench that stretched almost the length of the room.

He wore rubber gloves, safety goggles, and a clean laboratory smock (though patched to cover the rips from a giant centipede attack—those were the days!) A strip of electrical tape on the left breast covered the University of Doom Faculty embroidery.

Stainless steel pans rested end to end on the workbench.

The air brought a metallic lemony taste, from Dippel's Oil bubbling in slender glass cylinders standing at the opposite corner. Plastic tubing snaked from the cylinders to the source of the *putt-a-putt*, a Portaboy that chugged on the floor next to the workbench.

When had his father put this together? Alfonso had been so distracted by school and his friends that he forgot to nose around the house like a budding mad scientist.

Then again, Frankensteins had to be experts at working undetected, much like a colony of termites.

Black canvas curtains covered the windows. Beakers, test tubes, petri dishes, and pipettes crowded the edge of the workbench and the metal shelves along the wall behind his father. Frosty vapor feathered from the lid of a five-gallon plastic cooler on the shelf. The front of the cooler was stenciled with U.S. Lumber Accident Program: Amputation Services—Organ Donation.

Examination lamps on articulated struts dangled from the ceiling. At the far right, an autopsy table and sink were pressed perpendicular against the wall. The sink's pipes poked through ragged holes in the drywall to the bathroom next door. Water dripped from the drain line into a bucket.

Without looking up from the workbench, Dr. Frankenstein pointed to the right of the door.

Alfonso turned to see where his father motioned. Safety goggles hung from a coat hook by the light switch. Alfonso put them on and approached the workbench.

Human arms lay in the steel pans. Wires and plastic tubes connected a console to the severed limbs. Dippel's Oil leaked from catheters inserted into the arteries and pooled inside the pans. An open laptop on the workbench faced the doctor.

Alfonso gestured to the human parts in the pan. "Where did they come from?"

His father picked up a soldering iron. "I borrowed them from work."

"Borrowed? Or stole?" Alfonso didn't like asking the question.

Dr. Frankenstein pointed the soldering iron at him. "You know stealing is against the Evil Genius Code. You learned that back at the University of Doom. Article 7, Paragraph A. Only riffraff steal."

"Steal, borrow, what's the difference?"

His father brought his free hand close to his heart. "Borrowing is putting to good use materials otherwise neglected by their owners. Besides, the items will be returned...*eventually*. At least that's the intention."

"But didn't these people donate their organs?"

"Son, let me give you some mad scientist advice. Don't get too worked up about the ethics." Dr. Frankenstein touched a wire connection with the soldering iron. "What people don't realize is that as organ donators, most of their tissue ends up in places like where I work: the Bottomline Medical Research Facility."

He rested the soldering iron in a holder and clicked keys on the laptop. A beefy tattooed arm in the tray twitched. The doctor clicked more keys. The arm twisted, rolled over palm down and extended its fingers. They touched the end of the pan, curled to grasp the rim, and hauled the arm forward.

Alfonso asked, "Your work doesn't miss the parts?"

"Most of the *mano destre* are squeamish when it comes to handling dead flesh," his father answered. "No one ever checks the inventory against what goes into the bio-waste incinerator." He clicked more keys. The arm tensed and levered upward, holding onto the rim to perform a handstand.

"Ta da!"

"Nice trick, dad."

Dr. Frankenstein made a dramatic tap on the laptop. The arm relaxed and plunked back into the pan, splashing Dippel's Oil.

He plucked a roll of paper towels from the shelf and tore a length free. He wiped the drops of oil and tossed the towels into a garbage can by his chair.

Alfonso looked at the autopsy table again and picked up details he hadn't noticed before. Such as behind the bucket, jumper cables looped around a car battery. And wrist and ankle restraints that dangled over the edges of the table.

Jumper cables? Restraints on an autopsy table?

Alfonso pumped his fists. Happiness blasted out of his smile.

Dr. Frankenstein nodded enthusiastically. "You got it, son. I'm going to make a zombie so amazing that even Dr. Umpethe HooDoo would be impressed. Prove to the University of Doom they must bring me back."

"We can make already make zombies. This one better be *amazing* amazing. Will it have super powers?" Alfonso brought his hands to his eyes and cupped his fingers like binoculars. "X-ray vision?" He formed his hands into jaws and interlocked his fingers like teeth. "Maybe diamond ceramic choppers?"

"I haven't decided yet. Perhaps it will fly."

This was getting better and better. "Yeah," Alfonso replied, "you could stick a solid fuel rocket up its butt and *whoosh!*"

He studied the shelves. Glass jars with kidneys. Hearts. Spleens. Liters of whole blood. An aquarium filled with a coil of intestines.

"Where are the torso and legs?"

"On ice in the garage."

"Seems you got all the body parts."

"Except a head," Dr. Frankenstein replied.

"Can't you get one from work?"

"You'd think that with all the thoughtless morons killing themselves—car wrecks, hunting accidents, power boats and drugs—heads would be plentiful. But our cosmetic surgery department has dibs. They use the heads as teaching aids for eye lifts and nose jobs."

His expression got a faraway gloss. "If I could get into the cryogenics lockers. That's where those idiots who froze their heads have them stored while they wait for the Singularity."

"Singularity?"

"That's some point in the future when human brains will meld with a super Internet. One of the biggest scams yet propagated by the University of Doom and a big moneymaker for medical cryogenics."

"Seriously Dad, these people believe they can join their minds with the Internet? Have they spent any time online?" He made a face of disgust and pretended to shiver.

"Fools, I know." His father mimicked Alfonso's expression of disgust. "Is that where they want to meld their consciousness? With cheesy pop-up ads for easy credit and ring tones?"

"But with no noggin, we're a long way from success?"

"I prefer to think of my mad scientist beaker as half full. Son, I find a head, then consider our ticket out of here will be"—he pointed to the autopsy table—"that zombie."

CHAPTER
NINETEEN

For the Frankensteins, returning to the University of Doom was like a giant mountain they had to climb. Day after day, Alfonso felt they were getting closer to the top, and yet the summit still seemed so far away.

But right now, Alfonso had other problems. More urgent problems.

Like the baseball game against his nemesis, Jerry Tremont.

Alfonso used to wonder who his nemesis would be. You couldn't really call yourself an evil genius unless you had a nemesis, a sworn enemy who kept you scheming and looking over your shoulder.

There was Moriarty, but the professor was his dad's nemesis and an enemy too big for Alfonso to fight on his own.

He wanted a personal nemesis, perhaps a junior alien overlord or a bat-brain crazy chemist-in-training, somebody close to his age yet monstrously diabolical in the classical mad scientist sense. The closest he ever had to a nemesis was Lilith Vampira back at Dr. Moreau Junior Academy. But she wasn't a threat to him in a true ruin-your-whole-day level, just more of a smart-mouthed pain-in-the-butt.

So instead of an alien general or a crazy chemist, his nemesis was Jerry. A plain old bully who tormented Alfonso like a bellyful of rotten eggs.

How do you defeat a nemesis? By out-foxing him, preferably at his own game.

In this case: baseball.

Two baseball bats, an aluminum Easton Power Brigade and a wooden Louisville Slugger, lay on the workbench in the Frankenstein's basement. Even though Dr. Frankenstein had warned him against using mad science to cheat at baseball, Alfonso would try anything to humiliate Jerry, that muscled punk.

Still, a pang of conscience pricked him. He didn't want to defy his father.

Which was more important?

Obedience or getting back at Jerry?

But his dad had also told him: *Son, let me give you some mad scientist advice. Don't get too worked up about the ethics.*

If his father found out, what was the worse that could happen? A scolding? Loss of privileges...which were?

So what if he was put in the doghouse after whipping Jerry by cheating, the victory would be worth any punishment.

Now that his father was working extra late, no doubt scavenging body parts from the bio-waste bins at work,

Alfonso used his dad's absence to help himself to the laboratory equipment and high-tech junk in the house.

He had cut open the top of the bats and prepped the barrels to accept his newest secret invention, the Sure-Hit mechanism: a gyroscope, micro-servors, WiFi transceiver, batteries, and a tiny radar proximity fuse from an anti-aircraft artillery shell.

After replacing the tops, Alfonso tested the bats for weight and balance. They were identical to the original specifications with the seams painstakingly repaired under the gaze of his father's electron microscope and using a subatomic glue gun.

The radar of the proximity fuse would detect an approaching ball and send signals to the micro-servors to adjust the tilt of the gyroscope. The shift in gyroscopic force would move the bat in the direction of the ball.

Alfonso picked up a smart phone, one he had found discarded in an alley and repaired. He activated a custom app of his own design. The app controlled each Sure-Hit via the WiFi using virtual gauges and control switches.

He pressed the power button. The app cycled through the self-test procedure and showed all lights in the green.

He put his ear to the barrel of the Louisville Slugger and listened for the muted whine of the gyroscope spinning at ninety thousand rpm's.

Nothing.

He touched the barrel to feel for a telltale vibration.

Again, nothing.

Same with the Easton.

Perfect.

These bats weren't merely corked, they were hyper-corked.

Alfonso swung the Easton. He'd imagined chasing Jerry with the bat, the freckled toad whimpering and begging for mercy.

A tingle crawled up Alfonso's arms to the back of his neck. This game was going to be a thousand volts of awesome.

Provided the Sure-Hits worked.

He placed the bats at opposite sides of the workbench.

Here goes. He walked to the other side of the basement and picked up a baseball.

The tingle disappeared and his shoulders rounded with anxiety. This could be his only chance to get even with Jerry.

He lobbed the ball over the Louisville Slugger.

The bat jerked upward, as if swung by a ghost.

Pow!

The ball zoomed back at Alfonso. He ducked and it smashed against a metal locker.

Alfonso straightened. He studied the bat as it slowly rocked on the workbench and then he retraced the trajectory of the ball to where it had dented the locker.

The tingle returned. He gave an evil genius grin, a wide, toothy curve that dimpled his cheeks.

Jerry didn't know it, but the big oaf was standing on a railroad track and about to get run over by a train.

Alfonso tested the Easton bat.

Another *pow!*

The ball ricocheted across the basement.

Make that two trains.

Alfonso wrung his hands.

Mwua-ha-ha-ha.

The alarm function of his smart phone beeped. The game started in forty-five minutes.

Alfonso turned off the Sure-Hit mechanisms and slipped the phone into his pocket. He hefted both bats onto one shoulder, grabbed his glove, and clambered up the stairs.

The bats should be tested outside in real-world conditions but he didn't have time.

Because it was time for a baseball beat down.

Besides, what could go wrong?

CHAPTER
TWENTY

Alfonso scrambled into the dugout and plopped on the bench.

The score was 33 to 32. Bottom of the ninth inning.

His team was down by one run, but they would be last to bat. Certain victory shined as bright as the afternoon sun hanging over the ball field.

Somebody had clipped a homemade banner to the chain link fence surrounding their dugout.

Go Ravens.

Alfonso liked the name. Ravens were smart and sneaky, and the favored pets of many mad scientists.

These Ravens were a ragtag mix of neighborhood middle schoolers—skinny, chunky, tall, short. For uniforms they wore tattered jeans and baggy t-shirts in every shade of color but new.

So far, their opponents, Jerry Tremont's team, had played like the jocks they were—big and arrogant—getting solid hits and taking advantage of every error the Ravens made.

On the other hand, the Ravens played offense like they had cannons for bats.

Which they did, sort of.

Alfonso cut an admiring glance to their secret weapons, his Louisville Slugger and the Easton Power Brigade propped in the corner of the dugout. In his mind's eye, he could see their gyros spinning and the proximity fuses waiting to pound more homeruns and pound Jerry into the ground.

Alfonso tossed his glove under the bench and slipped the smart phone from his jeans pocket. He cupped the phone and rubbed a thumb along one side as if stroking a magic lamp. The Sure-Hits worked exactly as he had planned and his wish was about to come true.

Shove every insult that had come out of Jerry's mouth back down his throat.

Sarah slid beside him on the dugout bench. She swiped a twist of hair away from her face and tucked it under her ball cap. Sweat and dust mottled her face and clothes. The stripe of sunburned skin across her nose glowed like the burner on a stove. She tugged at the braided strings on her wrist.

"Can you believe it?" She smacked her fist into her glove. "Jerry's team of ringers thought they'd walk all over us. But we got 'em cornered like rats. Every inning we've gotten at least three runs." She held two fingers in front of Alfonso's face. "But two runs is all we need!" She barked like she was on a leash. "Then *bam!* Game! Over! We! Win!"

Sarah swiveled her head. "Crowd's gotten bigger. Word must've gotten out."

Good, thought Alfonso, *I want the world to see Jerry get depantsed.*

About thirty people sat in the bleachers behind the backstop, mostly neighborhood kids, a few adults. Candace was there, munching on a candy bar, cheering him on.

Alfonso looked again when he caught sight of a woman in jeans and a loose sweater taking a seat on the first row. His homeroom teacher, Ms. Humboldt.

It was odd seeing her dressed so casually and outside of school—as if she'd misplaced herself.

On the other side of the bleachers, a burgundy Cadillac Eldorado eased against the curb like a spaceship gliding in for a landing. The driver's window was rolled down, revealing a huge knot of dark muscle crammed behind the steering wheel. Otis Carroll, the school librarian.

He draped an immense arm along the bottom of his window. The sleeve of a rugby jersey hid his tattoo scars. With his wraparound sunglasses and blank expression, he appeared mysterious, like a spy.

Alfonso imagined Humboldt and Carroll congratulating him after the game while Jerry slinked away in defeat. Alfonso could see the scene, Humboldt's proud motherly smile, Carroll's gigantic hand embracing his, acknowledging his victory, never suspicious it was evil genius trickery that won the game.

Jerry's team filed out of their dugout. They trotted listlessly onto the field, as if in no hurry to reach their miserable destination. Loserville.

Jerry was on the mound again. His team had rotated through their pitching roster as Alfonso's team miraculously racked up run after run.

Actually, not so miraculous.

Next at bat, Sarah. She picked the Louisville Slugger. Even without the Sure-Hit mechanism, she was a dangerous batter. But thanks to mad science, in this game she was batting .738, with one home run and five RBI.

Alfonso touched his phone screen. Everything was ready.

Bells going *ring-a-ling* distracted him. A Merry Moo-Cow Ice Cream truck cruised alongside the ball field and rang the brass bells on its cab roof.

Perfect. The best way to celebrate beating Jerry would be with a banana split the size of a rowboat.

A sudden flicker on the smart phone snagged Alfonso's attention. The needles of the Sure-Hit twitched across the dials. An icy breath of disaster raised the hairs on the back of his neck. He tapped furiously on the virtual controls.

Sarah swung and connected. The ball arced over the fence on the right—foul—and bounced beside the ice cream truck.

She frowned and shook her head as if scolding herself.

Jerry allowed a tiny smile.

The phone gauges returned to normal.

Then the ice cream bells began again.

The Sure-Hit went haywire.

Alfonso pecked at his smart phone. Those bells must be creating an interference pattern that matched the radar echo of the Sure-Hit's proximity fuse.

Sarah cranked at the next pitch. Foul.

Alfonso stabbed again and again at the phone's screen, clueless and panicked about how to fix the problem.

Another pitch. Another swing. Another fly toward the truck.

The first baseman—Spike—shagged it for an easy out.

Sarah hung her head and shuffled back into the dugout. She tossed the bat against the fence and plunked next to Alfonso. "That was weird. The bat moved like it had a mind of its own."

He kept quiet and let the secret simmer.

The truck's bells rang again, the *ring-a-ling* mocking him with their festive irony.

Alfonso gritted his teeth. He wanted to grab a bat, run to the truck, and smash those stupid bells.

Turn off the Sure-Hit. He tapped the virtual off switch but it was of no use, the controls were frozen on the signal.

He removed the battery, and the screen went blank. He sighed, relieved like he'd just side-stepped a falling piano, and tucked the now useless smart phone into his glove.

Now it was Polecat's turn at bat. He selected the Easton, took a couple of loose swings, and strolled into the batter's box.

Come on, Polecat. All the Ravens need is one run to tie the game.

The ice cream truck started again with the *ring-a-linging*. Polecat swung and the ball ricocheted off the side of the truck.

Nooo! echoed in Alfonso's head, the word pinging from side-to-side like a ball bearing. The Sure-Hits inside the bats were still turned on.

Polecat connected with the next pitch, and the ball arced for the ice cream truck. The right fielder waited by the fence, jumped up and caught the fly.

Jerry clenched his fist. *Yes!*

Two down.

Polecat shook his head and dragged his feet into the dugout. Alfonso felt like those feet also dragged over him.

Jerry now had the ball. He raised it and taunted the Ravens' dugout. "Whatever mojo you guys had, it's gone."

Alfonso was up. He selected the Louisville Slugger and approached the batter's box. Polecat trotted from the dugout to coach first base.

The ice cream truck drove off and turned the corner into the neighborhood. The ringing bells grew mute in the distance, surely out of range.

Alfonso took a breath and wiggled his hips to settle into the stance.

The bells are gone. Just relax, aim, and swing.

Jerry leaned forward and his expression compressed around his eyes. Focused. Determined.

He curled into the wind-up.

The ball burned past Alfonso and he swung at air.

Strike one.

The Ravens clung to the dugout's chain link fence, faces darkened with impending doom.

Alfonso readied for the next pitch.

Jerry unwound with another heater.

Alfonso let go with a mighty swing.

Crack!

The ball skipped between the shortstop and third, catching the fielders by surprise.

The Ravens exploded with cheers.

Alfonso rocketed to first base.

Polecat tapped his shoulder. "Good job."

Heart racing, Alfonso stomped the base and gulped air.

Spike sneered at him.

Reginald stepped into the batter's box. So far, he had hit seven home runs. Another one, and the game was over.

A worried Jerry called Spike, the shortstop, and the catcher to the mound. They huddled, then returned to their positions.

An anxious silence descended over the bleachers, nerves stretched trip-wire taut.

Jerry set up for the pitch.

Polecat whispered to Alfonso. "Lead off."

He crabbed one step, then two steps away from first.

Jerry whipped around and fired the ball to Spike at first base.

Alfonso danced back to the base.

Spike missed the ball and it rolled against the fence.

Polecat pointed to second. "Go! Go!"

Alfonso galloped away. After sliding into second, he looked over his shoulder. Spike fumbled the ball like it was coated with butter.

The Ravens yelled. "Go Alfonso. Go."

He sprinted to third and slid into the base. Grinning, he picked himself up and sloughed dust from his pants.

The Ravens' dugout and the bleachers roared with celebration.

The noise stoked Alfonso, and his body loved the rush. If only his father was here to see another Frankenstein as a baseball hero.

Spike threw the ball to the shortstop, who…incredibly, dropped it.

Now. Now, Alfonso's brain commanded. *This is your chance. Steal home. Tie the game. Be the hero.*

Reginald hollered. "Hold up!"

Too late. Alfonso broke away at top speed, the rising cheers of the Ravens reeling him in like a chorus of sirens.

Alfonso glimpsed out the corner of his left eye. The bumbling error play of Jerry's team fell away and they suddenly clicked together with the precision of a gun.

The shortstop fired the ball at the catcher.

The ball popped into his mitt, and he crouched, facing Alfonso like a troll guarding his bridge.

The cheers turned into a shriek.

Alfonso's shoes plowed the dirt, his toes biting the earth, kicking dust, his heart seeming to shove against his chest in the opposite direction to escape the tag.

Jerry—that ape, that simple-minded bully, that muscle-headed moron—had baited him—a Frankenstein, an evil genius—into a trap and Alfonso had dived right into it.

As Alfonso turned back to third, the baseball blurred over his shoulder.

Jerry was on the baseline in front of him, red-headed, freckled and huge, the ball in hand.

White as a skull.

Round as a grenade.

Deadly as poison.

Alfonso's legs grew heavy and his insides collapsed into a lump of cold lead.

Jerry stepped forward and touched the ball against Alfonso's chest. It was like getting tagged by the Grim Reaper.

TWENTY-ONE

Something deep in Alfonso's brain snapped. Colors faded to gray, sounds muted to a low hum. His legs buckled like his bones were dissolving into powder and he slumped to the ground, kneeling along the baseline between third and home.

All Jerry had done was tag him with the ball, but the touch had brought such pain. A physical torment that scorched his heart and made his eyes water.

A blurry shape moved in front of him.

The image sharpened.

Jerry Tremont.

He stood huge, a colossus of vengeful wrath. "Get this straight, Franken-stupid, punks like you will always lose to guys like me. It's a fact of life. Get used to it. You're nothing but dirt under my cleats." He kicked dust and it spattered against Alfonso, clumping to the tears at the corners of his eyes.

Jerry bent his knees and leaned close. "Go ahead and cry. Boo-hoo. Show me and the whole world what a loser sissy-boy you are."

Alfonso hadn't felt such anguish since the time his mother had abandoned him. He thought he had grown thick calluses to protect himself, but Jerry had ripped them off and stabbed vicious words deep into his guts.

Everything had gone so wrong. Alfonso had disobeyed his father and used mad science to cheat. Then Alfonso got caught up in wanting to be the game hero and let himself get snared by Jerry's trap.

Alfonso was no genius, but a fool.

Jerry's fool.

Jerry straightened and walked off. A murmur of conversation droned in Alfonso's ears. Kids made plans for after the game, plans which didn't include him, and his teammates grumbled about how he had lost the game.

His mind looped through the final seconds of the game: Reginald yelling to stay put, the charge to home plate, the sudden appearance of the ball in Jerry's hand, the final tag, and the collapse of triumph into shame. Alfonso stared at the ground and wished himself dead.

Long shadows fell over him. Cool air crept over his skin. Alfonso blinked and realized the sun had long set. He swiveled his head left and right. The ball field was deserted and covered by dusky twilight.

He pushed himself upright, sloughed dust from his pants, and trudged to the dugout. The two corked bats lay beside the fence. His glove rested under the bench, the smart phone still tucked inside. For a moment

Alfonso wished his belongings had been stolen but they remained untouched, protected by the taint of bad luck.

The tears came back and he hurled the smart phone out of the dugout. The phone sailed into the street and shattered into a spray of broken pieces.

After wiping his eyes against the crook of an elbow, he tucked the glove under one arm and set the bats on his shoulder, consoling himself that worse things have happened in the world. A night's sleep and the world would look better in the morning. But home and tomorrow seemed so far away.

He ambled along, head down, watching his shadows stretch and shrink beneath the streetlamps. Two blocks from his house, someone came huffing behind him.

Sarah announced herself, "Wait up, why don't cha?"

Alfonso wanted to remain alone but when he saw it was Sarah, he was glad she had come to keep him company.

She fell in step next to him, her ball cap set low on her forehead. Dust marred her jersey top and sweat pants, souvenirs of one amazing catch after another.

"How are you doing?" she asked. "Dumb question I know, but I gotta start the conversation somewhere."

Alfonso kept quiet.

"So we lost. Big deal."

"It was a big deal to Jerry. And me."

"You're not going to get far letting b-holes like Jerry pull your strings. Let it go." Sarah elbowed Alfonso. "How come you weren't at Candace's pizza party? She might not be much of a baseball fan, but she knows her pizza. We were lookin' for you."

Alfonso shrugged. "Wasn't invited. Even if I was, don't think I would've gone."

"Hey buddy, if you're going to fit in around here, you never turn down free pizza. Unless you're dying?" She cocked her head to nail him with a stare. "You dying?"

"Of course not."

"There you go."

Sarah reached and took the bats from him. She yoked them behind her neck. "You know what's weird?"

The question sounded loaded. Like his bats. He didn't reply.

Sarah tipped a shoulder so the bats clunked together. "These bats. At first it was like they had a magnetic force they way they connected to the ball. Then at the end, it was like they still had a magnetic force, but opposite. You know, repellent."

Alfonso quirked an eyebrow.

"Don't look at me that way," she protested. "I may not like school but I like learning. It's that school takes all this interesting stuff and makes it"—she closed her eyes—"soooo freakin' boring." She opened her eyes and pointed to her feet. "Just think how awesome it would be to have that repellent force in your shoes. Isn't the earth one big magnet? How come no one's done it?"

Her comment knocked loose his despair, and his sadness flew away like an uncaged bird. The change in mood was so abrupt he chuckled. Many a mad scientist at the University of Doom had her idea. Problem was, anti-magnetic shoes kept failing when they reached an altitude of a hundred feet and for that reason they got the nickname suicide slippers.

"The last time I was at bat," Sarah said, "it felt like the Slugger was pulling away from me. And wasn't it weird that every ball kept going toward the ice cream truck?"

"I didn't notice."

Sarah levered the Louisville Slugger off her shoulder. "Maybe we outta look at these bats. Scientific like. Put them under an X-ray. Or an ultrasound. You should be good at that."

A shiver of worry pinged down Alfonso's spine. If he was found out, what would his friends think? Worse, his dad? And worse some more, Alfonso had corked the bats, like Moriarty had. So now he was as bad a stinker as that human skunk.

They turned the corner. Alfonso's house was at the end of the block.

Sarah halted abruptly and whispered, "Oh no."

Alfonso stopped and noticed that her face had gone pale. She lifted an arm and aimed a finger down the sidewalk.

He turned to see what she pointed at. His dad's Dodge pickup was in the driveway. A white sedan was parked along the curb. "What's the problem?"

"That's my aunt Natalie's Infiniti."

"So?"

"She's there to see your dad."

"Why?"

Sarah didn't answer. Instead she broke into a run toward his house, bats bouncing and clattering on her shoulder.

Alfonso started after her. "What's the problem?"

"Ever tell yourself that things couldn't get any worse?" Sarah huffed as she galloped along. "Guess what. They just did."

CHAPTER
TWENTY-TWO

Alfonso and Sarah raced toward his house. Midway down the block, she veered off the sidewalk and scooted along the hedges and bushes to stop and hide in the shadows cast by the corner streetlamp.

He halted beside her, gasping, and once he caught his breath, whispered, "So what's the big deal?"

Sarah brought a finger to her lips. She pointed to a scraggly hedge marking the property line of his home. "Let's ditch your stuff here so we can better sneak up on them."

They jammed the bats and glove under the branches. Sarah turned her cap backwards and picked her way to the Frankenstein house.

Alfonso kept two paces behind her. "What are we looking for?"

Sarah glared at him, put a finger to her lips and pantomimed an exaggerated *shhh!*

She crouched beneath the closest window, on the north side of the front room. The blinds were down and an interior light glowed through the slats. Rising on tiptoes, she put an ear close to the glass and kept still for a moment. She turned to Alfonso and shook her head. He didn't hear anything either.

They continued to the front of the house and at the corner, dropped to their hands and knees. After a quick glance around the corner, Sarah practically slithered onto the porch.

She stopped by the window next to the front door and peeked through a gap in the blinds. She whispered, "Your dad and Natalie aren't in the front room. Where could they be?"

"What's the problem?"

Sarah brought her mouth close to his ear. "Natalie is my mom's sister. The other day my mom was telling her about you and when she mentioned that your dad was a doctor, Natalie's eyes lit up like hitting the jackpot on a slot machine."

Her eyes popped wide. "Maybe they're already in his bedroom. Then we're too late!"

"Why would they be in my dad's bedroom?"

Sarah's face scrunched into an expression that said: *you're kidding?*

He hitched his shoulders. *What?*

She stepped off the porch and continued to the south side of the house. A conversation wafted through the screen of an open window of the den. Alfonso's dad and a woman were talking and laughing. Sarah halted under a small mulberry tree crowding the wall.

Alfonso and Sarah parked themselves beneath the window.

"Why is she here?" he whispered.

"My aunt's been married and divorced three times. Plus a string of boyfriends. There isn't a man with money she doesn't like."

"We don't have much money."

"When my aunt gets done with your dad, you won't have any. She'll talk your dad into buying her lots of expensive, shiny things."

This was like the business with Alfonso's mom all over again.

"What's a matter?" Sarah asked. "You're lookin' kinda sick."

"Just not feeling too good about this."

"A wise reaction."

"So what do we do? Maybe go in there and interrupt." He started to rise.

Sarah grasped his wrist. "No. We have to think of something that will stop this for good."

"Tell him the truth about her?"

"Fat chance that would work. The truth bounces off my aunt like rockets off Godzilla."

"So what do we do?"

"Wait. Like in the cowboy movies. Only we're the Indians."

They sat and leaned against the wall. A car rolled up the street and its headlights splashed across them. Sarah and Alfonso froze and their gazes followed the car as it rolled past. An exhale in relief, and a moment to relax. More cars proceeded back and forth along the street. More freezing in place. More music and conversation from inside. The minutes dripped by slow as cold syrup.

Alfonso's stomach growled.

Sarah said, "Should've gone with us for pizza."

"What are they talking about in there?" Alfonso was as restless as he was hungry. "Grownups sure are dull."

"As long as they keep talking, we're okay. It's when things get quiet that we're trouble."

"How so?"

Sarah gave him another *you're kidding* look.

"How do you suppose we get your aunt out of there?"

"Drag her out with a winch if we have to. She's that dangerous." Sarah perked her ears. "I hear glass tinkling. Your dad must've brought out his whiskey. That's not good."

The music inside was turned up. A deep voice singing about the night and love.

"Luther Vandross." Sarah dropped her head into her hands. "The trap is set."

"What trap?"

Another of those looks. *You're kidding?*

A new tune rose above the rest. Bach's *Toccata and Fugue in D minor.*

"What was that?"

"My dad's ring tone." The sound brought a thunderclap of hope. It was his dad's special chime for the University of Doom. *Why were they calling? About a job?*

Inside, Dr. Frankenstein excused himself and left Natalie.

Alfonso tracked his father's footsteps to the kitchen. Alfonso sneaked to the window over the sink and angled his head so he wouldn't be seen as he looked in.

His dad clutched a cell phone to one ear, and his face wrinkled with suspicion. "Moriarty," Dr. Frankenstein said the name like he meant dog poop. "What bad tidings do you bring?" He paused to listen.

Alfonso could barely hear his father through the window and it was impossible to hear the reply from the phone.

"Think I can trust you?" his father answered. "What happened? Did you shed your skin? Maybe fall on your head? Both?"

Alfonso's dad dragged a chair from the breakfast table. He took a seat and stretched his legs, a giveaway this might be a long phone call.

Maybe this was about a job at the university.

A job at the university! Alfonso wanted to shout but the words got choked behind another thought. If Natalie got her hooks into his dad, that might complicate moving away.

Alfonso scurried back to Sarah. "Are you serious about chasing your aunt out of here?"

"Absolutely."

"Then come along." *Time to think like an evil genius.* Alfonso dashed around her and to the front porch.

She followed. "What are you planning?"

"If the truth doesn't work on your aunt, then I'll use a big fat lie. Give me a minute." Alfonso carefully opened the door and crept inside. The front room was still cluttered from when they had moved in. He took slow steps toward a medical satchel, zipped it open, and withdrew a surgical mask that he slipped over his face. He stepped into the den. The lights were low.

A woman—Natalie, who else?—sat on the sofa. When Sarah had mentioned Godzilla, Alfonso had pictured a scary lizard-lady. But Natalie was pleasant looking. Swirls of blond hair that didn't match her eyebrows.

A print blouse swooped low to show off the deep crease in her bosom. Long legs stuck out from a frilly black skirt hiked over her knees. Two golden sandals lay heaped next to a matching purse. A thick old-fashioned glass sat on the coffee table, ice floating in whiskey. She held a similar glass in her hand.

Natalie had her legs crossed and bounced one bare foot, the toenails painted danger red. She had the impatient look of a high-school girl waiting for her date. How old was Natalie? Forty maybe? Did people that old still go for all that mushy kissing stuff?

Alfonso's dad continued to jabber out of sight with Moriarty.

Alfonso coughed.

Natalie looked up, surprised.

Alfonso raised a hand. "I'm Dr. Frankenstein's son. Alfonso."

Natalie mumbled a reply. Her gaze lowered from his eyes to the surgical mask.

"You're looking at this," he said, pointing.

She shook her head, embarrassed, and made the obvious effort of dragging her eyes to his.

"Just a precaution," Alfonso explained. "My dad's working in the Ebola lab—"

"Ebola?" Natalie uncrossed her legs and sat up straight.

"Yeah. Some of the bacteria escaped and infected one of the monkeys. But that's nothing compared to what happened in the flesh-eating virus lab." He faked a laugh. "Now that's a great story."

Natalie set her glass on the coffee table. "Do tell."

Alfonso paced close and extended his hand. "Pleased to meet you. And you are?"

"Going." Fingers shriveling from his, she chicken-winged her arms to her sides.

Alfonso brought his hand up and flipped it back-and-forth. "Relax. My rash is almost gone. What my dad was exposed to isn't *that* contagious."

Natalie spun the gold bracelet around her wrist and stared pop-eyed at a watch. "Oh my. Look at the time. I've completely forgotten my appointment." She snatched the sandals and yanked them on her feet.

"On a Saturday night?"

She stood abruptly like the sofa had suddenly grown thorns. "An Amway party." Natalie's look of horror sank with resignation. "They're the most fun ever." Purse tucked under one arm, she circled the opposite way around the coffee table for the door. "My regrets to your dad. Another time. *Perhaps.*"

Natalie disappeared out the den. The front door creaked open and banged shut. Sandals spanked the concrete sidewalk. A car door clicked open, slammed closed, and a motor cranked over. Tires chirped, and the car zoomed away.

Alfonso unhooked the surgical mask.

Sarah rushed through the front door and into the living room. She carried his glove and bats. "That was awesome. The last time I saw my aunt run that fast from a man was when his wife came home early. How did you do that?"

Alfonso mugged modestly. "It's a gift." He took the glove and bats.

"Well keep giving." She slugged his arm, "Later, gator," and vanished out the porch.

Dr. Frankenstein entered the dining room with a bucket of ice. "I apologize," he said absently. He caught sight of Alfonso and halted. "What are you doing here?"

Alfonso waved the bats. "I just got home."

His father glanced at the sofa, the cushions still dimpled from Natalie's bottom. "What happened to my guest? Natalie?"

"Is that who she was?" Alfonso crumpled the surgical mask in his fist. "She said something about an appointment and ran out. And you, Dad, who were you talking to?"

His father replied with a big shrug. "Nobody important. Nothing for you to worry about."

CHAPTER
TWENTY-THREE

Professor Moriarty sat in his office. Beelzebub was nestled on his lap. He caressed the vulture's head, its bald scalp smooth and cool as vinyl.

Moriarty projected a thought to the portal tablet on his desk to retrieve a recording he had made yesterday. The screen glowed and two Ken doll-sized holograms materialized above the glass screen.

The figure on the left was Greg Kaminski. On the right, Alfonso Frankenstein, perfectly reproduced in 3D.

Moriarty grinned smugly. Alfonso looked small, vulnerable, frozen in place.

Beelzebub turned its head toward Alfonso's hologram, hissed, and beat its wings.

"Easy. Easy." Moriarty gripped the bird and stroked its throat with a bent index finger. "Doom will come soon enough to the Frankensteins."

He congratulated himself on the cleverness of his trap. Alfonso and Greg had figured out how to talk online through the *Undead Siege* interface. They had spoken freely, unaware that anyone eavesdropped.

<play recording>

The two figures began to move.

Greg said, "Yo, it's so good to hear from you again. How's it going?"

"Okay," Alfonso replied without enthusiasm. "But every time I think I'm getting used to the neighborhood and school, something bad happens. Can't wait to get back to the University. How is it there?"

"Wish you were here. We're planning the semester field trip to the Mountain of Morbid Trials. The goal is to capture and tag an Abominable Snowman."

"Sure beats what my school has planned," Alfonso said. "Career day. So far they've scheduled beauticians and carnival ride operators."

"You mean like a Ferris wheel? Imagine mounting a Maybach 350 horsepower engine in that. Turbocharged."

"Greg. Greg. I'm not at Dr. Moreau Junior Academy. This is a public school. You have to scale back your expectations."

Beelzebub nuzzled Moriarty's chin. The bird's serrated beak scratched his jaw. It squawked softly for food.

The professor thought <pause>. The holograms froze in position, and he reached into a desk drawer for a carton of small predator kibble: live, defanged serpent-mice. Moriarty dangled a squirming mutant by its tails for Beelzebub to crunch. A cry followed by a spurt of blood that satisfied them both.

<play> The holograms started moving again.

"You might like this." Greg lowered his voice.

Alfonso's hologram stepped forward until the two virtual beings huddled with their heads together.

Moriarty cocked an ear and leaned closer, pleased that the boys thought their secrets would be unheard. <increase volume>

Greg said, "There's a rumor that Moriarty is looking to reverse your dad's termination."

Alfonso scowled. "Why would Moriarty help? He's the one who got my dad kicked out."

Moriarty smiled. Alfonso demonstrated the wariness he hoped for. Just more bait on the hook.

"I've heard," Greg replied, his voice low and wary, "the professor is having trouble with his cyborgs and needs your dad's help."

The comment prickled Moriarty. Even though he had planted that lie, it still rankled to hear anybody say he needed help to complete his cyborgs, and especially Eugino Frankenstein's help. Alfonso would tell the elder Frankenstein the outrageous lie, and the doctor, being so pathetically desperate, would swallow it— hook, line, and pole.

If Dr. Frankenstein heard the same information from two different sources, one of which was his own son, he'd surely lower his guard and make it that much easier to trick them both.

Alfonso stepped back from Greg and huffed. "Moriarty called my dad last night."

"So the rumor is true," Greg replied. "There's something else. The Undead Siege developers asked if I knew anyone who wanted the special game helmets."

"Are you kidding?" Alfonso said. "I thought you had to earn them by building points."

"I thought so too, but it seems they want to hurry their beta testing. I got a message from their tech department offering extra three helmets that I can give to anyone."

"Me for sure." Alfonso counted with his fingers. "My friend Reginald. And the spare for another friend."

Moriarty smiled and bared his teeth. *Excellent. Spread the wealth. The helmets performed brain scans of the wearer. With that information, he'd be able to choose the best candidates for his cyborgs.*

And who would they be?

Cross the Kaminski kid off any list. His father was Chair Emeritus for the West Point bio-weapons lab and ran their intramural robotics-bayoneting league. Mess with Greg, and Kaminski's dad would be sure to get even.

So Alfonso and his friends in the mano destre *would get special attention. Even if Moriarty lost points in the scientific portion of his dissertation for using such delusional and easily manipulated subjects, surely he'd get extra credit on evilness alone.*

"Yo, once you get the helmet," Greg taunted, "we're on for a tournament, right?"

"A tournament?" Alfonso laughed. "It'll be an annihilation."

Yes, yes. Moriarty cackled. *But it'll be you, young Mr. Frankenstein, who will be annihilated.*

CHAPTER
TWENTY-FOUR

Monday afternoon. The end of another school day. The first day back at Ty Cobb Middle School after the *Loaded Bats DEBACLE* against Jerry Tremont.

Nobody had said anything to Alfonso during homeroom science class. Ms. Humboldt did her lesson. Even Jerry acted like nothing special had happened. Alfonso could pretend the game had been a bad dream.

Then between third and fourth period, Jerry had ambushed him, and that's when the feud erupted again, which landed him here, ready to report for detention.

Alfonso paused outside Humboldt's classroom door, room 143. He was there with yet another black mark on his permanent record. If life was anywhere near fair, he should be on the way home and away from this prison masquerading as a public school. He opened the door and—head down—entered with meek little steps.

Ms. Humboldt stood at the back of the classroom. The door facing the school commons was open. A sunbeam brought out the yellow in her dress and sparkled across her hair.

Ever since Alfonso first met Ms. Humboldt, he had so wanted to impress her. Let her know he was the smartest student ever. Watch him humiliate that bully Jerry Tremont in baseball.

But Alfonso's plans had crashed and exploded like an out-of-control buzz bomb. He loved science—biology should've been easy as eating lunch—but school here was like constantly finding a fly in your guacamole. He wasn't doing very well in his classes. *Him! A Frankenstein.* The key to being an evil genius was the *genius* part. Kinda hard to call yourself genius with a C+ average, grades he'd kept a secret from his father.

Plus he'd heard about the Honors and Awards Banquet. He wasn't eligible because he hadn't been in the school for a year, and besides, the way his grades were tanking, he'd never make the honor roll. Yet another dose of sodium chloride in his wounds.

Humboldt said, "I am disappointed that you're here." She cocked an eyebrow and her mouth flattened into a grim line. "I thought by now you'd learn to make peace with Jerry Tremont."

Words boiled up Alfonso's throat. He wanted to launch into Why-is-this-my-fault?-Jerry-checked-me-against-the-hall-lockers-Called-me-Franken-loser-Told-me-to-stay-out-of his-sight-On-the-way-down-I-couldn't-help-but-grab-his-collar-(made him go *auwk!* like a seabird choking on a frog. that was awesome)-How-come-I-get-in-trouble-for-minding-my-own-business?

Alfonso stared at his shoes. "I'm trying, Ms. Humboldt."

"How are you doing?"

The guidance counselor had asked the same question. Did they really care?

He kept his eyes down. "Okay."

"You sure?"

Grown-ups always acted like they couldn't see the obvious. And if you did tell them the truth, so what?

Was Humboldt going to wave a magical wand and make everything better? Conjure a wormhole, puncture the time-space continuum, and send him and his dad back to the University of Doom? Summon witches, crumble that creep-o-zoid Jerry into flakes, and feed him to aquarium fish?

No.

She'd tell him to count his blessings, take advantage of opportunity—the usual menu of look-at-the-bright-side-crapola.

"Come on." She waved him closer. "Let's get this over with so you can go home. I've got a chore for you."

Clean the white boards? Scrub lab sinks? Disinfect the sponges? Alphabetize the tardy slips?

Didn't help his mood to have learned that since Jerry had baseball practice after school, his detention chores would be helping the coaching staff set up the batting machines and ball field. Some punishment.

Humboldt gathered the hem of her dress and crouched beside a big cardboard carton. She opened the flaps, reached inside, and pulled out a long slender cage made of sheet metal and wire screen.

A varmint trap.

Alfonso scrunched his brow and squinted.

"For detention," she set the trap on the floor between them, "I'm assigning you to squirrel patrol."

Squirrel patrol? Alfonso studied the trap. Primitive. Back at Dr. Moreau Junior Academy they would've used magnetic plasma containment units. "What do I have to do?"

"Help me with the traps." She pointed to another three still in the box. "To capture squirrels."

"For an experiment?" *To make killer bionic arboreal rodents?*

"No experiments. Principal Mulligan wants to get rid of them. Says they are a distraction."

Alfonso looked out the door to the oak and elm trees in the commons. What distraction? Squirrels chattered. They rustled through the trees. They ran across the grass. They were being squirrels.

A grin twitched Humboldt's lips. She spoke in a hushed voice. "I think the real reason is that Mulligan was leading a tour for the district staff. The squirrels bonked him on the head with some acorns."

So they didn't like him either. Score one for the squirrels.

She showed Alfonso how to set the trap and bait it with a pecan. She stood and said, "Bring the cages."

He tucked one under each arm and picked up the other two by the handles on top. He followed her out the door and into the commons, a horseshoe area framed by three buildings with the open end facing the gymnasium. During lunch, students crowded the commons, but after school, the grassy space was deserted.

Humboldt directed Alfonso where to set the traps. Squirrels watched from the tree branches. A comforting happiness warmed him as he armed and baited the traps, productive, his mood as shiny as the stainless steel of the cages.

A metallic pinging echoed from the ball field on the far side of the gymnasium. Had to be Jerry Tremont testing the batting machine. Jerry knocking baseballs all over the field. Jerry getting slapped on the back by the coaches, being told what a fine, upstanding young man he was, a champion. Jerry so perfect he probably thought he could pee soda pop.

A dark dullness settled over Alfonso, like the air had turned into a cloud of Venusian methane gas.

"Alfonso." Humboldt was talking to him. "You're getting that I-hate-the-world-face again."

"Sorry, Ms. Humboldt." He was sorry that she saw him but not sorry for feeling this way.

He hated this school. He hated not being in the University of Doom. He hated having to settle for so little and pretend he was grateful.

"Something you want to talk about?"

Alfonso tapped the side of the last trap. "It's stuff I have to figure out on my own." He looked up at her and smiled. "Thanks for asking."

"You're not alone, Alfonso. You have me. You have your friends. You have your father. I'm certain he cares about you very much."

This was the first time anyone had ever said this to him. Sure, he knew his father cared for him. And his friends liked him. The ever-cheery Sarah poked him with smiles and wisecracks that never failed to puncture his bubble of despair.

Teachers at the University of Doom had never been warm like this. But then, he had been so busy learning to be a mad scientist, he never gave it much thought.

He surveyed where they had placed the traps. "Now what? Do I have to get them in the morning?"

"No. Mr. Carroll collects them before school starts." Humboldt returned to her classroom. "We're all done. You can go home."

"What happens to the squirrels?"

"Mr. Carroll turns them over to Animal Control. They probably let them out in the woods."

On the walk from school, Alfonso thought about the complications waiting for him. What did Professor Moriarty want? Sure Greg Kaminsky had said Moriarty needed Alfonso's dad's help with cyborgs. And his father had taken the professor's call.

But Alfonso heard a dim sound far in the back of his mind, and that tiny noise shouted: Warning! Warning! You can't trust that vulture lover Moriarty.

Add Sarah's Aunt Natalie into the mix. Alfonso's dad hadn't dated anyone after the divorce. Maybe he was lonely. Maybe he'd ask Natalie to visit again. Suppose he started a "relationship" with her? Would that mean his dad might not try so hard to return to the University of Doom? If his dad had to make friends with a woman, Alfonso preferred it would be Ms. Humboldt. But even then, better that his dad remained unattached.

Life's problems piled around Alfonso like bricks falling off a crumbling building.

The driveway in his house was empty, meaning Dad wasn't home. A large cardboard box rested on the front porch. The express delivery label was addressed to him. The return address said: *Undead Siege.*

CHAPTER
TWENTY-FIVE

Alfonso studied the *Undead Siege* helmet. The spherical cranium shell made of carbon-fiber armor with a gray camouflage coating. A visor mirrored in gold and lined with a crystal matrix, most likely for the heads-up display. A foam liner was inlaid with a grid of some kind—a brain scanner? A thought reader?

A steel rail circled the bottom where the helmet clamped onto a space suit. Were these helmets real military astronaut helmets? If so, even better,

It looked major cool. He put the helmet on and admired himself in the dresser mirror.

Greg Kaminski had forwarded Alfonso's name to the *Undead Siege* people and the helmets had arrived overnight. Now that was service.

Eager to play and show off his new toys, Alfonso had invited Reginald and Candace over. They sat on his bed and unwrapped the other two helmets that had been in the box. Sarah should've been here but she was grounded. Had a fight with her oldest brother about kitchen chores that ended with her conking him with a frozen chicken.

"These are beyond awesome." Reginald fumbled with the visor latch of his helmet. "Look so real."

"They are real," Alfonso replied.

"I mean, they look like authentic astronaut helmets."

"Maybe they are," Candace noted. "Are you complaining? They're free."

"I could use more free stuff in my life," Reginald said.

She took off her glasses and screwed the helmet onto her head. "It's kind of small." She slipped her glasses through the visor port.

Actually, Alfonso had made sure to give her the largest size, but he didn't mention it.

The helmets came with a wireless hub that allowed them to connect all three to Alfonso's home computer. *The Undead Siege people had thought of everything.*

They all got ready, toggled to *Undead Siege* and the helmets automatically logged on. They played against the army of ferocious revenants for an hour, their avatars juking and scrambling in the virtual world of zombies and high tech mayhem. In real life, Candace moved like the chubby girl she was. In the game, her avatar sprinted and dashed leopard-like alongside Alfonso and Reginald.

Alfonso's skin tingled from the bio-feedback of his helmet. He had felt every blow from twirling axes, every splash of hot zombie goo striking his armor.

Soon a wall of dismembered undead corpses surrounded them. Their avatars waded through heaps of spent cartridge cases and body parts. Smoke curled from the red-hot muzzles of their assault grenade rifles. At any moment, another wave of zombies would attack.

Candace paused the game and worked her helmet off. Her hair fell around her head in a rumpled mess. "I gotta get home soon. My mom bought me a dress for the awards banquet Friday and I have to try it on."

The awards banquet. The HONORS and Awards Banquet.

Alfonso acted like he hadn't heard.

Reginald lifted his visor, his face a swipe of dark brown skin inside the helmet. "Yeah, I gotta go home, too." He pried his helmet off. His dense curly hair bore the imprint of the helmet liner.

Candace fished a protein bar from her backpack and tore the wrapper open. "You guys want some?"

Alfonso shook his head.

"Naw." Reginald slapped his belly. "I gotta save room for my mom's chicken cacciatore."

"I could eat a hundred of these, and it wouldn't ruin my appetite." She munched the bar in three bites. "I wish my metabolism would speed up so I could lose weight."

Alfonso was lucky to have friends like Reginald and Candace. Plus Sarah. He would hate to leave them. Hopefully, he and his dad might be returning the University of Doom. When it happened, he couldn't tell his friends why he was leaving because he and his father were *la mano sinistra*. They would vanish like they had never existed.

Alfonso logged off the game. He kept his helmet on and activated. His dad wouldn't be home for an hour, at least. Until then, he would experiment with the hand controller and watch what happened to the game interface. Lines of code trickled down on the monitor screen.

"What's that?" Reginald asked.

"It's the code for the helmet's driver to the interface."

"Shouldn't that be encrypted?" Candace asked.

"Should be, but apparently this helmet software has code running in the buffer that isn't encrypted." Alfonso scrolled through the code. "The game code is getting updates from the central server upstream. Plus it's streaming a lot of data the other way."

"Even now? The game is off."

Alfonso removed his helmet. "What's it sending?"

"Hold on," Reginald traced a fingertip across the code on the screen. "If you switch these two command lines, you should be able follow the link to the next code module. Find out where the data is going."

"Let's try," Alfonso readied his fingers on the controller.

"Would love to help," Reginald said, "but I better run."

Candace shouldered her backpack and plugged in a pair of earbuds.

Alfonso led them to the front door, sent them off, and returned to his room. He put the helmet back on. The lines of code appeared huge in his visor display, big as the movie credits at a theater. He used the hand controller to select the lines of code and swap them. He hit reset and another screen appeared. Instead of lines of code, 3-D objects materialized and floated around his avatar, like a cloud of corpuscles in a bloodstream.

Amazing! Too bad Reginald and Candace left.

Hundreds of the objects spiraled around his lower torso and legs like a tornado. The tornado's tail dipped and formed a highway of objects whizzing back and forth into the computer screen and receding into the distance. Some objects were cylinders in translucent green or orange, others floated like amoebas, still others resembled gems connected on a chain. Sometimes the cylinders bumped into each other. A glitter of electrified confetti would then puff from one to the next and the cylinders would sprout cilia like paramecium to scoot from one another. Some objects shuttled past in a blur. He wondered what they all were when the *A-ha!* hit him like a mallet.

The images were computer code controlling the avatar, reacting to one another like living cells. He had heard about this before—it was another example of reverse engineering the wreckage of the Roswell UFO.

Alfonso moved his cursor over the edge of the highway. An information balloon appeared with the caption:CPU Terminal Bus: RG46AA00567AG

Central Processor—Rhea*Rhea!* The University of Doom's computer system. This was a virtual conduit right into its brain.

Did this mean Undead Siege was a project of the University? Who was behind this? What information was being transferred?

He noticed that a tube undulated from the belly of his avatar like a transparent umbilical cord and connected him to the data highway. Grasping the tube, he stretched it between his avatar's hands. Inside the tube, he saw fleeting images of himself scrolling past. Recent images of himself. His memories.

The helmet wasn't just transmitting feedback to run his avatar. It was stealing his thoughts. *Undead Siege* was data mining his brain.

Not any more. Alfonso flattened his avatar's hand and karate-chopped the umbilical. The membrane broke and his thoughts spewed like beads into the nothingness of virtual space and melted away.

He rested his thumb on the power button of the controller to escape should an alarm activate.

The computer objects continued to whizz back-and-forth. His avatar floated in the void like an astronaut spacewalking on a tornado, thoughts feathering out the severed umbilical.

No alarm.

Alfonso grasped the umbilical cord and projected a thought into it. <stop>

His thoughts in the umbilical cord slowed to a trickle and stopped.

He still had a link into Rhea. Did he have access to the university's records?

Alfonso made his avatar snag a messenger cell. He squeezed it and one end opened like the mouth of a fish. He shook loose the stored information, which dissolved in a mini-cloud of data dust. He stuck the end of the umbilical inside the cylinder and projected:

<what is the purpose of using Undead Siege to mine data?>

A fresh glow of confetti flowed into the cell. He let go and the "mouth" shut. The cell undulated its cilia and swam upstream toward the memory core and central processor.

A moment later, a fresh messenger swam from upstream. It darted to him and halted, floating and waiting obediently. As before, he stuck his end of the umbilical inside the cylinder, only this time it absorbed the glowing haze.

The reply clunked into his brain: <unknown>

How could the status be unknown? Rhea knew everything on the computer system.

This sounded suspicious. And if there was anything suspicious at the University of Doom, Alfonso would bet Professor Moriarty was behind it.

What about the job Moriarty had discussed with his dad? Alfonso thought: <what is the status of the job position for Dr. Eugino Frankenstein?>

Message glowing within, the cylinder swam away. After a moment, it returned.

Alfonso repeated the procedure with the umbilical. The answer again clunked into his head. <unknown>

More suspicion.

If Moriarty offered the job to his father, the computer would know about the job...unless it didn't exist.

Maybe *Undead Siege* was Moriarty's scheme.

And what was Moriarty most obsessed about?

Becoming Doctor Moriarty.

Next thought: <what is the status of Prof. Moriarty's doctoral dissertation?>

The answer: <permission denied>

Alfonso had run into a firewall. He sent another question.

<is Professor Moriarty behind Undead Siege?>

<permission denied>

The reply made Alfonso smile. He had sent the computer a trick question. If Moriarty had nothing to do with *Undead Siege* the response most likely would've been "unknown." What was the professor up to?

Alfonso had to get past the firewall. To find the answer he had to go to the source of the information.

Moriarty's computer.

Which was at the University of Doom.

TWENTY-SIX

Friday.

The end of a week of squirrel patrol.

A week of lying low whenever Jerry Tremont was around.

A week of hiding the Undead Siege helmets from his dad. With his crappy attitude and dismal grades, Alfonso couldn't get caught playing video games instead of studying.

A week of waiting for his dad to work late.

A week of planning for a mission worthy of a mad scientist. He had to know if there really was a job for his dad back at the University of Doom. The only way to find out was to hack into Moriarty's computer, but that was impossible from the outside. Which meant, sneaking onto the university campus. A job Alfonso couldn't do alone.

And he had to know why Moriarty was data-mining his brain. He was sure it had to be the professor's doing. Who else from the university would focus an evil scheme on him? And Moriarty had also stolen thoughts from Candace and Reginald. Again, why?

Moriarty was certainly behind this twisted plot, and Alfonso would match him evil genius trick for evil genius trick and wreck the professor's plans. He'd do it for himself and his father.

Alfonso rushed out the entrance of Ty Cobb Middle School. He spied Sarah at the end of the block, strolling home, easy to pick out because of her blond hair, black and pink backpack, and bouncy gait.

He chased after her, calling her name.

Sarah halted, turned, and waited, looking so very tomboy in her olive green blouse and high-water jeans.

Alfonso caught up and paused a moment to catch his breath.

"What's new, zoo?" she asked. Her hair was pinned with skull and crossbones barrettes that matched the design decorating her backpack.

He found air for his words. "Are you're still grounded?"

"Nope. Got ungrounded last night. Mom got sick of me staying home. Said it was worse punishment for her."

"Good, I mean you getting ungrounded." Alfonso started walking with Sarah beside him. "I need you to come over."

"To play *Undead Siege?*" she chirped. "Finally."

"Maybe later. First, I need you to tell a fib."

Sarah made a face. "About what?"

"A sleepover."

"At your place?"

"Of course not. Why would I want to spend the night with a girl? Tell your mom you've been invited to a sleepover at one of your girlfriend's houses."

"What are you planning?"

"I need to break into where my dad used to work."

"What are you going to steal?"

"Nothing. I need to find out something."

Sarah crossed her arms and pulled them tight across her chest. "I dunno. Sounds like we could get into lots of trouble."

Definitely.

"Remember that guy Moriarty?" Alfonso explained in a dry tone. "He showed up in the big white limo the first day I moved here."

"The creep with the vulture?"

"Yeah, him. He's jerking my dad around about getting his old job back."

"Why would he do that?"

"Because Professor Moriarty is a world-class fink who's up to something rotten."

"So we're doing a *caper?*" Sarah went, "Oooooo... like on TV?"

"A caper. Yeah."

Sarah uncrossed her arms and wrung her hands. "A for real caper. I've always wanted to use that word."

"It's going to be an overnight thing."

"When?"

"Tonight."

"Might be tough. My mom hates getting news like this on short notice. It's gonna cost me extra chores."

"Like what?"

"The more disgusting the chore, the easier it will be to get permission."

"I can do disgusting."

Sarah raised a hand, palm toward him. "Hold on before you volunteer and then hate me. She's been after me to clean the bathrooms, especially the one upstairs."

"That's not so disgusting."

"You have older brothers?"

"No."

"Then you don't know disgusting. Especially after they reach puberty. Hair everywhere. *Gross!*"

Perhaps, thought Alfonso, but older brothers couldn't be as disgusting as cleaning up the entrails of an exploded brontosaurus clone.

"Back to your old haunts, huh?" Sarah added a lift to her step. "Must be pretty important. I mean, you and your dad haven't been exactly blabbing information about where you used to live and where he worked."

"You'll learn more than you should."

"What's that mean? Is it some top-secret government facility?"

"I'm not going to say anything more until we get there." Alfonso felt the pang of regret. He was about to violate the University of Doom's oath of secrecy. He took the oath seriously, but he had a bigger obligation.

Protect his father.

Besides, he had a way to protect the secret. A method he didn't want to use, especially against Sarah, his best friend among *la mano destre.*

He had to cover up one violation of trust by violating another trust. This caper was one ugly patchwork of treachery.

"How far is this place?"

"Upstate, I've told you that."

She rolled her eyes. "Yeah, like I could deliver a pizza with directions like that."

They reached the corner to his house and stopped. Alfonso replied, "Don't worry, I've got a ride figured out."

"We're not hitching a ride with strangers, are we? If so, I'm out."

"No, I'll be doing the driving."

She studied him. "Even if you have a car, you can't be driving."

"You'll find out. Right now, go and get your mom's permission to stay at a sleepover."

"What time should I be here?"

"Six o'clock."

"Your dad know about this?"

"What do you think? It's a caper."

"Six then." Sarah punched Alfonso's arm. "In a while, crocodile." She turned to the left and took off running.

Alfonso continued to his house. The family pickup was gone. His dad would be working late. Alfonso knew that Friday evening, when everyone else was in a rush to leave the office and start the weekend, was the best time to pilfer body parts from the bio-waste containers.

Now for the next step in the mission. Contact Greg Kaminski. Alfonso went to his room and put on the helmet to play *Undead Siege*. He'd be surprised if his friend wasn't deep in cyber battle against zombies.

This was the first time Alfonso had logged on since Monday. After hacking the code, he had decided to stay off the system and avoid the temptation of making more changes and getting caught.

He checked the buffer and saw that there hadn't been any maintenance work done to the software. Undoing the work of hackers should've been a priority. Alfonso got suspicious. Maybe the game had served its purpose, whatever that was, and Moriarty had moved on to the next phase of his evil scheme.

Alfonso switched to combat mode. Kaminski was already on and hailed, "Yo." They paired up and their avatars patrolled the castle ruins and sniped at zombies looming in the distant rubble.

Alfonso halted. To communicate with Kaminski, he needed to bypass any eavesdropping Moriarty might still have in place. He toggled the command cursor and entered the cheater code.

Instantly, the game dissolved into a black void, 3-D computer objects whizzing by. Alfonso's avatar balanced on its whirlwind cascading into the University of Doom's computer system.

Kaminski's avatar floated beside him, on a similar tornado, unaware that Alfonso watched from outside the game.

The umbilical cord to Alfonso's avatar remained severed. Good, this made his job easier.

An identical umbilical coiled from Kaminski's avatar. Images piped through the cord, his thoughts being sucked out of his head.

Alfonso grasped this umbilical cord and ripped it in two. Kaminski's brain junk spewed out like spilled glitter.

His avatar continued to move unaffected, shooting and ducking.

Alfonso took the loose end of his umbilical and jammed it against Kaminski's.

<resume thought transmission>

Alfonso's thoughts spewed through his umbilical, some leaking out the junction, but most pushing upstream into Kaminski.

His avatar jerked and groped at the air. <whoa. whoa>

<easy, easy, it's me. Alfonso>

Kaminski's avatar held its helmet. <what's going on?>

<Greg, it's me. now shut up and listen>

Kaminski's avatar spun around in spastic circles. <you're in my head>

Alfonso made his avatar kick Kaminski's in the butt and knock him over. The computer 3-D objects around Kaminski scattered through the void like a school of frightened minnows.

<settle down. I figured a way to stream into your brain. I got important news>

Kaminski picked himself up and dusted his knees. The computer 3-D objects returned and swirled around his legs.

<okay. what's the news?>

<I'm returning tonight>

<to the univeris—>

<where else? coming in from the north side of campus. meet me between Gatling Plaza and the Lake of Terror>

<how you gonna get here?>

<I got it figured out. once I'm there, I'm gonna need your help getting around>

<Alfonso, how much trouble is this going to get me into?>

Infiltrating the University of Doom would violate so many rules Alfonso would be surprised the faculty would let him live if they caught him. <megawatts, if we're lucky. gigawatts if we're not>

<kinda figured that. what's the plan?>

<sorta vague right now. we'll have to improvise>

Kaminski's avatar clicked its heels and saluted. <aye, aye captain. exactly what I expect from you. I'll be waiting>

Alfonso let go of the umbilicals and toggled back to the game. The castle ruins materialized around him. Kaminski's avatar remained at attention, the salute fixed in place.

He returned the salute. They bumped fists and reached up to click the power switches on their helmets. Their avatars and the world of *Undead Siege* dissolved into a gray static that morphed into Alfonso's bedroom.

It was a quarter to six. He zipped on his dark blue jacket and went out to the back yard. He tramped over dried grass and stringy weeds toward a large shed along the fence.

Next stop, the University of Doom.

TWENTY-SEVEN

Casa de Frankenstein was crammed with so much mad scientist gear the extra crap was heaped in the garage shed behind the house. The shed door should've been secured with at least a Grade 8 wolfram-steel padlock with a digital voice-command latching system. But as Alfonso's father noted, no point in that, as the walls were made of flimsy, weathered lumber held together with rusted nails. A single snort from a reanimated mammoth could blow it down.

Alfonso untwisted the wire coat hanger securing the door. He pushed it open and was smacked with a sharp chemical odor. Fading sunlight spilled into the shed's gloomy interior.

Most of the equipment was still in crates. Bottles, pipes, and drums of cables and hoses rested on sagging shelves.

He groped behind a box of revenant electrode bolts and found what he had hidden earlier, something heisted from his dad's *Do Not Touch Under Any Circumstances Super-Duper Secret Stash*—the Forgettor Gun. He pressed the *ON* switch and checked the power level. Fully charged.

Someone walked up the alley. "Alfonso?" It was Sarah.

Alfonso nudged the gun back behind the box. "In here."

The gate on the back fence creaked open.

"Leave it open," he said.

Sarah crunched over the dry weeds along the shed's threshold. Her ponytail was undone and her hair was tucked behind her ears. She wore a dark gray hoodie over her school clothes and carried her backpack.

He asked, "What's in the backpack?"

"Sleepover stuff. Remember?"

Alfonso gestured to a shelf. "Put it there until we get back."

She entered and halted, wincing. "What's that smell?"

Dilithium crystal solution. Alchemist stones. Venusian monster dust. "Fertilizer."

"So where are we going, Mr. I-Got-A-Big-Secret?"

"I'll tell you in a second. For now, gimme me a hand with this."

Sarah stowed her backpack and helped him uncover a long shape draped with a beige tarp, an object long as his dad's pickup. They peeled the tarp back, revealing a torpedo-like vehicle resting on tandem, spoked wheels with rubber tires. The vehicle sat low, just at Alfonso's hip, and was made of smooth aluminum with flush rivets. A red stripe swooped from the single vertical fin to the pointed nose.

"A motorcycle?" Sarah asked.

"Actually, it's a car."

"Car? With only two wheels, it's a motorcycle."

"Whatever, but it's known as the Rocket Fish."

Alfonso watched her examine the cockpit. A plain curve of glass for a windshield. An instrument panel crowded with dials, knobs, and switches. A steering yoke and levers. A spacious old-style bucket seat of green quilted leather.

She asked, "Where do I sit?"

"With me on the seat."

"Why do you need me?"

"This thing goes real fast. So fast I need someone to navigate."

"Is it street-legal?"

"There's nothing legal about this."

"So your dad stole it?"

"How can you steal something that doesn't exist?"

Sarah shook her head. "Honestly Alfonso, when it comes to stuff about you and your dad, your answers get pretty sketchy."

"This was one of my dad's first projects."

"I thought he was a medical doctor."

"Uhh...he's done lots of different research."

"So this Rocket Fish is here because he couldn't get it to work?"

"It works all right, I mean, it used to. What happened was that the Navy, the Air Force, and the Army got into a fight over who should own this. The Navy wanted it because it had fish in the name. The Air Force said anything with a rocket belonged to them, even if it had wheels. The Army said they wanted it because the Navy and the Air Force were too good at crashing."

"And we're riding in this...thing?"

"Once we gas it up." He looked around for fuel.

"What's it run on?"

"Hydrogen peroxide."

"Like what I got at home in the bathroom?"

"No. That stuff is diluted. I mean the hundred percent pure stuff. It's very explosive."

Sarah took a step back toward the door. "You keep that in here?"

"Relax, it also runs on lawn mower gas." He used both hands to haul a heavy metal gas can from under a shelf and drag it toward the rear of the Rocket Fish. He opened a small hatch along the spine of the car and unscrewed a filler cap. "Gimme a hand."

Sarah helped him hoist the gas can and pour into the tank. When the spout quit going *glug-glug* they set the can back down. He fit the cap back in and closed the hatch.

"Now what?"

"We push it out of the shed." Alfonso reached under the seat and retrieved a pair of vintage leather football helmets with boom microphones. He gave her the helmet with goggles.

Sarah took it and brushed away the dust. "This is way cool."

Alfonso put on his helmet, fastened the chinstrap and climbed into the cockpit. He flicked switches, reading the faded labels and going by trial-and-error.

Battery on. Primary fuel pump on. Secondary fuel pump on. Burners set to preheat.

The needles on the gauges crept upward.

One more check. He tapped his jeans pocket and made sure he'd brought a cell phone. When he discovered Moriarty's plans, Alfonso might have to contact his dad super quick like.

Sarah spit on the lenses of her goggles and used the sleeve of her hoodie to rub them clean. She smoothed her hair back and pulled on her helmet. "Where's the kickstand?"

"There is none." An oversight. Mad scientists couldn't think of everything. "What you gotta do is push me from the wall. It'll take the gyro-stabilizers a moment to activate."

Which reminded him. *Gyro-stabilizers, on.*

Sarah grasped the vertical fin. Soot from around the nozzle smudged her pants. She leaned against the car, dug her toes into the dirt floor, and pushed with a grunt.

The Rocket Fish scraped from the wall. The car rolled out of the shed and thumped over the threshold. Alfonso steered toward the alley.

The gauge for the gyro-stabilizers reached fifty percent and he could hear them whine.

"Okay," he shouted over his shoulder, "let go."

The Rocket Fish rumbled into the alley. He pushed the brake pedal and the car remained balanced.

Sarah closed the shed and the gate. *Good thinking.* Make it less obvious the Rocket Fish was missing. She had evil genius potential.

Alfonso scooted forward in the seat to make room. "Get in."

The car rocked like a canoe when she climbed aboard and settled behind Alfonso. He yanked a video tablet from the left side of the cockpit and touched the *ON* switch. The tablet's screen illuminated and showed a map like those on the Internet. "Here, steer with this. It's called a Navi-Brain." He passed it to her.

He groped for the lap and shoulder harness and snapped the buckle, but kept it loose so he wouldn't squish her against the seat. He handed her a cable connector for the helmet intercom, and she clicked in.

He adjusted his microphone and said, "Put your goggles on."

"What about yours?" Her voice sounded tinny through the headset.

Alfonso reached under the seat for a pair of goggles with long binoculars fitted to the lenses.

"Why do those look different?"

"These are special goggles that focus my eyes using tunnel vision. I'll use them before we get to cruising speed."

He blew dust from the optics and fixed the goggles so they rested against his forehead, the binoculars angling upward like the eyestalks of a crab. Their unbalanced weight strained his neck.

"When are you going to tell me where we're going?"

"Soon." He ratcheted the handle of the manual pump to dump fuel into the combustion chamber. Grasping the steering yoke with his right hand, he wrapped his left around the throttle lever, thumb resting on the button marked *Ignite*. "Ready?"

"Is this caper dangerous AND stupid?"

"Kinda late to ask. You gonna chicken out?"

"I can handle dangerous. I just can't handle stupid."

He pressed the button. Flame whooshed out the tailpipe. The Rocket Fish surged forward.

Sarah shifted behind him. "How fast does this thing go?"

"Depends on traffic but we should be able to cruise at Mach one point five."

"Mach one point five? How fast is that in regular human talk?"

"Supersonic."

"You mean like a bullet?"

He inched the throttle forward. "Faster."

CHAPTER
TWENTY-EIGHT

"**B**oss," Toulon announced, "we are home."

"Quit calling me boss," Moriarty snapped. "We're back on campus and my title is *Professor*."

"Stretch" Toulon, the only lab tech available from the Minion Pool, drove the delivery van. He was folded over the steering wheel, and still, his head pushed against the roof lining. Moriarty resented the seven-foot beanpole working for him, loathing having to look up to anyone.

They had returned from Greenville, the closest town to the University of Doom, and were now cruising between warehouse-type buildings, the faculty laboratory complex on campus. Moriarty needed dogs, specifically dog brains in the next step for his new batch cyborgs.

"So we were out in public, doing God knows what 'evil genius work'," Toulon made air quotes. (Minions did that a lot when ordered about by their superiors.) "And you use your for-real name?"

Good point but Moriarty couldn't acknowledge that Toulon might be right. If there was grand evilness to be done, Moriarty wanted his name involved.

Toulon backed the van toward Moriarty's laboratory. The robotic sensor scrolled the bay door open and let them enter.

Back home, safe. Moriarty's pet vulture, Beelzebub, climbed from his lap to his shoulder.

Toulon halted the van beside the remains of Moriarty's previous cyborgs, a pile of blasted and twisted metal scrap heaped on a pallet. The door rattled closed.

Moriarty got out, Beelzebub riding his shoulder like a pirate's parrot. The professor's latest versions of his most diabolical creations—three military cyborgs, eight-foot tall automatons of brushed black steel—stood on magnetic immobilization platforms to the left of the scrap heap. He had learned one lesson—never animate a cyborg with a brain you can't control.

Which led to the beauty of this new scheme. A double-whammy of diabolical monstrosity.

Whammy nummer eins. Put dog brains in the cyborgs.

Whammy nummer zwei. Have the dog-brained cyborgs crash the Ty Cobb Middle School honors and awards banquet and kidnap the preselected students to take their brains. Candace Wolcott. Reginald Thompson. And of course, Alfonso Frankenstein. With kids' brains in the cyborgs, they'd be the perfect military machines.

Moriarty salivated as he relished his mad scientist evil strategy. The *Undead Siege* game worked exactly as planned. Data provided by the helmets had identified Alfonso and two schoolmates as worthy brain donors.

However, the data mine processor had raised an alert during Alfonso's thought transfer. Some misgivings about the honors and awards banquet.

Moriarty dismissed the red flag. Most likely a glitch, and the fault of the minion software engineers. Overpaid, scatter-brained rabble. From Harvard. Stanford. MIT. Rensselaer Polytechnic. Mere trade schools compared to the University of Doom. And don't get him started on DARPA[1]. You'd be better off giving rocks and sticks to monkeys.

All the smartest kids would be at the awards banquet and wasn't Alfonso, a Frankenstein, the smartest of the smart? Of course he'd be there.

And so will I. Yes. Yes. Moriarty rubbed his hands together and smacked his lips. The meddlesome brat would probably be getting the highest award. Which would make ruining the banquet even more delicious.

Toulon brought a shop towel. "Boss, you're drooling. It's kinda gross."

Moriarty wiped his chin. "Just bring the dogs."

Toulon ambled to the back of the van and returned with three Golden Retrievers. They strained against their leashes, barking and yelping.

"I gotta give you props, boss. Sheer genius using Craigslist to advertise a boutique dog sitting service."

Genius goes without saying. Moriarty stretched his arm to a skull-shaped perch jutting from the wall.

1 Defense Advanced Research Projects Agency

Beelzebub hopped from his shoulder, up his arm, and fluttered to the perch, where it sat facing the laboratory.

Moriarty plucked a smock from the coat rack by the perch and fit his arms through the sleeves. Can't do mad scientist work unless you've dressed the part.

Toulon brought the dogs to the operating dollies. Each dolly held a brace for one dog, used to hold the dog upright facing a reanimation console at the front of the dolly. Bundles of tubing swayed from under the consoles to a PortaBoy embalming machine connected to the glass bottles of stasis fluids beneath: Keep-Fresh, Omni-blood, and Dipple's Oil. A hologram touch screen flickered above the console.

Moriarty snapped on latex gloves. As soon as the mission was over, he would replace the brains, and the dogs would be back to normal.

Funny how these things worked, even at the University of Doom. Plan for thermonuclear warfare—the annihilation of millions—and the biggest concern was, *Can you do this on budget?*

But harm a dog and even the viliest of evil geniuses would turn on you.

He and Toulon coaxed the dogs onto the dollies, cinched them into the braces, and fed them kibble laced with Kanine Koma. The retrievers snarfed the kibble and stared at Moriarty, tails wagging, panting for more.

A minute passed. Their radiant eyes dulled with slumber, their tails drooped, and their heads lolled into the jaw cradles. Toulon inserted a catheter into the first dog's neck and Moriarty made sure the other end of the clear tube was seated into the reanimation console.

He commanded: <begin stasis>

The PortaBoy whirred. Pink fluid bubbled from the console, through the catheter and into the dog. Pins in the support brace sent feedback from the dog's cardio-vascular system to the console. A life-support module circulated the proper mixture from the bottles.

Moriarty read the vital signs on the hologram. When the signs achieved stasis, the console rang *bing!*

He and Toulon repeated the procedure with the other two dogs.

Bing!

Bing!

Toulon massaged Zombie-Mousse into the first retriever's scalp and molded the hair into a point so it looked like a furry cone. He used a black marker to draw a line in the exposed skin circling the skull.

Moriarty rolled a gang box to one of the cyborgs. He touched the cyborgs' remote in his pocket.

<activate>

Servos inside the first cyborg hissed and it hunched forward until its head was level with Moriarty's chest. He flipped the top of the steel skull open so it hung like a wind-blown toupee and then readied the connectors inside the brainpan.

<skull lubrication>

Dipple's Oil gurgled through the mesh lining of the skull.

Toulon pushed one of the dollies with an unconscious retriever to the cyborg.

Moriarty opened drawers along the front of the gang box and selected tools needed to complete the brain transfer. An electric bone saw, a chrome brain scoop, and a shaker of reanimation nanobots. He and Toulon put on safety goggles.

The minion held the dog by the muzzle to steady its head. Moriarty placed the spinning blades against the skull and followed the marker line. When he'd circled all the way around, he lifted the upper skull by the moussed tuft of hair and handed it to Toulon. He rotated the top of the shaker and measured a pour of nanobots on top of the exposed brain. The nanobots—smaller than grains of sand—scattered to vanish into its furrows.

He followed the progress of the second hand on the wall clock while the nanobots prepped the brain for removal. At twenty seconds (what was taking so long?) the hologram flashed big red letters: READY

Using the scoop, he lifted the brain out of the skull, the gray mass quivering like pudding.

Beelzebub squawked *Yum!*

Toulon spritzed the inside of the dog's empty brainpan with Keep-Fresh and replaced the top of the skull.

Moriarty shook a dash of nanobots into the cyborg's skull. He slid the brain off the scoop into the skull where it landed with a gooshy plop. He handed the scoop and shaker to Toulon and grasped the medulla oblongata, which he connected to the wiring harness. He arranged the lattice of piping for Dipple's Oil over the brain.

<AWARENESS switch from OFF to STANDBY>

Oil bubbled through the piping. The lights inside the cyborg's eyes flickered. Toes and fingers flexed.

It's alive!

He swung the cyborg's skullcap closed and used a cordless drill to insert and tighten the retention screws.

<AWARENESS switch from STANDBY to ON>

The cyborg threw its shoulders back and straightened to its full magnificent height. The eyes burned red. The mouth opened, revealing rows of titanium choppers, and clamped shut. Those jaws could chew through an M1 tank. This machine—this quarter-ton monster of crafted steel—represented the apex of mad scientist creation. On looks alone, this cyborg should earn Moriarty his coveted doctorate.

He took a moment to close his eyes, clench his fists, and congratulate himself for being the most brilliant evil genius ever. *I'm so lucky to be me.*

They readied the other two cyborgs. All he had to do now was load up the van and leave.

"Toulon, go to the first cyborg and unfasten the restraints."

"Why me?"

"Because you're the minion."

"What if this thing attacks me?"

"Then we'll know something went wrong, won't we? Besides, the magnetic anchor is on. He's not going anywhere."

"Should've been a plumber," Toulon grumbled. He crouched at the base of the cyborg's platform and unfastened the steel safety straps from around its ankles. Eyes alert with caution, he loped backwards on his gangly legs. "Boss, when do you need these cyborgs?"

"Friday night."

"This Friday? As in tonight?"

"What are you talking about?"

"Today is Friday."

Moriarty felt the pinch of worry and took a paper note from his trouser pocket to read:

Honors and Awards Banquet

Friday the 13th

Ty Cobb Middle School

"Today can't be the thirteenth." He became queasy with doubt and growing panic. Tuesday I had to tweak the nanobot recipe. Or was that Wednesday? Thursday I had my "Evil is as Evil does" lecture. Which meant...

"Tredici," chirped Toulon. "Ju san. Wa'maH wej. Pick any language you want. It's the thirteenth. If these cyborgs are supposed to be ready for whatever 'evil schemes'"—air quotes—"you got up your smock, then it's now or never."

If Moriarty wanted kids' brains as planned, he had to leave within the hour. He folded the note and shoved it into his smock's breast pocket. "I don't have time to tweak the cyborgs. Besides—"

"Yeah, I know," Toulon raised his hands and rolled his eyes. "What could go wrong?"

One big detail remained.

Toulon.

He knew too much and could squeal to his minion friends, who might then alert the faculty, spoiling Moriarty's plans.

Time for a workplace accident. But it was going to be such a bother expensing Toulon's demise to the department's overhead.

The professor aimed a thought at the cyborg.

<species profile?>

The reply: <Golden Retriever>

<switch to Timber Wolf>
<Timber Wolf obtained>
<Behavior index status?>
The reply: <Tame>
<switch to Rabid>

With its eyes blazing at 500 watts of power and a wavelength of 648 nanometers, the cyborg bent forward and growled, hind legs straining to lift from the platform.

Toulon lunged for the office door, screaming.

Moriarty glanced to the Environmental Control Unit on the ceiling. Some mood music. <Queen's Bohemian Rhapsody—loud>

Moriarty stared at the platform. <magnetic anchor—release>

The cyborg sprang off the platform and arced over the floor. It shoveled Toulon into its arms, crushing the rangy, shrieking minion into a wad of mangled limbs like a ball of pipe-cleaners.

Beelzebub jumped from its perch and skidded under the cyborg. The vulture hopped about with its beak up and open, gobbling Toulon's spurts of blood and gore.

Moriarty smiled at the cyborg. If his creations worked this well with dog brains, imagine how much better they'd be with kid brains.

Song blaring from the speakers, Moriarty ticked through a mental checklist of what still needed to be done for his mission. He'd better hurry.

He had an appointment to keep. With Alfonso Frankenstein.

CHAPTER
TWENTY–NINE

T he Rocket Fish rolled down the alley, flame spewing out the tail nozzle.

Sarah's voice came through Alfonso's helmet speakers. "There's a good chance we're going to burn down the neighborhood."

He glanced over his shoulder. Embers swirled from the tail and floated over the Dumpsters. Fortunately they arrived at the street before anything caught fire. He checked for traffic and steered left. The Rocket Fish leaned into the turn.

"How far will we get before the police stop us?"

"All the way," he answered. "And they won't stop us."

"Come on Alfonso, this thing practically has 'arrest me before I blow up and kill someone' written all over it."

Alfonso flicked the blue switch on the steering yoke. Something like heat waves shimmered over the vehicle and it disappeared.

"Holy smokes," Sarah exclaimed. "Are we—"

"Invisible. Yep."

"Like no one can see us?"

"That's what invisible means."

She conked his head. "I was being rhetorical." She fidgeted behind him. "Jeez, Alfonso, you sure have a bony butt. Make room for me already."

Alfonso inched forward in the seat. He drove the Rocket Fish past Ennuyeux Lane and away from his house. His big worry was someone colliding into them. "Now guide us. Turn on the Navi-Brain."

"How? I can't see it. We're invisible, remember?"

"Feel for a round button on the top. Push that one." In a shiver of panic, he remembered a possibly fatal detail. "But not the square button."

"I'm feeling around. I found the square one."

"Don't push it!" That would activate the self-destruct mechanism. A lock-out safety on the button would probably be a good idea.

"Okay, I heard you, quit yelling. I'm leaving that button alone." She fidgeted some more and the edge of the Navi-Brain creased into his back. "Okay, I think I found the *ROUND* button."

"Press it."

She whispered, "Whoa."

Since the Rocket Fish and everything in it were invisible, the driver needed a way to get information. The Navi-Brain would send maps directly into the user's mind. Right now Sarah was a body-less eye swooping over a topographic landscape.

She leaned into Alfonso and her breath puffed against the back of his neck. "This is so awesome."

SUVs and a sedan drew close. The light at the intersection turned red. Alfonso glanced left-right to see that the way was clear and darted through.

The ramp to the interstate was up the street.

"Once we get on the highway, I'm going to light the afterburner and we'll go supersonic. At that speed, all I can do is stay on course and do my best not to hit anything."

"Do your best? I need better than that. Maybe I should drive."

"You stay back there and give me directions."

"I need to know where we're going."

"There should be a little icon labeled Home."

"Searching. Searching. *Wow!* This is fun flying around like a ghost."

A red SUV flashed past in the opposite lane. In the instant it drove by, Alfonso recognized Jerry Tremont in the front passenger's seat. No doubt on his way to the awards banquet.

Alfonso pulled a tight U-turn, and the Rocket Fish leaned almost horizontal. He wove through traffic and got even with the SUV.

"What are you doing?" Sarah asked.

"Change in plans." He surged ahead of the SUV. When he gained a hundred feet, he goosed the throttle lever. The Rocket Fish kicked forward. A ball of flame burst from the back end of their inviso-shroud. The fire flared for an instant in front of the SUV. It jerked from side to side and screeched to a halt.

Heh-heh-heh. Having a hot time tonight, Jerry?

Alfonso swerved again to the left and got back on original course.

"Things are dangerous enough in this bomb," Sarah scolded. "Let's not tempt fate, okay?"

A green highway sign said: Upstate. Ramp Ahead. Merge Right.

Alfonso slid to the edge of the shoulder and passed traffic.

A silver tanker-trailer wobbled back and forth in front of them. The safety placard on the back read: Flammable High Octane Gasoline

Great. He and Sarah were riding a blowtorch up the butt end of fifty-thousand gallons of gasoline.

The tanker drifted left enough for Alfonso to juice the throttle lever. They shot past and onto the highway.

"The way looks clear enough." *Sorta.* "Have you found Home?"

"Finally. I didn't know there was a university there."

And neither does the public. El escudo de ignorancia— the shield of ignorance—*guarded the university from all detection. Satellite observation saw nothing. Search for the area on an Internet map and a super algorithm cut a hole around the campus and stitched the edges together. Accidentally walk there and you'd find nothing but bramble and a dense hedge. Sneak through, and well, the hyena-scorpion sentries were kept hungry for a reason.*

Alfonso lowered the bino-goggles over his eyes. The only way to traverse the road at supersonic speed was to focus completely on what was in front of him. He touched the side of the goggles and pressed the switch for Tunnel-Vision.

The world collapsed into concentric rings, going from foggy gray on the outside, to blurry, less blurry, to a center circle where everything was illuminated in razor-sharp focus and moved in super-slow motion.

"Ready, Sarah?" He draped his hand over the throttle lever.

"Ready, Freddy."

Alfonso nudged the throttle forward. The rocket motor rumbled loud. He was pushed against Sarah.

Alfonso kept his eyes forward and concentrated on the highway in front of him. He swerved around the cars and trucks, the Rocket Fish pivoting from side to side.

The readout in the goggles said:

SPEED 125 MPH

THRUST 31 PERCENT

He advanced the throttle to 50 percent.

The Rocket Fish cruised along the highway and threaded through traffic.

SPEED 372 MPH

"This is fast," Sarah said. "How come there's no canopy?"

Another design oversight.

"Uhhh...just keep your hands and head inside the cockpit and you'll be okay."

Alfonso kept his eyes locked forward. At this speed, one careless instant and they'd be a smear of roasted hamburger.

But they had to go faster. Who knew what Moriarty was up to? Alfonso kept pushing the throttle.

440 MPH.

500.

550.

The Rocket Fish began to shimmy.

"Wh...what's that?" a worried Sarah asked.

"Turbulence. We've reached the sound barrier."

"So what happens?" For once, she sounded scared.

"We push through." Supersonic speed would over-heat the Rocket Fish's skin and tear it apart. Alfonso clicked the Skin Coolant switch to *ON*. And there was that pesky Sonic Boom. Sonic Boom Suppressor—*ON*.

He nudged the throttle lever until it hit the after-burner detent. His thumb slid over the release catch. "Hang on."

He depressed the catch and rammed the throttle all the way forward.

Flame roared out the exhaust.

They were slammed backwards in the seat. Alfonso was squashed against Sarah, her knobby knees smacking the outside of his thighs.

He concentrated on what appeared in Tunnel-Vision. The cars in the center ring moved like they were in crystal syrup where they slid to the perimeter before getting sucked to the outer rings.

SPEED 973 MPH

MACH 1.3

"Road goes left," Sarah said.

He tipped the steering yoke to the left.

"Now right."

Alfonso aimed for a gap under an overpass.

The Rocket Fish kept accelerating.

SPEED 1146 MPH

MACH 1.5

Alfonso and Sarah streaked along the highway, slaloming through traffic and eating the asphalt at over sixteen hundred feet per second.

After several minutes of more directions, Sarah said, "Up ahead. The turn off."

Alfonso eased back on the throttle.

The Rocket Fish wobbled as it slowed through transonic speed. At 300 MPH, Alfonso lifted his goggles. He blinked at the sudden and overwhelming rush of peripheral vision.

The speedometer read 120 MPH.

He sluiced along the shadowy, twisting road.

"I'm cutting the motor to hide our heat signal." He pulled the throttle to the rear stop and mashed the *KILL* switch on the yoke handle. He slapped the fuel switches to *OFF*.

The growl of the exhaust nozzle faded, replaced by the hum of rubber tires on the pavement.

A line of trees formed on the right, growing denser and taller until they formed a dark and seemingly impenetrable wall. On the other side—the University of Doom.

Alfonso's throat went dry and his pulse hammered in anticipation. Finally, almost back home. His real home.

He veered off the pavement. The Rocket Fish bounced over the grassy dirt and made Alfonso jiggle like a bobble head.

Sarah chirped through the intercom. "We're gonna sneak through that forest, right?"

"Not sneak, exactly."

She said nothing, then, "No way! You're going to crash through the trees?"

"Have to. If I slow down, we won't get past the Obfuscation Misters."

"And then, piece o' cake. Right?"

"Well...no. There are guards patrolling the other side."

"*Guards.* Like they could stop me." Sarah's reply was a gob of sarcasm.

"Don't be too sure of yourself. Wait until you meet them." Alfonso leaned forward and scanned the opaque mass of trees until he spied a purple gap in the dark tangle.

SPEED 90 MPH. Plenty of velocity, what fighter pilots called *smash.*

He aimed for the purple shape, a triangular opening framed by thick oaks. He jerked tight the safety harness, cinching him against Sarah. She wrapped her arms around his waist and squeezed. A nervous gulp remained stuck in his throat.

The Rocket Fish bounced along. Alfonso's eyes rattled in their sockets, making his target a purple blur. He focused on its center and held steady.

Tiny droplets spattered the windshield. The Obfuscation Misters were working.

Alfonso got light-headed. He tightened his grip on the yoke and kept the Rocket Fish on course. At walking speed, people would get so turned around they'd never reach the trees. But at this clip—*whoosh,* he was through the mist, his mind already clearing.

A hundred feet to the gap.

Alfonso hunched his shoulders and pulled into the steering yoke.

Fifty feet.

Smash!

The blow slammed through Alfonso. The bino-goggles flew from his helmet and ricocheted against the inside of the windshield. The Rocket Fish lanced between massive oaks. Branches raked its aluminum skin in a raucous symphony of snapping and breaking. The inviso-shroud flicked off and the Rocket Fish shimmered into view.

Twigs and leaves whapped Alfonso's helmet. The crackling of tree branches changed into the *crunch, crunch* of busting through gnarly brush. Sets of leafy jaws mouthed the sides of the Rocket Fish and slipped away.

"What was that?" Sarah blurted.

The perimeter of man-eating Venus Flytraps.

A ceiling of stars opened above them. The front wheel snagged on something and jerked to the left, tearing the steering yoke from his hands. The warning lights on the instrument panel flared then went dark. The Rocket Fish spun around and careened onto its side, scraping for a hundred feet before sliding to a halt.

Dust settled on Alfonso. He remained tense, muscles wire tight.

From his vantage in the crashed Rocket Fish, the world looked off kilter. A dim light barely illuminated the area, light from the stars and a half moon. They were inside a meadow surrounded by brush and clumps of taller grasses. He flexed his fingers, then his wrists, arms, ankles, and legs. Nothing broken.

"Sarah," he said, "you okay?"

She squirmed behind him. "I survived." Her voice sounded muffled with the intercom not working.

Alfonso studied what he could see of the Rocket Fish. The sides didn't look too mangled. Greg Kaminski could help him repair the damage though it was doubtful it could go supersonic for the trip back home.

He scanned the gloom for landmarks and guessed they were somewhere along the northern border of the university campus.

A soft hiss pressed into the silence. The coolant tank was depressurizing, or one of the tires must be going flat.

Sarah shifted position and pressed against his back. "There's a welcoming committee behind us. Please tell me they're harmless."

Alfonso turned his head.

The hissing didn't come from the Rocket Fish but from two hulking dog-like creatures that stalked them from the forest. Huge segmented tails, like bowling balls strung together, arched over their spotted backs, each tipped with a sharp poisonous stinger glistening in the moonlight.

Hyena-scorpions!

CHAPTER
THIRTY

"Get out!" Alfonso struggled with the catch on the safety harness. It clicked open, and he fell from the seat. Sarah tumbled over him.

Alfonso scrambled to his feet. Sarah was behind him, pushing away from the Rocket Fish.

Yanking off their helmets and tossing them aside, they sprinted toward the forest.

Giant Venus Fly Traps waited along the brush, mouths gaping.

"We can't go that that way." Alfonso dug his heels into the dirt and stopped. Sarah ran into him.

Turning around, Alfonso saw the two hyena-scorpions creep after him and Sarah. The monsters' segmented tails arced wickedly over their muscular backs, poison seeping from the hooked stingers.

"I guess we have to fight them off." Sarah snatched a fist-sized rock from the dirt. She cocked her arm back and aimed for the closest hyena-scorpion.

The rock ricocheted off its forehead. The mutant beast blinked, snarled, and tensed its legs.

"Unless you think of something pronto," the defiance had leaked from her voice, "we're about to be K.I.A."

The second monster banged at the Rocket Fish with its paws and tails, dimpling the car's aluminum side with scores of holes. Gasoline spurted out. The monster reached into the cockpit and groped.

Something flipped out and landed in the dirt between the hyena-scorpions and Alfonso.

The Navi-Brain.

The means to escape gruesome destruction—if he could get to it.

Alfonso measured the distance to the device. Thirty feet feet. And the hyena-scorpions ten feet beyond. To get the Navi-Brain would be a race against certain death...but he had no choice. "Get some rocks and cover me."

"What are you going to do?"

"Just start beaning those mutants. Keep them distracted." He crouched and readied to sprint, eyes locked on the Navi-Brain.

A rock sailed at the first hyena-scorpion and struck it squarely on the nose. Hopping backwards, the beast stabbed the rock with its stinger tail.

Alfonso darted forward, legs cycling like pistons in a racecar engine.

The glistening rectangle of the Navi-Brain lay on the grass, beckoning.

At the edges of his peripheral vision, he noted the twin sets of glossy hyena-scorpion eyes snap toward him.

He snatched the Navi-Brain and juked to the left in a tight circle.

A dark blur stoked the air to his right. The segmented tail and stinger spiked the grass where he had just been.

Still running at full speed, Alfonso slid his hand across the Navi-Brain, found the square button, and mashed it hard.

The Navi-Brain shouted: "Warning! Self-destruct initiated. Ten."

Alfonso tossed the Navi-Brain over his shoulder.

"Nine."

If this didn't work, he expected to get skewered by those enormous stingers.

"Eight."

He clutched Sarah's hand as he raced past. "Run!"

They tore into a sprint, splitting the difference between the Venus Fly Traps and the hyena-scorpions.

"Seven."

Alfonso glanced back to take mental snapshots of what could be his last moments alive. The beasts stared transfixed at the squawking Navi-Brain, growling and waving their stinger tails.

"Six."

Alfonso and Sarah let go of each other's hands so they could run faster.

"Five."

His heart and feet pounded in desperate rhythm. Weeds and tall grass slapped his shins.

"Four."

Keep going! The hyena-scorpions could suddenly lose interest in the Navi-Brain and renew their attack.

"Three."

Alfonso's throat burned and his lungs seemed on fire.

"Two."

A stitch in his side stabbed at him.

"One."

A bright flash painted the dark meadow in harsh, yellow light. The blast lashed his back with superhot air. Pieces of flaming wreckage ricocheted past them. The booming concussion knocked him and Sarah flat.

They lay face down side-by-side, grimacing and gulping for air.

A fireball rose from the torched remains of the Rocket Fish. Both hyena-scorpions were on their backs, legs curled, smoke and fire swirling from their charred bodies.

She picked herself off the ground. "Somebody definitely heard that"—the fireball lifted high into the night sky, perched on a tower of flame and smoke that corkscrewed upward—"and saw that."

Alfonso stood and scanned the south side of the meadow that led to the center of the campus. Light from the burning Rocket Fish flickered across the meadow and into the shadows. They were within the university perimeter and unless the administration had added another ring of security, it should be a clear path forward.

As he brushed the grass off his clothes and felt around his pants pocket, he discovered that his cell phone was in pieces. Yet another complication. He scattered its useless remnants on the ground. "Let's go."

Sarah trotted alongside him, glancing back to the blasted hulk of the Rocket Fish. "Alfonso, how are we getting home?"

Alfonso's eyes flicked back to the burning wreckage. That was a good question.

CHAPTER
THIRTY-ONE

Alfonso and Sarah raced out of the meadow. They darted around random hedges and ran up a slope. Huffing up the incline drained the last of their stamina, and they stopped.

Bent over, hands on knees, they studied the smoldering remains of the Rocket Fish down the hill. A halo of orange light reflected off the trees and brush about them. Above, the fireball dissolved into a cloud of embers and black smoke.

When Alfonso had fully recovered his breath, he climbed to the top of the slope, backlit by the glow of the distant university campus. Sarah had gone ahead and was already scoping out the reverse side. She kept repeating, "Wow. Wow."

At the crest, he halted again, stunned by the panorama of the University of Doom before him, a woodsy rolling campus threaded by ribbons of pavement connecting imposing structures incorporating every architectural style from Ancient Egypt to Classical Roman to Gothic to post-modern sweeps of gleaming steel and angles of concrete, the vista jewel-like from the sparkle of countless lights.

The Museum of Horrific Failures. The Cassandra Library of Forbidden Knowledge. The Torquemada Administrative Center. The assorted classroom buildings surrounding RJ Gatling Plaza.

On the east side of campus, the Forest of the Damned. In the middle, The Lake of Terror. To the west, Judgment Knoll. Farther west, Hindenburg Airfield. At the far side of the lake, miles to the south, the ordered confusion of lights marking the faculty laboratories and resident housing.

Tears itched Alfonso's eyes. He missed this place so much. Now he was back. But as an unwelcome trespasser.

Sarah bumped into him. Her eyelids were peeled back so far that her eyeballs looked ready to pop from their sockets. "O.M.G," she whispered, "this is better than Disneyland."

"Oh please," Alfonso replied.

"Is this place for real?"

"Weren't the hyena-scorpions enough proof?"

"Why didn't you ever tell me about it?"

"In case you haven't figured it out, this place is secret."

"So where are we?"

"The University of Doom."

An explosion deep within the campus flared into the air. The blast rumbled toward them.

"What was that?" Sarah jerked in surprise.

"Mid-terms. And it's Friday night. A good way to celebrate the weekend is to blow stuff up."

To the left, a second explosion sent showers of sparks tearing into the sky.

"Might explain why security didn't investigate the Rocket Fish blowing up. They must think it was a student project. Not too many folks make it through the hedge and onto the campus. Actually, I think we're the first."

Sarah pointed past the plaza, to a building made to resemble a French Renaissance palace, complete with hipped tile roofs, dormers, ornately decorated cornices, and rows of multi-paned windows. Gigantic Tesla coils on the conical spires of the turrets buzzed and crackled and then discharged bolts of lightning.

Alfonso didn't wait for her question before explaining, "That's my old school. The Dr. Moreau Junior Academy."

"No. Freakin'. Way. Compared to that, Ty Cobb Middle School must seem like a dump."

"You noticed?"

Hands on hips, Sarah turned her head left to right. "This is something." She punched Alfonso on the upper arm. "So what now, Kemosabe?"

"We find Moriarty's computer."

"Which is where?"

As much as Alfonso had dreamed about the university, his recollection of the layout remained etched in his mind. Professor's Moriarty's lab was...to the far side of the Lake of Terror.

He pointed. "We gotta get over there."

"Across that big ol' lake?" Sarah released a grumbling sigh. "Figures. And what's the story, Cory? Are you going to hack into Moriarty's computer? And he's going to let you?"

Alfonso had been so focused getting here that he realized a little more planning might have been useful.

Where was Moriarty? In his lab? Maybe Alfonso would have to fight him hand-to-hand. Alfonso squeezed his hands into fists. If he wasn't afraid of Jerry Tremont, he wouldn't let himself be afraid of any pasty-skinned dumpy professor.

"We'll have to wing it," Alfonso said. "But first, we get to the other side of the lake. I've made arrangements to meet a school friend between the academy and the lake. He'll know how to get across."

A quarter of a mile to the south, streetlamps illuminated the paved mall leading to R.J. Gatling Plaza, the bronze dragon statue, and the adjacent lawn. A trolley glided along the mall, the robotic driver at the front—a stack of metal barrels—scanned the path with its green Cyclops eye. Students in dark clothes and faculty in white lab coats rode on the benches.

"We're gonna hitch a ride on that?"

"No. We might run into somebody who knows me."

Alfonso motioned to the gloom beneath a line of trees to the right of the mall. "That way. The dip in the grass will hide us from anyone on the plaza."

She clasped his arm and motioned left. "We'll get better cover if we sneak along the buildings."

He pulled loose. "Trust me. The buildings are all wired."

"This place has a problem with *burglars*?"

"Of course not. But students are always sneaking in to do lab work. Midnight studies. And to borrow stuff."

"Then let's get going." Sarah scooped a long stick from the ground and started for the trees.

"What's that for?" He stepped beside her.

She waved the stick menacingly. "Just in case. I prefer a Louisville Slugger but this will do."

They crossed over the hilltop in low crouching footsteps, stepping faster, then faster, until sprinting down the other side. Their feet seemed to fly over the soft grass. They entered the darkened woods, ducked under a low branch and halted, panting, leaning side-by-side against a tree trunk.

Alfonso's heart pounded so loud he was sure the university's seismic detectors would hear him. He craned his neck and reached to part the leafy branches.

The trolley disappeared between the closest buildings.

No other signs of activity. No alarms.

He led Sarah through the gloom. They wove through the trees and paused behind the next bush.

Sarah wheezed and yanked on his arm. "Something slithered over my ankle."

"Did it bite?"

"If it did I'd be screaming my head off."

"Then forget it. The woods are crawling with snakes."

"Since when are snakes furry?"

Alfonso thought for a moment. He couldn't remember if the university had ever created furry snakes. He couldn't think of anything furry that slithered.

Sarah jumped. "Alfonso, I'm not afraid of snakes or any other creepy crawlies as long as I know what they are." She jabbed the stick at the ground.

Something furry slithered away. Definitely snake-like. And really long.

Alfonso followed the shape to where it blended with a mass of mossy fur ten feet away. Light glinted over an object round and big as a dinner plate.

Make that two objects.

Eyes?

The mass of fur began to undulate and hairy tentacles uncoiled from under its belly.

Terror clanged down Alfonso's spine, a raw metallic emotion that drew his throat tight and made him shrink against the brush.

The tentacles looping toward them belonged to a huge wooly octopus.

CHAPTER
THIRTY-TWO

The wooly octopus lifted off the ground, its tentacles quivering like taut springs.

Alfonso bounded away, Sarah at his side, the stick in her hand.

The octopus sprang into the brush where they had been, filling the air with the gnashing of branches being ripped apart.

Alfonso and Sarah rushed through the darkness, stumbling over rocks and exposed roots. As long as he kept the moon aligned with his left shoulder, they were heading in the correct direction. South toward the campus buildings.

They reached the edge of the grove and halted. The way was clear to the mall sidewalk and a bridge over Iguanadont Moat. Dr. Moreau Junior Academy was on the other side. The Tesla coils on its roof sparked and sizzled.

"We can take a short cut through the school," Sarah noted. "Scale the fence. Put it between us and that *thing*."

Alfonso gestured to a pole inside the front gates. A spotlight at the base of the pole illuminated a red flag hanging from the top. "See that flag? It means the really dangerous creatures are out of their pens to forage and exercise."

"What do you mean, 'dangerous?'" She cocked a thumb over her shoulder. "More dangerous than what's hunting us?"

"That's the reason the wooly octopus is out here. In there, it would be lunch." He pointed to the school grounds.

"And that's a school?" Sarah asked. "For kids like us?"

"The monsters are rounded up before class starts. High-explosive mines keep them inside the fence."

"Monsters? Mines? And parents let their kids come here? Doesn't anyone get killed?"

"Not the students. It's the adults who forget to be careful. You gotta pay attention and respect unexplained science."

"I don't understand how people can live with such dangerous beasts on the loose."

"Folks in the mountains live with wild bears," Alfonso answered. "Swamps have alligators. Oceans have sharks. What's the difference?"

Sarah chewed her lip, clearly too nervous to argue. "So what now?"

"We have to get over the bridge. Then find a way to cross the Lake of Terror. We'll need a boat with proper weapons."

Sarah brandished the stick. "I got this."

"Lake monsters would use that for a toothpick. We need electric-harpoons. Vulcan cannons. Fusion catapults."

He scouted for signs of Greg. No doubt dressed for the occasion with gadgets all over him. The only instructions had been to meet between Gatling Plaza and the lake.

Nada.

Maybe he got held up. Or forgot altogether. When Greg was in the mode of creating a device-not-to-be-created, he'd get lost in his work.

A light rose in the west, stopping at a height of about a hundred feet. The light remained motionless for a moment, then glided toward them.

"What's that?" Sarah asked.

"Hopefully a friend." Maybe Greg had jury-rigged an impulse thruster to a go-cart.

The wooly octopus crashed through the thicket.

Alfonso and Sarah scrambled toward the bridge. The water in the moat seethed with unseen creatures sensing a quick meal.

Once on the other side, the way to the lake looked clear. Shadows and sparkles of moonlight crosshatched its broad expanse. The mysterious light floated closer. They would have to hike along the western shore for about two hundred meters before meeting it.

A white beam shot down and fell across Alfonso and Sarah. He brought his hands up to shield his eyes.

"If that's your friend"—Sarah blinked and looked away—"he isn't being too subtle that he found us."

The light moved closer to the lake. A reflected glow from the water illuminated three struts scissoring beneath a sinister saucer shape. The saucer wasn't levitating but was supported by those three struts, a giant tripod advancing daddy long legs-style. Any hope that the approaching light was Greg's doing evaporated into fear.

"Alfonso, you look scared."

"I am. That's a Martian war machine." From their ill-fated invasion of 1898. The world governments had purged all public records of the attack, commissioning H.G. Wells to retell the catastrophe as outlandish fiction. The surviving machines had been turned over to the university to reverse engineer. The only known working example was operated by Campus Security.

The war machine's search lamp remained locked on them.

"This isn't good, is it, Alfonso?"

"Let me put it this way," he groaned. "Ever wonder what a roach is thinking when it's caught in the middle of the kitchen floor?"

They couldn't go left toward the school grounds. They couldn't go right toward the war machine. Or go back because they'd have to face the wooly octopus.

Alfonso pushed Sarah toward their only escape. Straight toward the Lake of Terror.

THIRTY-THREE

Alfonso and Sarah split up and zigzagged, lost the war machine's light, and sprinted closer to the lake. Bones littered the muddy beach.

When Sarah joined him, he glanced back to the bridge over Iguanadont Moat. A dark lump slithered between the bridge railings. The wooly octopus was hot on the chase.

To the west, the war machine ambled on its gigantic stilt legs, churning car-sized feet through the woods towards them, the blazing white circle of light from the search lamp groping across the ground like a hand.

Along the fence behind the school, eyes—some in pairs, others in triple—glimmered menacingly in the gloom.

"So we get close to the lake," Sarah asked, "then what?"

"We stick close to the water's edge. Hopefully lose the war machine." He stepped into gloopy mud. "We should only run into little critters, and you can take care of those with your stick."

"What about bigger animals? Like that octopus?"

"He gets close to the water and a fire-breathing squid will eat him."

"But not us?"

Alfonso decided not to answer.

They stepped into the muck. Putrid vapor burbled and puffed up from the mud.

Sarah gagged. "A Porta-Potty smells like roses compared to this."

To the right, the war machine tottered closer. Behind them, the mossy hump of the octopus reflected the school's lamps. To the left, those eyes bunched along the fence, the monsters risking the explosive mine barrier for a taste of human.

It was becoming a contest to see who would snag them first.

Alfonso led Sarah in a low stoop along the lakeshore. Once they reached the water's edge, they'd hide in the reeds.

He stopped, a new chill paralyzing his muscles. Up ahead, something big as a railroad tie cruised through the reeds.

Sarah halted beside him. She panned the reeds with the stick like it was a rifle. "What's there?" she whispered.

"Alligator rat. A big one," he answered, regretting that he had said it.

"Listen Alfonso," Sarah's voice cracked, "I'm not about to go all girlie on you but I hadn't planned on being part of any menu."

Something else broke the surface of the water.

Another alligator rat?

Alfonso and Sarah crouched back-to-back and scanned around them. He felt her tremble as much as he did.

The wooly octopus had crawled to the edge of the muddy shore and was now about two hundred feet away. The war machine trampled through the brush, an eerie low-pitched moan humming from its Martian engine. To the left, an assortment of ghastly eyes pressed against the fence.

An eyestalk rose from the water. It rotated in a small arc then fixed on them, the lens red as though smeared with blood.

There was nowhere to run that had a welcome ending.

The eyestalk lifted higher. It grew from a hump that broke the surface, like the back of great aquatic beast. Water cascaded off its metallic hide.

Doom seemed ready to crunch Alfonso and Sarah.

The water thing surged toward them. It stopped abruptly as if hitting the brakes. Its wake rolled onto the beach and lapped over Alfonso's shoes.

Sarah raised the stick. "I guess we die fighting."

A sliver of light grew across the top of the creature's hump. The sliver grew into a long curve until it outlined a hatch lifting open. This was no creature but a submarine.

The wooly octopus seemed to have sensed it was losing its prey. The monster scrolled through the mud in a confusion of hairy tentacles, huge eyes shining with hunger.

An obscene wooden sound clacked from the fence. The clusters of eyes moved out of the shadow, where the ghostly light revealed rhino-sized tarantulas smacking their mandibles.

The submarine beached its metal snout. The ship's girth was ten feet in diameter. Measles of thumb-sized rivets covered the hull plates. A handrail along the spine of the boat ran from a ring on the bow to the hump.

The hatch clanged open, and a round head with a burr haircut popped up to greet them.

Greg Kaminski. "Yo, you two." He spread his arms. "I'm here!"

Alfonso's heart leaped at Greg's unexpected promise of salvation.

Sarah flung the stick at the octopus. She and Alfonso galloped over the muck and lunged for the handrail.

One leg of the war machine lifted from the shore and splashed into the water, levering the infernal contraption closer. A camera-like heat gun jutting from the front whined as it built up energy for the discharge. The spotlight circled around Alfonso and Sarah—so glaringly harsh that he felt the light scour through his skin—and then shifted to lock tight on the wooly octopus.

The creature's enormous pupils shrank to points. It braided its tentacles into a mask over its eyes.

Sarah grabbed the railing and hauled herself hand-over-hand toward the hatch. Greg dropped inside. Alfonso jumped and skittered monkey-like for the hatch.

The searchlight went dark.

There was a monstrous crack of thunder. Night became day for an instant, then night again. A wave of heat blasted over him. The air stank of burnt meat and wool. Pieces of smoldering octopus rained into the lake and pelted the submarine.

Sarah dove through the open hatch and disappeared. The submarine rocked and lurched back into the lake.

Alfonso fell against the dorsal hump. Legs pumping against the slick hull, breath frozen at the back of his throat, he grasped the rim of the hatch and strained to hang on.

The war machine loomed over the submarine, standing close enough to straddle the hull. The heat gun whined again to reload. This time, its stubby muzzle fixed on him.

Alfonso yelled, "Get us out of here!"

"I'm trying but we've run into something." Greg's voice echoed from inside.

The submarine's engine groaned. They pitched forward, making Alfonso swipe across the hull like a wiper blade. His hands ached from the effort of holding on.

Sarah popped back out the hatch and seized Alfonso's wrists.

The submarine pitched backwards. A huge shape grew from the water, gigantic tentacles unfurling over the stern of the submarine. A volcanic cephalopod!

Alfonso's breath recoiled down his throat. His heart banged against his ribs like the hammer of an undertaker beating nails into a coffin.

The squid spread its telephone pole-thick tentacles to reveal a beak the size of a Dumpster.

The whine of the war machine's gun grew into a shriek.

Caught in the crossfire between a fire-breathing monster squid and a Martian heat-ray, well, with luck, it would be a quick death.

THIRTY-FOUR

The cephalopod folded its upper tentacles back and pointed its beak at the war machine.

A giant tongue of fire shot from the beak, engulfing the war machine. The stream of flame was brilliant, yellow, and hot—as if a slice of the sun had fallen from space.

Sarah screamed, "Yikes!" and tightened her grip on Alfonso's wrists.

The heat passed over them. Alfonso glanced upwards. The war machine teetered from side-to-side, fire clinging to its circular hull.

A white beam shot from the heat-gun and barely missed the squid. A cloud of steam burst from the water in a demonic hiss and blurred everything with a gray shroud. The squid knocked into the submarine, bouncing Alfonso and Sarah against the hull.

One of the war machine's legs telescoped toward the submarine. A pair of enormous squid tentacles slithered around the gigantic metal strut. A second set of tentacles, metal and segmented, dropped through the hot mist and intertwined with the squid's.

The squid loomed from the steam and grappled tentacle-a-tentacle with the war machine. The two behemoths beat the water, and the submarine sloshed from side to side.

Sarah's eyes spread wide, mirroring Alfonso's terror.

The submarine pitched forward, then back. The propeller bit into the water and the submarine shuddered backwards, beneath the squirming tentacles writhing in mortal combat.

Alfonso's toes found traction along a set of rivets. Sarah heaved backwards and yanked him up the dorsal hump and into the hatch.

He slid through the opening, collapsing on top of Sarah and they tumbled down a chimney-like tunnel. They came to rest on steel plates at the bottom of a metal ladder.

Alfonso pulled loose from Sarah and took in the submarine's cramped interior.

Greg stood at the helm, dressed in his blue school shirt and baggy khaki cargo pants. He grasped an upright wheel on a pedestal and faced a console crowded with levers and dials, all surrounded by a maze of pipes. The rainbow glow from dozens of instruments silhouetted him.

"Close the hatch," Greg barked over his shoulder. "We're going to dive."

Sarah scuttled up the ladder to the submarine's hatch. The hatch banged shut and the latching bolt squeaked into place. She dropped down the ladder and joined Alfonso.

The submarine pitched violently, a reminder of the giant squid and war machine still fighting above. Alfonso and Sarah grasped at pipes to hold steady. Greg swayed at the helm and pulled a lever.

The submarine zoomed backwards. With one hand on the helm wheel and the other grasping the lever, Greg kept his attention fixed on a compass mounted overhead.

Another wave bashed against the submarine. Then another wave, this one weaker. Still another. And another. Moment by moment, the waves lessened in violence as they retreated from the brawling squid and war machine. The chug-chug of the engine hummed through the deck plates.

Greg tore his gaze from the compass. "We're clear." He spun the helm wheel. The submarine leaned and pivoted to the left. Greg straightened the wheel, pushed the lever, and the boat righted level and smoothly accelerated forward.

"Gotta admit," Sarah looked upward, eyebrows perked, "that was an awesome fight. Wonder who won?"

Greg turned from the controls and gave her a dirty look. "Who is she? Someone from the outside?"

"Greg," Alfonso said, "this is Sarah Baker. Sarah, this Greg Kaminski."

"If you two are worried about me spilling the secrets about this place, forget it." Sarah zipped her lips. "Locked. Besides who would believe me?"

He cut a suspicious glance from her hand to Alfonso. "We don't need any dead weight."

"Dead weight?" Sarah brandished a fist. "Better not be talking about me." She opened her hand and extended it to Greg. "But no hard feelings cuz we barely met."

Greg grimaced. People in general made him uncomfortable and that explained why he spent so much time working on mechanical gizmos. He smiled reluctantly and took her hand.

After they had let go hands, she waved her fingers. ""You're safe. No cooties."

Alfonso cleared his throat and when Sarah made eye contact, signaled with a head shake that cooties were a taboo subject with the Kaminski family. His parents had been the first to invent self-replicating nanobots, which ended up making people itch and break into hives, and so had created the first artificial cooties.

Alfonso stood and bumped his head against a low ceiling crisscrossed with a tangle of pipes and valves that extended along the narrow hull. Water bubbled through glass tubes. Electricity arced inside transparent domes. Pointers rotated on dials inscribed with lettering and numbers in Italic script.

Sarah squinted at the instruments. "This looks old-fashioned."

Alfonso asked, "Isn't this the Nautilus Junior?"

Greg nodded. "Captain Nemo's test submersible."

Alfonso looked at Sarah. "*20,000 Leagues Under The Sea.*"

"No duh," she replied. "I've seen the movie."

"The only example," Alfonso said proudly, "is in the university's Gallery of Undersea Exploration and Calamities."

"Was," Greg corrected.

His footing secure, Alfonso advanced from the pipes. "How did you get this boat?"

"Same as last time."

"Wouldn't the school have improved security?"

"Alfonso, you've been among *la mano destre* too long." Greg shook his head. "Build a better mouse trap and what do you get?"

"A smarter mouse," Sarah replied. Hands on hips, she cocked an eye at Greg. "So you stole this submarine?"

"I"—Greg began.

"He"—Alfonso interrupted.

"...didn't steal," they answered simultaneously. "Borrowed."

Greg turned back to the control console and adjusted the levers. "I figured you'd make it to the lake. The submarine would be the sneakiest way to get to Moriarty's laboratory."

"Does anyone know you're here?" Alfonso asked.

"Are you kidding? My mom and dad think I'm in a subatomic particle displacement workshop."

"Do you know where Moriarty is?"

"No. I was too busy getting the Nautilus Junior." Greg mashed a large faceted crystal button in the center of the console. A hologram map of the campus materialized in the air over the console.

Sarah stepped forward and put her fingers through the ghostly image. "This is movie stuff."

A red dot glowed along the north edge of the Lake of Terror. "That's us." Greg tapped the dot and a line of red dashes zippered in a roundabout course from their location to the south side of the lake.

Alfonso studied the route. A direct path would have been quicker but that meant sailing through the Shoals of Misery and certain death. He checked his watch. 7:21PM

His pulse quickened at the certain race against Professor Moriarty.

Greg sniffed. "What stinks?"

"Hate to admit it, but that's us." Sarah lifted one of her cross-trainers, caked with mud. She frowned. "These were brand-new. Now look at 'em." She pulled the front of her hoodie, covered with stained blotches. "How am I gonna explain getting this messy at a sleepover? Don't suppose you got a Laundromat at this school?"

Alfonso saw that he was just as filthy. They should've brought a change of clothes. Another oversight. "We'll figure something."

Sarah wandered within the tight confines of the bridge. She'd reach for a knob or a lever, touch it delicately, then pull her hand away.

Alfonso wanted to chat with Greg about life here in the university. But his friend concentrated on keeping the Nautilus Junior on course, adjusting levers, twisting valves, tapping instruments.

Speed: 22 knots.

Depth: One hundred ten feet.

The bottom of the hologram showed the undulating green wave of a sonar scan, fleeting spikes on the wave confirming the echo return from obstacles ahead.

Alfonso would've simplified piloting the submarine by connecting the helm to a video game controller and a heads-up display, but Greg seemed to relish this busy hands-on manipulation.

The red location dot marking the submarine's position advanced to the mouth of False Hopes Lagoon.

Greg pulled a lever, and the submarine stopped. He watched the depth gauge and turned a wheel.

Compressed gas hissed into the buoyancy tanks, displacing water. The submarine rose. Alfonso's ears popped. They floated upward to a depth of ten feet and held in place.

Sarah gazed over Greg's shoulder. "What now?"

"Electrified anti-monster nets." Greg opened a cabinet to the right of the helm. A shelf folded out with an old-fashioned typewriter device made of bronze and steel with round ivory keys. A circular dial with three concentric rings of letters was fixed to the back of the machine.

He scrunched his eyes in concentration and the tip of his tongue poked from the corner of his mouth. He jabbed the ivory keys and metal arms spanked the platen. The outer ring of the wheel spun until the letter *K* clicked beneath a barbed pointer.

Greg slapped the returned lever and typed another string of characters, repeating until he had spelled out: KNOCK KNOCK

He yanked a crystal knobbed lever. Hydraulic pistons groaned from outside. The anti-monster net was opening.

He returned his attention to the controls and the sonar scan to guide the Nautilus Junior through the gap. He pushed the lever. The pistons groaned again, closing the net behind them.

Up ahead, the hologram map showed their destination, Devil's Island Landing.

Greg cranked a series of valves, whisking his hands from the ceiling pipes to the hull pipes and back up again. He cross checked a battery of gauges along the front of the console.

Greg pressed a lever and the steel vertical pipe beside the console telescoped upward. An eyepiece module at the bottom of the pipe rose from a hole in the deck. The module stopped at head height.

"A periscope," Sarah exclaimed. "So cool."

"Alfonso," Greg directed, "scan the surface."

"I got it." Sarah nudged past Alfonso. She flipped the side handles of the module to horizontal, grasped them, and brought her face against the eyepiece.

Sarah pivoted in a circle. "Range mark," she mumbled. "Bearing mark. Open the bow caps. Stand by to launch torpedoes."

"What are you saying?" Greg asked.

"Submarine battle drill." She kept her face against the eyepiece. "Don't tell me you can't learn anything from watching old movies."

"We don't have torpedoes."

"Maybe you should."

"Just see what's ahead of us." Greg reached under the eyepiece module and flicked a switch. One half of the hologram repeated what Sarah viewed through the periscope.

The image of the shore scrolled before them. The water's edge was a ragged white line. Dozens of lights shined from behind the wood line bordering the lake.

Alfonso's chest tightened with an ache of nostalgia.

So many sweet memories and bitter regrets flooded into him that he was torn between smiling and crying.

Sarah toyed with buttons on the handles and cycled through the different scanning functions: thermal viewer; ambient light amplifier; electromagnetic sensor; psychic aura reader. She focused on the dock and zoomed to an upright spot, a pale form against the background.

"Greg, are you working alone?"

"Yeah, why?"

"Because there's someone on the dock waiting for us."

Alfonso's heart clenched. Could it be Moriarty? Security? He and Greg crowded before the ghostly virtual image. Sarah twisted one handle of periscope and zoomed to maximum gain.

A girl's face filled the screen, her slender image in shades of green. Wisps of hair feathered from around her head.

Greg moaned. Alfonso moaned. His mission might as well be over.

Sarah screwed her face tighter against the eyepiece. "Who is that?"

"The biggest snitch on campus," Alfonso answered. "Lilith Vampira."

THIRTY-FIVE

"**W**ho's she?" Sarah turned from the periscope.

"A classmate," Alfonso snapped.

"She looks kinda creepy."

"Kinda?"

"What should we do?" Greg squeaked. "Abort the mission?"

That was the problem with Greg. Things got complicated—more than the usual—he wanted to chicken out.

Alfonso crossed his arms and set his jaw. "No. I have to find out what Moriarty is up to."

"And stop him," Sarah added. "You forgot to add that part."

Alfonso looked at her and was glad she had come along. Lilith seemed to be expecting Alfonso and Greg, and she was used to intimidating boys. But how would she do against another girl, especially an outsider as stubborn and tough as Sarah?

Sarah mirrored his stare. "What?"

He hid his thoughts behind a smile. "Can you help us dock the boat?"

She cracked her knuckles. "Watch me, sailor boy."

Greg retracted the periscope and made minute adjustments to the helm wheel. The Nautilus Junior broke the surface and water splashed overhead. Sarah climbed the ladder and cracked the hatch open. Cool humid air puffed into the bridge.

Alfonso was next up the ladder. Sarah had crouched on the bow. He climbed out and joined her, the two of them clinging to the hull railing.

Lilith Vampira waited at the far end of the dock, impassive as a statue on a crypt and pale as granite. Her black hair and lace fluttered around her reedy form like smoke. The hem of her gown batted against the tops of pointed boots.

"I hope your friend keeps her distance," Sarah whispered.

Alfonso liked her defensive tone. *You've met your match, Lilith Vampira!*

Greg appeared in the hatch and piloted the submarine from controls inside the cupola. The Nautilus Junior bumped against the dock. Sarah jumped off. She gathered a rope from the dock and tossed it to Alfonso. He lashed the rope to the bow ring, and Sarah pulled it tight against a piling.

The submarine's engine went quiet. The light from the hatch dimmed and went out. The abrupt darkness swallowed Alfonso and seemed to magnify the distance between him and the lights behind the far side of the dock. The wind rippled across the Lake of Terror and moaned through the trees. Fallen leaves rustled over the ground, as if kicked up by specters. The University of Doom had never seemed so eerie.

He hopped onto the dock.

Greg crawled out of the cupola. He had looped a school bag looped over his neck and scuttled down the curved hull for the dock.

They marched side-by-side to Lilith, Alfonso in the center, Greg on the left, Sarah on the right, like a trio of gunslingers ready to kick butt. They halted close enough to read Lilith's face in the gloom.

She was a mean one, mean as the spiders in her hair. He was glad Sarah was along.

"Alfonso." Lilith lingered on the *s*. "Can't say I've missed you but it has been boring around here. Just the usual fires and random explosions. Nothing that reeked of foolish catastrophe."

"Can't say I missed you either. How did you know I was here?"

A nighthawk fluttered past her head and swooped back into the darkness. "My spies." She brushed a stray lock of hair from her face.

She acted so cool while his heart raced. "I'm surprised you haven't ratted me out."

"Can't do that. Not until I learn what you're up to."

"So the university can catch me red-handed?"

She lifted a shoulder. "Depends on what it's worth to me."

Alfonso advanced a step across the narrow dock. "I'm not telling."

Lilith didn't budge. Alfonso could've easily pushed her aside but he didn't want to get too close, not unless he wanted a face full of spiders.

He held a glare, making his expression a rigid mask to hide his nervousness. "We can't stay here all night, Lilith."

"You can't. I can."

"What do you want?"

"I've told you. Tell me what you're doing here."

Alfonso could lie, but his plan was already a cobbled mess. If Lilith found out he had fibbed to her, then she had a good reason to sabotage him.

"I have to get into Professor Moriarty's lab."

"Why?"

"Geez, Lilith. I can't tell you everything."

"I'm not asking you to. I'm only asking enough to see if it's worth helping you."

"Help me? What for?"

"Alfonso, things have been too quiet without you. The faculty is keeping us occupied with busy work when they should be scrambling to keep you from destroying the place."

"You got some rep," Sarah quipped.

"Who is she?" Lilith's brow furrowed, and her eyes slit, pressing her long eyelashes together. "An outsider? *La mano destre?*"

Sarah stepped past Alfonso.

"Wait, Sarah." He clutched her arm but she broke free.

She stood sneaker-to-boot with Lilith. "Name's Sarah."

Lilith spread her arms, and a fuzzy penumbra surrounded her head.

Alfonso blurted, "Watch out, Sar—"

Sarah threw her shoulders back in surprise. Then she pointed at Lilith's hair. "Are those spiders?"

Lilith replied through clenched teeth. "Very deadly spiders."

Sarah leaned close. "And you have them in your hair? As pets?"

Lilith's face relaxed. "Of course."

Sarah swiveled her head toward Alfonso, her mouth open. "Did you know this?"

"I know more about Lilith than I want to."

Sarah raised her hand. "No need to share." She turned back to Lilith. "This is so freakin' amazing. Can you show me how to do this?"

"Do you like spiders?"

"Depends on whether they bite."

Lilith pointed her gold-tipped fingernail at the spiders and ordered, "Behave." She offered her hand to Sarah.

They clasped fingers. Spiders marched down Lilith's arm and onto Sarah. The arachnids hopped into Sarah's hair and danced across the crown of her head.

Greg winced. "Gross."

Sarah rolled her eyes upward, and her pupils followed the parade of spiders. "This is awesome. A trick like this might get me a passing grade in biology."

Alfonso's nervousness stuttered into irritation. Sarah and Lilith were not supposed to become friends.

Lilith let go of Sarah's hand. "What are you doing here?"

"I'm the muscle of this here operation." She slowly raised her arms and flexed her biceps. "I would like to say I'm also the brains but I have no clue what's going on."

Lilith tilted her head in Alfonso's direction, and the sarcasm returned to her voice. "So what's the plan, Einstein?"

Seeing as how she and Sarah were now acting like true blue buddies, Alfonso decided he might as well try to recruit Lilith as an ally. She was as stealthy as a snake and that could prove handy. "Sneak into Moriarty's lab."

"You already told me that."

"Uh..." The next part was difficult to share. "Hack into his computer."

Lilith went, *hmmm*, then said, "That's a huge infraction. Could get you expelled."

"I'm already expelled. So are you in or out?"

"Don't rush me. I'm still thinking. Word gets out that the Provost's computer got hacked, and Moriarty would be the laughing stock of the university."

"I suppose he would."

"Then I'm in," she replied. "I never did like the jerk and his nasty little vulture."

Sarah said, "That makes two of us." She hooked her arm around Lilith's elbow.

Alfonso's irritation became peppered with envy. Lilith was supposed to be evil and unpleasant and how did she get Sarah to chum up so quickly? Did girls share a secret language?

"Would you know where Moriarty is?"

Lilith answered, "I can look."

"And I've got another problem," he offered.

"Just one?" Lilith slanted an eyebrow.

He gestured at Sarah. "When we're done, she and I need a way to escape the university before we're caught."

"How did you get in?"

"The Rocket Fish."

Both of Lilith's eyebrows jumped. "And you lived?"

He added, "But the hyena mutants destroyed the car so we're stuck."

"That is going to be tough," she answered. "The Martian war machine was deployed which means that campus security has clamped a Level Three Quarantine around the perimeter. Shoot to kill and all that." Lilith tapped her chin. "How much time do we have?"

That was the problem. Alfonso didn't know. He guessed, "All night I suppose."

"Let's divide responsibilities," she replied. "You and Greg get into Moriarty's lab. Sarah and I will look for a way to escape."

"I'll scout ahead," Greg offered.

"How?" Lilith's question was smeared with scorn.

"Easy." Greg reached into his book bag and pulled out what looked like a divers mask, crudely fashioned out of metal and festooned with knobs and tiny disk antennas. He fit the mask over his head.

"With these reconnaissance goggles that I made." Greg adjusted the strap. It looked like he had a saucepan squashed against his face. "Detects the full range of the electromagnetic spectrum. Nothing can get by me." He touched a knob and the antennas rotated back-and-forth. He extended his arms, fingers outstretched, and inched his feet forward.

Alfonso and the girls followed him off the dock and onto the narrow asphalt road leading into the woods.

"You guys stay here." Greg shambled up the road far enough to disappear in the darkness. A moment later, he returned and removed the goggles. "The way looks clear."

"I could've told you that," Lilith said. The nighthawk circled over them. She started up the road, gliding over the ground like a column of smoke.

Sarah rose on tiptoes and craned her neck to scan darkness. "Any more of those wooly octopus things?"

"Not on this side of the lake," Alfonso replied. "Having your faculty eaten alive makes it tough to recruit new staff."

They followed the road through the darkness until it made a T with a wider road curving into more dense forest. Greg stopped and faced to the left.

Lilith pointed to the right. "Sarah and I will go this way. I'll keep in touch using my portal tablet." She parted the lacey folds of her dress and revealed a leather purse with shiny buckles.

Greg tapped his bag. "I got mine."

She clasped Sarah's hand. They began walking and their feet rose to barely brush the pavement. Alfonso watched in amazement as the two girls floated away, levitating an inch above the pavement, Sarah going, "This is so cool."

He blinked and they were lost in the murk.

Greg put the goggles back on. He reached blindly for Alfonso's arm, grasped it and pushed him forward.

They crashed through the brush and stumbled over the weeds. After traveling a hundred feet, Greg yanked Alfonso's arm and pulled him to the ground, the movements abrupt and urgent.

"Down, down," Greg warned.

They lay prone, facing the road.

Bright lights flared around the bend. The lights dazzled, forcing Alfonso to squint. There were several lights, clustered into two groups that rose above the tree line.

A soft whine grew into a shriek. Alfonso could just make out two bodies floating toward them.

Security guards. Wearing jet packs.

THIRTY-SIX

Alfonso and Greg hunkered down in the weeds. The search lamps fixed on them, and the brilliance of the light seemed to press Alfonso to the ground.

The security guards passed overhead, their jet packs deafening, the thrust nozzles raking hot blasts over the ground, billowing leaves and dirt.

A projectile smacked the ground beside the boys. When the dust settled, Alfonso raised his head and stared at a coffee can-shaped shell, hoping it had been a dud.

The top popped off. A thin vine snaked out. Then another. The vines curved along the ground, growing stems that grew into branches that grew into more branches, the tendrils crisscrossing and forming a mesh that stretched to the left and right of the two boys.

The sight fascinated Alfonso and it took him a moment to realize the danger. "Kombat Kudzu!"

But too late. The writhing net of kudzu tendrils was all around them, snagging their arms and legs, tripping them, flexing and pinning them to the ground. Alfonso clutched at the ropy vines, each as thick as his thumb.

The guards circled back. "Got 'em," a man's voice echoed from the sky.

Alfonso struggled but the vines were too strong. He and Greg gasped and groaned, and traded looks heavy with desperation.

The guards in their jet packs descended before them, blasting clouds of debris from the ground. The shrieks of the turbine engines dropped to low whistles. The dust scattered to reveal hulking guards encased in armored exoskeletons made of dull titanium. The nozzles of the jet packs jutted from behind their shoulders like a second set of outstretched arms. Panels on the exoskeletons *zitt* opened, allowing the minion guards to step free. They marched forward in their sleek black uniforms and helmets with mirrored visors.

"Remain still," one the guards said, his voice blaring from a loud speaker, then muttered, "Like you fools are going anywhere."

The other guard added, "Catching these guys is going to get me a day off. Sweet."

Alfonso's pulse measured the cadence of their approaching steps. Beat by beat, his mission was over.

At least Sarah and Lilith were still free, and maybe they could get into Professor Moriarty's computer.

One of the guards hopped and screeched. "Spiders!"

The other joined him, his manly voice rising to a high-pitched squeal, "Get them off me."

"I hate spiders."

"Yikes! They're biting! I'm not getting paid enough for this."

"Owww! It burns!"

Hands slapped clothing. Boots scuffled over the grass. The minion guards stampeded in crazy circles, screaming and pawing at their bodies, then sprinted to the road and disappeared around the bend.

Something else materialized from the gloom. Something gauzy and delicate.

Alfonso craned his head around to see.

Sarah skirted between the abandoned jet pack exoskeletons. She wore a lacey wrap around her street clothes. "Good thing we doubled back. Figured it wouldn't be long before you got in trouble."

Lilith approached from the other direction. She crouched between Alfonso and Greg. She extended her index finger and used the razor-tipped fingernail to slice through the kudzu.

"You shoulda seen it. Lilith went like this." Sarah raised her arms and wiggled her fingers. "Then those spiders started—"

"I've seen it before," Alfonso interrupted. "Anyway, thanks you two."

Sarah's hair was fluffed with curls instead of hanging straight. Spiders crept between the locks. And that wrap was a frilly Vampira touch, very untomboy. One of Sarah's string bracelets hung from Lilith's wrist. Alfonso had thought the two girls might have gone after each other's throats and instead, the girls were bonding big time.

"Aw man," Greg grumbled. He turned his goggles over. Pieces tumbled free. He dropped the goggles and whisked dust from his shirt and pants and from his book bag.

Lilith announced, "I found out that Moriarty isn't on the campus."

"Where is he?"

"Once he leaves the university, my spies can't track him."

If he wasn't here, where was Moriarty? Was that good news...or bad news? Alfonso pivoted to get his bearings and spied in the distance, beyond the trees, the bell tower marking the entrance to the faculty laboratories. "That way. Back to my plan."

"Which was?" Lilith asked with a pronounced sneer. "We rescue you again?"

"No. This time Greg and I won't get caught."

"How's that?"

Alfonso stepped to the exoskeleton on the right. "We'll fly."

Sarah trailed him. "No fair. You get to do the fun stuff."

"Stick with me." Lilith hooked an arm into Sarah's and led her into the woods. "Within ten minutes we'll be hauling them out of another screw up."

Alfonso tried to fit his body into the inside of the exoskeleton frame but it was contoured for a grown man. He wormed his arms into the sleeves and barely touched the control buttons inside the armored gauntlets.

His left pinky flicked a switch. The exoskeleton trembled. A list of disasters ran through his mind. Explode in place. Shoot upward and explode. Shoot downward, get buried, then explode. The panels around the torso, his legs, and arms clamped shut and shrank around him.

It was going to squeeze him to death!

The exoskeleton went quiet. It conformed to his body, from foot to hand, as if it had been custom tailored. He examined himself and thought he looked like he'd walked out of a comic book.

He was about to tell Greg what to do when a thunderous din billowed over him.

The second jet pack exoskeleton lifted, flames shrieking out the thrust nozzles. The jet pack hovered in front of Alfonso, Greg hollering from the exoskeleton, his words swallowed by the turbine engine howl. No surprise a master gear head like him figured out how to fly these machines.

Alfonso fumbled with the controls inside the gloves. A head-up display would be nice but those were inside the helmets, long gone along with the minion guards.

Something clicked, then the engine mounted behind him went *tick, tick, tick,* then the turbine spun up and growled. Flames whooshed from the nozzles on either side of his shoulders.

He made fists and moved his thumbs. With a hellacious scream, the jet pack yanked him off the ground.

The exoskeleton yo-yoed from side-to-side. Swallowing his panic, he made slow movements with his hand. The exoskeleton hovered steady. He pushed his fists forward and glided beside Greg.

They cruised the treetops and aimed for the bell tower.

The woods parted for another road separating them from a lawn and a finger-shaped pond that ran parallel to the chain-link fence behind it. Rows of single-story warehouses stood inside the fenced perimeter. Moriarty's laboratory sat alone, a plain concrete box at the end of the closest row. A lamppost illuminated a trolley stop at the right corner of the fence line.

The headlamp of a trolley appeared down the side road.

Alfonso goosed his jet pack upward, Greg staying right with him. They arced over the trolley as it passed below. A robot steered at the front, the light shining Cyclops-like from its head. The trolley was crowded with passengers—older students, from the college—who looked like they were partying. Probably celebrating a lab experiment that had failed with spectacular results.

The trolley continued down the track toward campus housing.

Alfonso and Greg were now inside the fence and circled for a recon. The place appeared deserted, and the windows of Moriarty's lab were dark.

Alfonso chose a landing spot behind Moriarty's lab, hidden from the road and the trolley rail. Slowly, carefully, he adjusted the movements of his hands and guided the jet pack to the ground. The exoskeleton's legs flexed to absorb the touchdown.

Now to shut the engine.

Greg was already on the ground and climbing out of his exoskeleton. He yelled at Alfonso. "Push down with your thumbs."

Alfonso did. The engine coughed and the jet nozzles went quiet, the whistle of the turbine growing softer and softer. He flexed his legs, pressing his knees forward, and the exoskeleton panels parted to let him out.

Greg waited in the shadow along the building. They crept around the corner for the front of Moriarty's lab and passed a garage-sized door and approached a regular door, made of steel.

Alfonso drew close to the cyber-tumbler above the knob. His fingertips tingled with anticipation.

A red laser light speared his hand.

Alfonso froze.

"Halt!" commanded a mechanical voice.

Alfonso and Greg slowly turned their heads.

A robot stood behind them. A diamond-shaped head covered in optical sensors. Spindly arms. Barrel-shaped body. Flexible legs attached to separate hips. A Model 14 Alpha Meka-Mann. The laser shot from a lens in the center of its head.

"Greg," Alfonso whispered, "I know this model. It has a design flaw. Drop on all fours."

He lowered to his hands and knees. Greg followed his example.

Alfonso continued to whisper. "It can only recognize upright shapes as human. Now act like a dog."

Alfonso crawled in a circle. Greg chased after him. *Sniff. Sniff. Woof! Woof!*

The Meka-Mann stepped closer and raked its laser across their bodies.

"I don't think it's buying our trick."

"Not if you keep talking," Alfonso scolded. "Now act more dog-like."

Greg turned around.

"What are you doing?" Alfonso asked.

"Maybe we should sniff each other's butts."

"Get your nose away from me. *Arf. Arf.*"

"*Bow-wow.*"

The Meka-Mann turned off the laser. The robot remained still, the lights of its omni-eyes flashing in a dim random pattern. The symptom of a very confused machine. The Meka-Mann scratched its head and clanked away.

Alfonso and Greg waited on hands-and-knees until the robot turned the corner.

Greg started to get up.

"Stay down," Alfonso ordered.

Greg got back on all fours.

The Meka-Mann poked its head around the corner, laser shining.

Alfonso and Greg sat on their haunches, panting.

The robot shut off the laser and slid behind the corner.

Alfonso counted to sixty. The Meka-Mann didn't return, and he was certain they were safe.

"Now for the next step," Greg whispered. "Getting into Professor's Moriarty's lab."

CHAPTER
THIRTY-SEVEN

Alfonso stepped to Moriarty's lab door.

"Careful," Greg cautioned, "his lab must be rigged with the most advanced security on the planet. Subatomic-motion detectors. Infra-red disruptor field. Brain-wave scanners. DNA sniffers."

"It is," Alfonso replied.

"Then how are you going to get inside?"

"Trust me. What I've learned about Professor Moriarty is that he's as lazy as he is diabolical." Alfonso extended his right arm to reach over the doorframe. He groped for a moment. "Found it." He brought his arm down, a key in hand.

"The professor connected all his security systems to one central mechanism." Alfonso inserted the key into the door lock. Then again, maybe the professor had learned his lesson. Too late to back out now. Alfonso held his breath and turned the key.

The lock clicked. Alfonso pushed the door open and was engulfed with the smell of Dipple's Oil

No alarms.

The room was dark. Tiny lights flashed along computer consoles and instrument panels. A chorus of pumps puttered. Reanimation was in process.

Once inside, Alfonso closed the door and flicked on the light switch. Rows of overhead halogen spotlights burst on, blinding him for a moment. Computer and lab equipment was neatly arranged throughout the room.

To the left, a heap of broken and twisted cyborg parts lay on a pallet. Tire marks led from the garage door to a spot in the middle of the floor. Just past that, three magnetic immobilization platforms rested at the base of the wall, the type used for military cyborgs.

In the center of the lab, three Golden Retrievers were supported upright in cradles mounted on reanimation dollies. A bandage circled each of their skulls. Tubes and wires taped to their necks led to reanimation consoles.

Tongues lapped from each dog's mouth, which were open in a retriever's signature grin. Their tails wagged in relaxed arcs, as if the dogs were in slow motion.

"What gives?" Greg asked.

Alfonso noticed brain transfer tools on a gang box beside the dollies. "Moriarty must've taken the dogs' brains."

"Ick. What for?"

"I'm guessing to put them in something else." Alfonso searched through the gang box. He pulled open a bin drawer and found a cardboard box. The box contained a packing slip from the university fabrication shop:

Mark-86B Brain coupling unit. Quantity Ordered: 3. Quantity Shipped: 3.

Three brain couplings delivered. Three Golden Retrievers in stasis. Three magnetic immobilization platforms. 3 + 3 + 3 could only equal three cyborgs.

"Dog-brained cyborgs?" Alfonso thought aloud. "Why? To play fetch?"

He walked to the professor's workstation. The hologram projector screen was dark.

Now that he looked at this computer, he admitted to himself that hacking it would be tough. He not only needed the access code, he needed to match Moriarty's brain pattern. Plus, who knew what cyber traps the professor had left.

Alfonso circled the laboratory for clues to tell him what Moriarty had been up to. The trash compacter at the end of the sink counter went *slurg, slurg* like a washing machine. The Read Out said: BIO MATTER—DIGESTING

What was Moriarty getting rid of?

Alfonso noticed a spot, maybe six by six feet, near the door that appeared lighter in color than the rest of the floor. Why was this spot so clean? He crouched and counted dots of blood past the edge of the spot.

Dog blood? The three dogs were in stasis at the other side of the room. Nothing told him there had been a fourth dog.

Then what?

Skin pimpling into goosebumps, he looked back at the compacter. Maybe it wasn't what, but who?

"You see this?" Greg pointed to a metal skull jutting from the wall at shoulder height. "And this?" He gestured to a wrinkled smock hanging from a coat rack. The sleeves were spotted with blood. "If this was a routine brain transfer, it was awfully messy."

Alfonso inspected the smock. He lifted one sleeve. The breast pocket opened, revealing a slip of paper. He plucked the slip, unfolded it, and read:

Honors and Awards Banquet

Friday the 13th

Ty Cobb Middle School

Alfonso blinked as he read and reread the note. His throat drew tight, and his mouth went dry. Why would Moriarty be interested in his school?

"Yo," Greg said. "Look it this." He had opened another cabinet and lifted a gray astronaut helmet. An *Undead Siege* helmet.

The details of Moriarty's plan snapped together. The professor's infernal EVIL-ness sprawled before Alfonso. Immense, foul, and disgusting.

Moriarty's calls to his dad? Bogus sympathy meant to dull his father's suspicions.

Beelzebub trying to steal the thumb drive with information about Alfonso's schoolmates.

Undead Siege? A complicated scheme targeting Alfonso and his friends. Now he understood why the game siphoned his thoughts. It was Moriarty boring a hole into his mind to steal information. That was how the professor must've known about the banquet.

Three dogs in stasis; brains missing. Three cyborgs missing. Three helmets had been shipped to his house. One for him. One for Candace Wolcott. One for Reginald Thompson.

Alfonso couldn't prove it, but he was certain Moriarty was planning to crash the banquet and attack them with the cyborgs. Why? Kidnap them? Bring them back here? Take their brains?

Alfonso put his hands to his temples. His head spun in outrage, and he sank to the floor.

One thought hammered his mind. *Stop Moriarty. Stop Moriarty. Stop Moriarty.*

Alfonso read his wristwatch. 7:32PM

The banquet had started at seven. Moriarty could already be there.

If Alfonso still had his cell phone and could bypass university security, he'd call his father and tell him to get Moriarty. But the cell phone was in pieces and long gone.

He rose to his feet. "Greg, lend me your portal tablet. I need to make a phone call."

"To who?"

"My dad?"

"Are you nuts? An outside call will pinpoint us to campus security."

"That doesn't matter." Alfonso started to explain but the words bottlenecked in his throat. He took a deep, deep breath and sorted through his thoughts, then told Greg what he had figured out. His friends Candace and Reginald were in great danger.

Greg listened, mouth drooping more open with every detail. His freckles darkened as his face went pale. He reached into his book bag and handed Alfonso the portal tablet.

Alfonso tapped his fingers on the portal's screen. The brain scanner was coded for Greg so he used a simple bypass. He hit the firewall portal, and fingers dancing on the virtual keyboard, hacked his way to the external portal to the public phone system.

"See, that was easy."

From outside, sirens and warning bells screamed across the campus.

The portal tablet spewed glowing crimson letters that floated in the air, pulsating with the message:

System shutdown.

Intruder on campus.

RED ALERT!

THIRTY-EIGHT

"What happened?" Greg yelled. When things went really bad, he wasn't good at keeping a cool head.

"Don't see how I tripped the alarm." Alfonso's voice cracked. He didn't have the chance to call his dad. So much had gone wrong all night long.

"What do we do now?"

"Now that I know what Moriarty is up to, we get out of here and stop him. We don't have much time."

Alfonso shut off the portal tablet. Greg took it and dropped it in his book bag.

They dashed to the door, and Alfonso yanked it open. Sirens echoed from every direction.

The Meka-Mann waited outside, arms raised, a pair of electro-cuffs in each metal hand. "Aha. It's you, little lying fiend." The voice blared from a mesh panel at the top of the body. "You are under arrest."

This model of Meka-Mann was discontinued for a good reason. They were diligent but not very smart.

"Get out of my way," Alfonso commanded. "There's an intruder alert in progress."

"I know." The Meka-Mann shook the cuffs. "That's why I'm here."

"Do you know who I am?"

The Meka-Mann lowered his arms. The comprehension light bounced from eye facet to eye facet. The laser scanner beam swept from the top of Alfonso's head to his feet and back up.

"You are Alfonso Frankenstein."

"Wrong," Alfonso scolded. "I am Professor Moriarty. In disguise."

The comprehension light bounced slower. "That does not compute."

"I'm not asking you to compute anything. I'm telling you to get out of my way." Alfonso thumped the robot's metal chest. "Unless you want me to report that you interfered with my attempt to capture the intruder. You know what will happen?"

"I do not."

"You want to know?"

The Meka-Mann slumped his shoulders. The electro-cuffs dangled from his steel fingers. "Not especially."

"Well then, let me pass. In the meantime, guard this lab." Alfonso whispered to the Meka-Mann. "I've heard the intruder is a tricky fellow. If he comes here"—Alfonso clutched his fingers into claws—"you can catch him. Imagine the reward."

Alfonso and Greg stepped around the Meka-Mann. The robot took his place in front of the door, arms crossed, electro-cuffs at the ready.

Alfonso and Greg walked around the corner and once out-of-sight from the Meka-Mann, bolted to the alley.

"Greg," Alfonso huffed, "when we reach the jet packs, take off and return to the Nautilus Junior and get ready. I'll look for Sarah and Lilith. When you see us approaching, shove off."

"Leave you on the dock?"

"Just get a head start. We'll find a way to catch up. I got a feeling security will be in super hot pursuit, and we'll be cutting it Occam's Razor close."

The two exoskeletons stood waiting where they had left them in the alley, the entry panels on the arms, legs, and torso open.

Something green and glowing whirled over Alfonso's head. An electro-cuff. It sparked against one of the exoskeletons.

"Intruders, halt!" the Meka-Mann hollered. His voice bellowed through a loud speaker jutting from around his back and towering over his head. He sprinted at them, his steel feet clanging against the pavement.

He was too close. They didn't have enough time to start the jet packs and lift off before he caught them.

Alfonso pushed Greg toward the left-most exoskeleton. "Get going. I'll delay this guy." He turned and sprinted toward the Meka-Mann, then juked right, left, and ran out of the alley around the front of the lab and toward the perimeter fence.

The headlight of a trolley appeared up the street. It could be carrying a squad of security minions or more Meka-Menn.

The buildings across the street were draped in shadow. Beyond them, the woods, and then the

Lake of Terror. Maybe he could reach the Nautilus Junior on foot.

The Meka-Mann ran toward him. The robot reached into his chest and pulled out another pair of electro-cuffs.

Alfonso rose to full height and acted as indignantly as he could. His only chance for escape was to fool the robot one more time. "I told you to guard the door."

"The jig is up, short round." The Meka-Mann slowed and walked closer. The headlamp of the oncoming trolley outlined him in silhouette.

The trolley wasn't slowing. It rushed at them at emergency speed. Meaning it had to be carrying a security detail.

Alfonso could run, but where? The end was here.

The Meka-Mann approached him. "You can make this easy or painful." The electro-cuffs sprang open. "Why am I lying? *Heh-heh*. This only has a painful setting."

The trolley rumbled straight at them.

Alfonso took off running along the trolley track. If he could make the Meka-Mann fixate on capturing him it might miss the obvious.

The Meka-Mann stamped behind him, shouting that he halt and surrender.

The trolley hurtled down the track, an avalanche of steel. The robot was behind him, gaining with every step of its clanging feet.

The trolley's horn shrieked, and Alfonso felt the trolley practically on top of him. He sensed the Meka-Mann's metal hands reaching for him.

Get this wrong, and Alfonso would be sliced-and-diced into human cutlets.

He dove to the left, directly across the tracks in front of the trolley. The oncoming trolley seemed huge, its horn loud as the crash of a mountain, the headlamp as dazzling as a meteor burning through the atmosphere. The twin trolley tracks flashed beneath him, and the next sensation was of his hands and knees scraping into the ground.

The Meka-Mann lunged after him.

The trolley smacked the robot like a swatter smashing a fly, the loud speaker breaking off and skittering down the road. The Meka-Mann bounced along the pavement, sounding like a tin can clattering down a drain spout.

The trolley's brakes screeched. Sparks flew from under the wheels.

"Come on." It was Sarah yelling from the trolley.

Alfonso pushed up and hobbled toward her. Lilith waited onboard and grasped his arm. "Get on. Where's Greg?"

Alfonso pointed to the sky after he'd jumped on the trolley. Greg in the exoskeleton jet pack roared overhead.

Sarah was straddling the shoulders of the driver-bot. The top of his head was missing and Sarah had jammed two steel bars into its metal cranium and used them as steering levers.

"All aboard," she called out and levered the bars forward.

The trolley lurched and accelerated down the street.

"Thanks," Alfonso said.

"No thanks yet," Lilith replied. "We're still on the run. I found a way back home for you and Sarah. Go to the airfield and borrow one of the flying machines.

An X-craft. Scramjet. Flying saucer. Whatever. But first we have to get around the Lake of Terror."

"Perfect," Alfonso said. Another glance to his watch. 7:45PM

"What do you mean, perfect?"

"I have to get back as fast as I can to stop Moriarty. A scramjet might do the trick."

"Didn't you hear me? First we have to get around the Lake of Terror."

"Or across it," Alfonso replied. "On the Nautilus Junior. Greg will be waiting."

More lights converged on them. Hover cars from campus security.

The trolley leaned around a corner and tipped on one set of wheels. Alfonso started to slide off until Lilith grabbed his wrist.

The trolley landed on all sets of wheels with a bang.

He looked to the left. More hover cars. Above them, jet packs. Behind them, a platoon of Meka-Menn at a dead sprint. Straight ahead. A beetle-shaped armored car hunkered on the trolley track, its plasma cannon aimed at them.

"They've got us surrounded," he yelled.

"Not quite." Sarah twisted the steering levers for a sharp right turn. The trolley jumped the track and smashed through the fence. The trolley wheels clattered on the pavement, sparks skirting from underneath.

A nighthawk zoomed close and alighted on the seat next to Lilith wheel. It squawked at her, then flew off.

She yelled, "The hawk said it's clear to the Lake of Terror."

"Good," Alfonso replied. He held onto a pole as the trolley rattled down the road. They rounded a bend to the right, another to the left, the tree line broke and the Lake of Terror sprawled before them.

Two Meka-Menn jumped out of the shadows ahead of them. They locked hands and pulled apart, their arms stretching like strands of steel taffy to create a blockade ahead of the trolley.

Sarah gunned the trolley.

The Meka-Menn shook off their feet and plunged their legs into the pavement. Anchored in place, they hunched over, ready to absorb the impact.

They stared at Sarah.

She stared back, teeth gritted.

Alfonso steadied himself for the impact.

At the last instant, Sarah zoomed around them, the trolley teetering and about to fall before settling back on all wheels.

The Meka-Menn struggled to unlock arms and yank their legs from the ground.

Lilith cackled. "Suckers."

The road curved to the pier.

Sarah gripped the steering levers to hold the trembling trolley steady. "Alfonso, what next?"

He grasped the driver-bot's shoulder to keep from getting shaken off. The road aligned with the dock.

The husk of the exoskeleton stood empty at the end of the dock. Beyond the dock, in the liquid blackness of the lagoon, a cylinder bobbed in the liquid blackness. The cupola of the Nautilus Junior.

If they didn't stop right *NOW!* they'd run off the end of the dock and into the water.

"Stop!" Alfonso hollered.

Instead, Sarah pushed both steering levers forward. "Banzai!"

THIRTY–NINE

Lilith and Alfonso grabbed Sarah's arms. "Stop! Stop!"

She shook them loose. "Can't. Don't have time. I'm going to drive this trolley off the dock and ride the submarine piggy-back out of here. Once we're in open water, we'll climb inside the submarine and vamoose."

Alfonso's brow wrinkled as if he had never done anything crazy in his life. "You okay with this?" He cocked an eyebrow at Lilith.

"Don't look at me." Her eyebrows climbed high up her forehead. "She's your friend."

The trolley's wheels screeched, spinning, smoking, when the steel rims whirled against the wooden planks. They barreled straight toward the exoskeleton at the end of the dock. The front of the trolley bashed into the exoskeleton, ragdolling it into the water at the right. Then all went silent.

Yee-haw!

And *splash! Clang!* Right on top of the Nautilus Junior. Alfonso's stomach flattened against the pit of his abdomen.

The trolley tipped from side-to-side. Water lapped over the floorboards of the trolley, first the left, then the right. The left. The right. After a worrisome moment, the trolley settled upright.

Lilith climbed on a seat and folded her legs beneath herself. "I hate getting wet."

The submarine shifted beneath them, snagging the trolley's chassis, locking tight, and dragged it forward.

Sarah leaned over the steering levers and studied the water. "I could totally handle this evil genius stuff if it wasn't for the math and science."

The trolley-topped submarine cruised through the lagoon, stopping to open the anti-monster nets, then past the Shoals of Regrets and into the open lake. The moon added its meager glow. Far behind them, headlamps from Meka-Menn, the hover cars, and the jet packs lanced across the dock and toward the open water.

Alfonso and Lilith lowered themselves behind their seats and peaked over the tops, as if the act hid them and the trolley from view.

The beams scissored over the water, parted, turned back for the road and went out.

Alfonso and Lilith rose from behind their seats.

"Why don't they follow us?" Sarah asked. "Those jet packs could easily catch up."

"Monsters," Alfonso whispered, "we are in the Lake of Terror," careful to keep his voice low so he wouldn't summon a jinx.

"If this place is so advanced," Sarah pressed, "how come they don't follow us using some sort of radar or infra-red doo-dad?" She tapped her foot against the driver-bot. "Maybe this guy has a tracking device."

"The lake is littered with abandoned experiments. Security can't get a lock on us. But it won't be long before they send out aircraft or zoom on us from one of their special satellites. Maybe find us with a psycho-tronic projector."

"What about your tablet thingees? If they work like cell phones, security could easily track you."

Alfonso and Lilith laughed. "When you get one," Lilith explained, "the first thing you do is learn how to disable the tracker. What evil genius likes someone looking over her shoulder?"

The submarine veered to the right. Weeds clumped along the trolley and made it pitch and roll.

"Greg. Greg," Sarah shouted, "you're taking us through the lake weeds."

"He can't hear you." Alfonso ran to the front of the trolley. A ropey heap on the bumper dragged the nose of the trolley into the water.

Sarah climbed from the driver-bot and reached beside Alfonso to help him tear at the weeds but they couldn't yank them away fast enough.

The trolley listed to the left. Alfonso clutched the front of the trolley to keep from falling. Lilith scrambled to the right side and hung from a pole for leverage, all eighty pounds of her. Alfonso felt himself flying, then splashed into the lake. The cold water seized his breath. Weeds wrapped around his waist and legs.

He bobbed upward, flailing his legs and arms until he broke the surface and could holler into the gloom. "Sarah! Lilith!"

"Over here." Sarah was just a shape in the inkiness.

Alfonso half-swam, half-crawled through the weedy water. Sarah pushed a seat cushion toward him. He clung to it, grateful for the buoyancy.

He called out, "Lilith?" and imagined her sputtering to the surface like a drenched cat.

"This way." She stood on top of the upside down trolley. Her gown billowed around her, magically crisp and dry.

"Where's the Nautilus Junior?" Sarah asked.

Alfonso studied the wet empty murk. "Maybe it sunk, damaged by the trolley." That meant...he yelled, "Greg. Greg."

"Now we're screwed." Sarah blinked water from her eyes. "Screwed with a capital S."

Alfonso found himself wishing for security to rescue them. Soon. Before the lake creatures arrived. With an appetite.

CHAPTER
FORTY

Water bubbled from under the inverted trolley and it slid further into the water.

Lilith danced up the exposed chassis, hopped over the axles, and balanced on the back bumper.

Sarah readied a cushion. "Better jump before you're a goner."

Lilith raised her arms and stepped off the bumper. She floated like a ghost and landed so gently on the cushion the water barely rippled. She crouched and sat cross-legged.

All safe for now...

Until Sarah shrieked.

An eyestalk burst up between the cushions. Its red pupil rotated on them.

She grabbed a lily frond and whacked the eyestalk.

"Easy, easy," Alfonso said, relieved. "That's the submarine's periscope."

Sarah's eyes cut from the periscope to Alfonso. "Oh yeah. Silly me. Imagine that it might have been a monster. A monster in the Lake of Terror."

Alfonso looped a weedy vine over the periscope. "Now each of you, hold on." He mouthed to the periscope lens. *Turn around. Keep going.*

The periscope lens dipped once. *Understood.*

It turned around and surged to the north. The slack in the vine went taut, strained against the mass of weeds, and towed Sarah, Alfonso, and Lilith forward.

After floundering in the water, all they had to do was hang on and wait. If Greg kept the submarine underwater, they'd be harder to spot. Soon, they should be on the other side.

"Is it just me," Sarah quipped, "or am I the only one who feels like she's trolling for sharks?"

"Just don't kick," Alfonso replied. "Or splash around."

"Which I'm not doing."

"Heads up," Lilith said.

To the near right, a tall fin knifed through the water.

"Oh God." Sarah's voice trembled.

"It's a grizzly-shark," Alfonso noted, his voice dry as dust despite him being soaking wet.

"Of course," Sarah replied. "No way could it be something cuddly like a panda or a honey bear. And I bet this thing feeds at night."

"Only in the spring."

"Alfonso."

"What?"

"It's spring."

The fin circled back, its rolling wake lifting Alfonso and crew.

Lilith clutched the sides of her cushion. "Alfonso, I get wet and boy will you be in big time trouble."

"More than we already are?"

"Oh yeah. I get done with you, you'll beg that monster to come after you for seconds."

The periscope shuttered and a commotion rippled through the water.

Sarah pointed. "The grizzly-shark is bumping against the Nautilus Junior."

A blue light flickered in the water. Alfonso's skin tingled. "Greg's activating the electro-shield."

"With you two in the water," Lilith remarked, "once he goes to full power, you'll boil like sausages."

Sarah and Alfonso locked eyes and shared the terror. They tore the weeds and threw them at the periscope.

Together they yelled, "Greg, don't go to full power."

The blue light flashed again.

Alfonso's muscles jerked in spasms. Sarah quivered and slipped off her cushion.

Alfonso's eyes vibrated, everything became unfocused. He dipped beneath the surface. Water filled his mouth and nose.

The electric shock stopped. His muscles unlocked and he splashed for air. He surfaced, sputtering, gasping, coughing.

After a deep breath and checking that he was okay, he looked for Sarah.

She was gone.

He called her name and jerked his head this way, that way to find her.

The submarine continued to drag him and Lilith, pulling them farther and farther from where Sarah had disappeared.

Lilith was kneeling over the edge of her cushion and calling out. "Sarah! Sarah!"

Her name echoed in Alfonso's heart. He had made a lot of mistakes in his short life but never had he caused someone to lose theirs. And this time it was Sarah.

He was cold and wet, yet tears scorched his eyes.

The water exploded in front of him. The back of the grizzly-shark broke the surface.

Sarah clutched the dorsal fin.

Her face was pale as a fish belly, her soaked clothes plastered to her body. She sputtered, "Help me, Alfonso."

The creature dove back into the inky blackness and vanished.

Alfonso blinked, like he had been hallucinating. Sarah was here, then she was gone, she was back, and now gone again.

The grizzly-shark broke the surface again, Sarah still clinging to the fin. The creature was fifty feet away and swimming from the submarine. The grizzly-shark dove again, to resurface a hundred feet away, Sarah stuck to the fin.

The grizzly-shark surfaced—Sarah's pale form still on the fin—then dove. The process repeated until the monster and Sarah were lost in the distant glimmer of the lake.

The air grew quiet. The drone of the Nautilus Junior's engine sounding loud against the backdrop of silence and despair.

Scattered emergency lights and search lamps lit up along the shore of the lake.

"We're over the deepest part of the lake," Lilith mentioned in a solemn low tone.

Alfonso read the shore lights and got his bearings. She was correct.

Which meant...

The Kraken.

CHAPTER
FORTY-ONE

There were many ferocious monsters lurking in the Lake of Terror. Creatures even worse than grizzly-sharks or even volcanic cephalopods.

Like the Kraken.

No one was sure where it came from. Some speculated it might have been the spawn of the Loch Ness Monster altered with tissue from the frozen creature recovered by the UFO surveillance team at McMurdo Station, Antarctica.

The behemoth simply appeared one day, fully formed, rising from the water and wrecking havoc.

At first, the University tried to capture the beast. Forty minions later, the administration turned to a sterner approach: depth charges.

The Kraken ate them like Pop Rocks.

A plan to launch a fifty-megaton homing torpedo was scuttled at the last minute when an intern noted that the detonation would incinerate the entire campus and turn the lake bottom into a giant glass bowl.

After a moment of frantic discussion, the anti-Kraken team relented and—disappointedly—returned the atomic torpedo to the Nuclear Physics Department.

So the Kraken remained.

"How long do you think it will take to get into shallower water?" Lilith whispered.

Alfonso measured their progress against the distant shoreline. He whispered, "Twenty minutes," though if anything, the Kraken would certainly hear the submarine engine.

His watch read, 8:26PM. Alfonso felt the tightening grip of time. By now, Moriarty was certainly deep in his evil scheme. And Sarah was gone.

The periscope accelerated, and it tugged hard against the cushions.

Lilith clung to her cushion as it bounced on the water. "What's this about?"

Alfonso gulped nervously, "The submarine's sonar must've detected something bad."

"Bad as in—"

A mountain of water burst upward. Torrents of water fell on Alfonso, the humongous deluge pushing him under.

He wrestled to hold on to the cushion and sputtered to the surface. His shoulders hurt like the falling water had beat him with fists.

Lilith, dry as a cactus in the Mojave desert, remained balanced on her cushion, rocking on the turbulent water.

The Kraken towered over them, its house-sized head extending from a serpentine neck that stretched six stories into the night sky. Water cascaded off its shoulders. Gigantic teeth filled a mouth large as a two-car garage. Tentacles long as a city block writhed through the air, suckers the size of tractor tires lined the bottom of each sinuous limb.

Alfonso's heart crawled into his throat and seized in mid-beat. Lilith turned whiter than white, becoming translucent.

This was the end.

In the water before them, the Nautilus Junior flashed bright blue. Jolts of current shook Alfonso, and he held to his cushion with trembling claw-like fingers.

How could the submarine's puny electro-shield stop the Kraken? If anything, the flashing attracted the monster.

The Kraken's enormous eyes scanned downward. The hideous creature bent forward. Two of its tentacles speared the water, gripped the Nautilus Junior, and lifted the ten-ton submersible.

The weeds tightened around the periscope, hauling the cushions, and Alfonso and Lilith were yanked upward. They swung beneath the submarine, close to its spinning propeller.

Alfonso's hands were frozen to his cushion, and he watched the whirling bronze blades fan the air by his nose.

The Kraken pulled the Nautilus Junior toward its mouth, which gaped as if to devour a big metallic hot dog.

The submarine glowed neon blue. Sparks arced from the hull to the monster's lips.

The Kraken's eyes seemed to spiral in agony. Its grotesque face withered in alarm and pain.

The monster let go of the submarine and let it drop. Alfonso and Lilith fell after it, arms locked in terror around their cushions.

The Nautilus Junior splashed in the water, plunging deep, pulling Alfonso with it, then bobbed to the surface. Alfonso gasped alongside, shivering like a freezing, waterlogged dog.

Lilith floated on her cushion, dry as ever.

The Kraken bellowed, bent its mountainous torso to the lake, and scooped water into its mouth.

"It looks really mad," Lilith said.

The gargantuan head swiveled and the enormous eyes fixed on the submarine.

A terrific roar bellowed from its throat—the air stank of rot and gore—and the Kraken reached again for the Nautilus Junior. The behemoth loomed over them big as the sky, the half moon appearing like horns on its head.

This time, there was no escape.

Suddenly, a red laser beam hovered on the crown of the monster's head. A second laser quivered on the left cheek, a third laser on the right.

A fire-tailed Nike Hercules missile streaked through the air, a giant white dart screaming at supersonic speed.

The missile exploded dead-center on the Kraken's head. A second missile sucker punched it with a left. The third with a right.

The explosions boxed Alfonso's ears. The over-pressure slapped his lungs. Heat lashed his face.

But he shrieked with joy, "It's the anti-Kraken rocket batteries!"

The Kraken stumbled in the water, and waves crashed over the submarine and Alfonso. More lasers locked on its head and torso, forming a red net of impending high-explosive mayhem.

Lilith cupped her hands around her mouth. "Greg, get us out of here!"

The Nautilus Junior pitched in the waves, its propeller churning. With a groan, the submarine bit into the water and darted forward. Alfonso and Lilith tagged behind.

More missiles shrieked at the Kraken, blasting, smacking it one-two-three, punching it down.

The monster humped over and slid beneath the surface, in search of a meal less troublesome than a shrimpy submarine.

Two Hercules missiles boomed from the launchers. The rockets arced high overhead, becoming points faint as tiny stars, then looping back, falling to Earth, getting bigger, like meteors burning through the atmosphere.

"Hold on," Alfonso screamed and hugged his cushion.

The missiles speared the water where the Kraken had disappeared.

Two enormous geysers blasted upward, their waves tossed Alfonso about. The Nautilus Junior rolled on the surface, its propeller foaming the turbulent water.

The lasers crisscrossed the air above them, searching, then one by one, turned off.

Alfonso, Lilith, and the submarine rocked on the surface, the water lapping against them. The air grew quiet.

"The Kraken," Lilith said, "explosions, murderous chaos, yeah it hasn't been the same since you left, Alfonso."

He clung to his cushion and looked to the east, the direction the grizzly-shark had taken Sarah. He was so cold his bones felt they were breaking. But what chilled him most was despair. What were the chances Sarah hadn't drowned or wasn't eaten? He couldn't return home without her.

Moriarty had it in for the Frankensteins, and in a roundabout way, he had exacted his revenge. Alfonso would remain miserable for the rest of his life, tormented by guilt for losing Sarah.

The Nautilus Junior settled in the water and turned toward the northern shore, chugging for a spot east of the fence line behind Dr. Moreau Junior Academy. The slack in the weeds pulled tight and dragged Alfonso and Lilith. She remained on her cushion, still dry as ever.

Approaching the shore, they noticed a line of white shapes, the reflections off the domed heads of the security-bots. Not clumsy Meka-Menn but state-of-the-art Robot-Kommandoes.

Their welcoming committee.

CHAPTER
FORTY-TWO

The six Robot-Kommandoes stood in line facing the shore, stiff, as if at attention.

For the last few hours, Alfonso had fought off the grip of dread but this time it held him fast like the hand of a pitiless colossus.

He had struggled so hard and now all seemed lost. Moriarty had won.

"This is the end," he said.

"Don't be too sure," Lilith answered. She sounded confident but Alfonso was too depressed to ask why.

He studied the robots. They were close to eight feet tall, with angular lines defining their armored heads, torsos, arms, and legs. Rocket-grenades were clumped to one arm of each robot, the other arm equipped with a 23 millimeter electric Gatling gun.

Alfonso expected the robots to break ranks and spread out in a semi-circle along the beach. But they didn't move.

Getting close—fifty meters from land—he noticed that the entire line was covered in a vapor-like substance. *Smoke?*

He leaned forward to sharpen his focus. The substance resembled gauzy shrink-wrap. Like a huge spider web.

He glanced at Lilith.

She cocked a shoulder. "I have my ways."

The submarine slid up the shore and beached itself. Alfonso's toes dragged across the sandy bottom. He planted his feet and stood in the knee-deep water.

Lilith let her cushion bump against the shoreline and she stepped onto dry land. All that turmoil in the lake and not a drop of water dampened her clothes or hair.

Alfonso waded onto shore, waiting for the Robot-Kommandoes to yell *Boo!* and attack. But they remained silent and eerily wrapped beneath that cobweb.

"What's keeping them paralyzed?"

"You ever heard of bugs in the system?" Lilith wiggled her fingers creepy-crawly fashion. "I've got spider mites creeping inside."

Alfonso waved his hand in front the left-most robot, the one with sergeant chevrons on it upper arms. "Can they see us? File a report?"

"Nope. The webs in their computer brains are thick as cotton candy. Nothing is working in those metal skulls."

Lilith walked from the lake to the wooded crest of a slope. Alfonso followed her.

She stood on tiptoes and pointed through the trees to the distant Snt airfield. An assortment of exotic rocket planes stood on their tail fins, ready to get "borrowed."

All they had to do was sneak around Dr. Moreau Junior Academy, cross through RJ Gatling Plaza, over Judgment Knoll, and navigate the woods teeming with wooly octopi. Avoid the security patrols. Simple.

Alfonso looked back to the eastern side of the lake. He couldn't leave Sarah.

Greg jumped off the prow of the Nautilus Junior.

"Get back on board," Alfonso said.

"Yo, what do you mean? We made it."

"We have to go back out in the lake and find Sarah."

Greg didn't move. "Sorry, Alfonso, but no can do. The Kraken damaged the hull. The bilge pumps were working max volume on the way here and they finally seized. That tub's been taking in water like it was made out of chicken wire."

As if on cue, the submarine hissed and moaned. It shuddered and slid backwards into deeper water. Moment by moment it sank lower into the water—burbling—first the hull, then the dorsal fin, and with a final burp, the cupola.

When the periscope dipped into the murk, Greg's head hung down, chin pressed against his chest. He wiped a tear.

Alfonso read his watch. 9:07PM

By now, Moriarty was deep into his nefarious plot. The brains of his friends—Candace and Reginald—could be on ice to be inserted into cyborgs.

The appearance of the Kraken seemed to have kept anyone from following them across the lake. Maybe security was certain they had been eaten by the many lake monsters. The only place that looked quiet was to the east, where Sarah was last seen headed.

The eastern side was mostly rocky beach. Subterranean tunnels beneath the granite cliffs. The favored grounds of the larger mutants to nest.

A map would help. He turned to Greg. "Still got your portal tablet?"

"Yeah." Greg tapped his book bag. "But the system is locked down, remember?"

Options? None, except to start walking east.

"Where are you going?" Greg trotted after him.

"To find Sarah." Alfonso halted. Lilith stayed on the slope. He asked her. "You coming along?"

She shook her head. "I wouldn't do much good."

"You going to rat on me?"

"Should I? Sarah is in trouble. The sooner someone rescues her, the better."

That was true. What was more important? Saving Sarah or escaping the campus?

"Maybe you can find some way to help," Alfonso said. He wanted to walk with his head hung low but didn't let himself. There was no time to feel sorry. He had to be vigilant and resolute, though he had no idea where he was going except east along the Lake of Terror.

Greg walked beside him. They entered the gloomy wooded path that bordered the water's edge. Alfonso swatted away curtains of moss and spiny vines and kept his eyes searching ahead. Greg kept a nervous lookout to the sides and rear.

He stumbled on Alfonso's heels.

Alfonso didn't break stride.

"It might help," Greg whispered, "to think like a grizzly-shark. Where would it go to...er...um—"

"Eat?" snapped Alfonso.

"I was gonna say, sleep."

"Either way, let's hope Sarah is with it."

"And then what? The only reason that monster didn't devour us was the Kraken scared it away."

"I'll think of something." Should they find Sarah and have to fight the grizzly-shark, with what weapons?

So many problems. He always thought that as a mad scientist his problems would remain neatly bottled to be dissected in the lab. His father had warned him. Surprises were part of the romance of being an evil genius.

The flip side was the unexpected consequences. Really bad unexpected consequences. In this case, the grizzly-shark taking Sarah.

Unexpected consequences. He was practically an expert at those. Like what happened when he had cheated at baseball and lost.

This time he couldn't lose.

Alfonso trudged ahead, determined to find Sarah, escape the campus, and stop Moriarty.

The rocks around them scattered. Alfonso stifled a cry of surprise. Greg bumped against him.

The rocks flashed greenish-yellow and stopped about six feet away.

These weren't rocks but round, flat lizards the size of a hand. They bared their teeth and an intense interior glow outlined their tiny organs and skeletons like they had each swallowed a chem light. The luminescence highlighted the spikes jutting from their heads and the circumference of their flattened bellies.

"That is so awesome." Greg reached for one.

Alfonso held his arm back. "That's a Hiroshima horned toad."

"From Japan?"

"Actually, from New Mexico."

"Is it radioactive?"

"No, that glow comes the concentrated capsaicin in its blood."

"Capsaicin?"

Greg was a typical Kaminski—a talented mechanical engineer but a mediocre biologist and chemist. What mad scientist didn't know about capsaicin? "That's what makes chili pepper so hot. One bite from this little dude and you think you've eaten an atomic bomb."

Greg stepped around the lizard. "Some weapon."

Weapon. Alfonso halted. "Gimmee your book bag."

"What about my portal tablet?"

"Put it in your pants cargo pocket."

"And my tools?"

"Stuff everything in your pockets."

Greg frowned at Alfonso and scooped his portal tablet and tools from the bag: screwdrivers, pliers, wire strippers. He stuffed them into pockets in his pants and shirt.

Alfonso searched the ground and found a long stick. The lizards backed out of reach. He selected the largest lizard and tapped the ground in front of its head. The horned toad hissed and puffed, swelling its body and glowing bright as fire.

"Now sneak up behind it and catch it with your bag," he said to Greg.

"Are you crazy?"

"When we find Sarah—"

"If she's not already dead."

"Think positive, will you? When we find her, we'll need a weapon to fight off the grizzly-shark."

"This lizard?"

"Just help me. I'll figure the details later."

"Isn't that what always gets you in so much trouble?"

Alfonso beat the stick on the ground to chase away the other lizards. He dragged the stick in front of his prey and jabbed at its nose. The horned toad lunged forward—its color bursting a louder neon hue—and snapped its jaws in warning, before retreating a step. Greg circled behind it. He slowly crouched and opened his bag inches behind the lizard's stumpy tail.

Alfonso bumped the stick against the lizard's nose. It hissed and clamped its jaws on the stick. "Got him."

Alfonso raised the stick. The horned toad remained on the end, wiggling, glowing like a spiky glop of radium. He eased the lizard into the bag. Once inside, Greg tossed the flap over the stick and lifted the bag.

Alfonso shook the stick. The lizard writhed inside the bag and chomped the stick. Alfonso pulled it free. The gnarled end of the stick looked it had been jammed into a garbage disposal.

Greg held the bag at arm's length. "What if it bites through the bag?"

Alfonso gave him the stick. "Tie it to the end and carry it that way."

Greg cinched the bag's strap over the end of the stick and rested it on his shoulder. He kept the handy bag far from him and minded it with worried glances.

Alfonso shooed the remaining lizards by stamping his feet and cleared a path.

The trail curved against the rocky shoreline, the narrow path dipping and climbing as it wended along beneath a steep, craggy cliff overlooking the lagoon and the large rugged rocks jutting from its surface.

A gyrocopter skimmed the lake far beyond the rocks. A searchlight hunted left and right. Alfonso and Greg crouched, just in case.

The gyrocopter abruptly shot upward, a tongue of fire climbing after it, a volcanic cephalopod trying for a snack.

The boys kept motionless until the gyrocopter's navigation lights shrank against the dazzle of lights at the far shore.

Alfonso pointed to the rocks. "That's where the grizzly-sharks nest.

"Yo, there must be dozens. How can we search them all?"

"We try, okay!" Alfonso replied, too tired, angry, and frustrated to argue.

Greg lowered his head.

Alfonso tapped his friend's shoulder. "Sorry, Greg. Didn't meant to take it out on you."

"So-kay. I'm not exactly bubbling with cheer myself."

Alfonso's mind flipped between all of tonight's disasters: the rocket car getting blown up; the attack by the first wooly octopus; near miss after near miss with university security; sinking the trolley; almost getting eaten by the Kraken, then almost getting blown to pieces by the Hercules missiles; capsizing the Nautilus Junior; knowing he was too late to stop Moriarty...and worst of all—losing Sarah.

Worries and regrets bouldered around him.

But he couldn't give up. He had to find Sarah.

The trail narrowed to a thin ledge along the bottom of the cliff. The closest rocks in the lagoon were thirty feet away, others as far away as a quarter mile.

Triangular fins of various sizes cut through the water in random patterns. This was the home turf of the feared amphibious monsters.

At a rock about a hundred feet away, a black shape crawled out of the water. The moonlight was just bright enough to illuminate a bear-like face, thickly muscled forearms, with triangular fin on its back—most definitely a grizzly-shark.

The monster seemed so close. Alfonso's breath froze.

The grizzly-shark dragged something in its left paw. Alfonso didn't want to believe it was Sarah...

...and it wasn't. It was a wooly octopus.

The monster climbed higher on the rock, perching on a outcropping, and curling its finned tail. It gripped the octopus in both paws and tore through the hairy hide. Ropey strands of flesh draped from the grizzly-shark's teeth.

A thought lanced through Alfonso's brain. A thought so dark and terrible that he became nauseous. Maybe Sarah had been devoured like that.

He pushed the gruesome image out of his mind. She was alive. *Had to be.*

They proceeded up the trail. The cliff wall towered menacingly over them, and the trail narrowed to a thin ledge a foot above the lagoon. There were square miles of water surrounding them but Alfonso felt claustrophobic with fear.

Rather than walking further toward salvation for both of them, he could be leading Greg and himself right down the throat of a mutant monster. He imagined his chewed bones—either regurgitated or buried in monster poop—displayed in posters warning about the Lake of Terror.

Alfonso Frankenstein, last of the infamous reanimators, turned into monster chow.

Alfonso stumbled, lost in worry and fear.

Greg grabbed his arm. "Listen."

Alfonso stopped. He cocked an ear toward the water.

A soft moan rolled toward them like a whisper.

A human moan.

A girl's moan.

Sarah!

CHAPTER
FORTY-THREE

Alfonso cupped a hand behind each ear and swiveled his head like a radar antennae to pinpoint Sarah.

He and Greg gestured at the same time in the same direction.

A tall rock fifty feet away. In the lagoon. Filled with monsters.

Fifty feet. Might as well been fifty miles.

Another moan pierced the gloom.

Sarah was alive. And in pain.

Alfonso's mind pinballed through the worst possibilities. Had a grizzly-shark chomped off a foot? Maybe broken her legs and jammed her in a nest as a snack for shark-cubs? Was Sarah so near to the end that she was about to die?

Another moan raked his nerves.

"We're so close," Greg whispered.

"Close enough to rescue her."

"But the monsters?"

"Like we didn't expect any?" Alfonso steadied himself against the cliff wall and eased a foot into the lake.

The bottom was smooth rock and sand. He stepped into the water and it inched up past his ankles. He helped Greg climb down and cautioned, "Whatever you do, don't lose the lizard."

The water rose to their thighs, then to their waists. It was cool and smelled of algae and dead fish.

They waded slowly to keep from splashing. All around them, unseen creatures slapped and snicked the lagoon's surface, the gurgles and slithering bringing the nightmare image of teeth and jaws ready to devour them.

Another moan.

Greg grasped a handful of Alfonso's shirt. Alfonso touched his friend's hand to reassure him. And himself.

The water about his waist began to recede. The rock looked suddenly closer.

The water was at his knees. At his shins. His wet trousers became stiff and icy cold. His feet groped for steady footing.

When he stepped onto dry rock, he turned around and helped Greg out of the water. They held still and listened, their pants going *drip, drip*.

Another moan. To their front. Alfonso studied the rocky island, which was not much bigger than his yard at home. The hard ground sloped to a cone-shaped, rocky peak.

Eyes wide open, ears on maximum gain, skin electric with awareness, he stalked forward.

Ten feet from the peak, an eye-watering stink smacked them, an odor worse than ripest of summer Dumpsters.

Alfonso stared into a cave. Something moved along the bottom.

He tapped his foot and waited, hoping nothing lunged out to eat him. Stepping forward, he braced his hands on either side of the opening and leaned in, feeling like a mouse sticking its head into a trap.

Even with his eyes accustomed to the night, the darkness remained thick as goo.

"Greg, bring the bag."

He crouched beside Alfonso and opened the bag's flap.

A greenish glow illuminated the cave. Large bones and mats of hairy flesh filled the bottom. Piles of rice dotted the layer of body parts.

Rice?

The piles of rice boiled with movement.

Not rice, but maggots!

Alfonso gagged and fought to keep from retching. Sarah moaned.

Something moved. A hand. With a bracelet of braided thread.

Sarah!

Alfonso used his foot to rake aside the maggots. He reached for the hand. The slender fingers recoiled, then groped for his.

He wrapped both of his hands around the wrist and pulled. Sarah's arm came from under a torn pelt of fur. Then her shoulder.

Finally her head.

"I got her." Alfonso's voice cracked with excitement. He kept pulling until her torso was free.

Grimacing, gagging, sobbing, she rose to her feet and stumbled against the wall. Maggots dropped from her hair.

Her skirt and top were stained and bunched to look like rags. But her skin looked okay. No cuts. No blood.

The glow of the horned toad made her eyes shine. She pushed from the wall and staggered against him, crying, mouthing the words, "I knew you'd make it," between sobs.

Greg threw the flap back over the pouch, and they were swallowed by the gloom. "Let's continue the reunion when we get off this rock and away from the monsters."

Sarah hooked her arm around Alfonso's neck and sagged into his shoulder. They stepped out of the cave and toward the lagoon.

On the opposite side of the little island, a dark hump rose from the water. The hump lifted, becoming the head of an immense grizzly-shark.

Alfonso wanted to melt and sink into the cracks of the rocky ground. Or turn invisible. Anything so the monster wouldn't see them.

The grizzly-shark lumbered up the slope, shook water from its broad head and neck, and dragged itself toward the cave. Sniffing, the grizzly-shark stuck its head into the opening.

Alfonso, Sarah, and Greg remained still as the stone beneath their feet. With luck, the monster would not see them.

They stepped backwards into the water, carefully, as if they were treading through a cemetery filled with open graves.

Snorting and snarling, the grizzly-shark shimmied backwards out of the cave. Its beady gaze swept the tiny island and fixed on Alfonso, Sarah, and Greg.

A mighty bellow erupted from its throat, a ferocious sound that promised pain and death. Fangs long as railroad spikes glistened in the mutant's open jaws. It balanced on its shark tail, rising twenty feet into the air and spread its thick arms, tipped with claws long as butcher knives.

The grizzly-shark dropped down and charged, bellowing again, a locomotive of fury and destruction.

"Get ready," Alfonso shouted to Greg. Sarah shrank behind Alfonso.

But Greg was paralyzed, eyes brimmed with terror.

The grizzly-shark approached, snarling and bellowing.

Alfonso tore the stick from Greg's hands.

"W...What's that?" Sarah stammered.

"Our only chance against that monster." Alfonso hoisted the stick before him, the bag swaying from its tip.

Sarah twisted the stick from his grasp. "Then let me do this. That chump and me have unfinished business."

Alfonso clutched for the stick. "No, Sarah."

The grizzly-shark bolted down the rock at them. It rose again on its tail, its claws extended and ready to slice them to pieces.

Sarah cocked the stick over one shoulder like a spear, advanced a step and chucked it, bag end first into the grizzly-shark's toothy maw.

The monster chomped on the stick, mashing it to splinters. It started another bellow, then stopped. A luminescent foam frothed around its mouth.

The grizzly-shark let out an ear-piercing cry, the glow of the horned lizard pulp smeared inside its mouth, and charged the kids.

They jumped out of the way.

The creature's great bulk whooshed by. The grizzly-shark plunged its head into the water and held it there for a moment. The head came up, tongue hanging out, glowing water cascading from between the teeth of its open jaws. The monster bellowed again.

Thanks to the capsaicin, that grizzly-shark would be in misery for many hours, if not days.

"If that monster thinks he's in pain now," Greg said, "Wait 'till he does his business tomorrow and the chili burns his butt."

Alfonso nudged Sarah and Greg. "Here's our chance."

They waded around the monster as it tended to its misery. They scrambled across the lagoon to the bottom of the cliff. Alfonso helped Sarah out of the water, then Greg. He climbed onto the ledge, and the three scrambled along the narrow trail like mice. The grizzly-shark's pained cries echoed across the cliff above.

Greg froze on the trail, looking back to the lake, moonfaced with dread. He whispered, "Oh no."

Alfonso knew it was pointless to turn around. Their best chance to escape was to keep running. But he had to look.

A shape bigger than the rock, a mountain of boneless flesh, lifted from the water and unscrolled tentacles long and thick as lamp posts. Two huge eyes fixed on the grizzly-shark. Water gushed from man-hole sized gill siphons.

A volcanic cephalapod! The fire-breathing giant squid must have heard the grizzly-shark's cries and had come to eat.

The grizzly-shark was now the hunted. It greeted the squid with a defiant howl.

The cephalapod reared back and parted its tentacles. The squid's beak opened and a jet of flame splattered against the grizzly-shark. The mammal-fish withered inside the tornado of fire.

The squid extended its tentacles, wrapping the burning grizzly-shark in enormous leathery coils. The cephalapod's wagon wheel-sized eyes slanted with the effort of smashing its prey. The tentacles parted, making a gruesome ripping noise, and each length grasped smoldering hunks of freshly roasted grizzly-shark carcass.

The cephalapod lingered on the surface. The tentacles fanned above its head—dripping embers of flesh—and one by one they looped toward the squid's beak to dine on the cooked grizzly-shark.

Sarah watched, hands on hips. "Man, what I wouldn't give to post that on YouTube. You'd get like a bazillion hits."

"Let's keep going," Alfonso advised. "While the squid is busy eating something besides us."

The trail wound into the brush, away from the lake and deeper into the thicket. They halted in an opening, gasping, legs aching, wet clothes itching.

Alfonso wiped muck from his trousers, glad to be alive. The weight of terror lifted from his shoulders.

Sarah patted the greasy patches on her clothes and picked maggots from her hair. She crawled through a gap in the thicket. "Let's not waste time."

They crept in single file under the branches, Sarah leading, Alfonso next, Greg trailing.

Branches creaked to their right. Alfonso studied the inky darkness.

Branches creaked to their left. Whatever it was, there were two of them.

Something wheezed behind them.

Make it three.

"I know that sound, unfortunately" Sarah whispered. "Wooly octopi."

Greg shoved against Alfonso's butt. "Get going."

Sarah tore away from Alfonso. He scrambled after her, his hands and knees scraping over the hard dirt, rocks, and roots. Alfonso swatted little creepy crawlies from his face and the back of his hands.

Sarah tumbled into a shallow hole, black as the sky above. Alfonso fell over her. Greg wiggled after them. They huddled along the bottom.

"Which way?" Alfonso asked.

"Why are you asking me?" Sarah replied.

"Cuz you were leading?"

She craned her head out of the hole. The creaking and wheezing drew closer.

Greg flattened himself to the side of the hole. His eyes glistened as they nervously panned the sky. "Can we make it any easier for these mutants? We might as well be waiting in a soup bowl."

Alfonso wanted to bolt—every teenager for themselves—but he had to be the good example. He tamped away his fear and panic. He needed a clear mind to think of an escape.

The creaking and wheezing got closer.

A tiny firefly appeared in the gloom between two hassleberry bushes. The glowing bug was so pretty and dainty, as if it had no place in this moment of impending doom.

A second firefly appeared behind the first. Then a third farther back. And a fourth. A fifth. A sixth. And more. They formed a straight line pointing through the brush.

"That way," Sarah perked up and pointed at the fireflies. "Lilith Vampira is showing us how to get out of here."

FORTY-FOUR

Sarah scrambled to get out of the hole.

Greg grabbed her ankle and pulled her back down. "What if it's another trick?"

Sarah kicked free. "I'll take my chances." The creaking noises got closer and she cocked her head toward them. "You wanna get munched by a wooly octopus, then be my guest."

A tentacle slithered over the rim of the hole.

Greg, Sarah, and Alfonso scurried away, jostling one another, and sprang onto the trail. Sarah, the fastest, took the lead, Alfonso right behind her. Greg shoved from behind, panting and choking, tools clinking in his pockets.

They busted through the thicket, the fireflies scattering. Sarah stumbled through a confusion of branches and leaves. Alfonso and Greg fell against her and they were swallowed in darkness.

Where were the fireflies?

Sarah and Alfonso thrashed at the brush, tearing through the leaves and branches and found the trail. Up ahead, a line of fireflies stretched across a meadow.

Sarah plunged ahead and once clear of the thicket, sprinted along the line of fire flies.

Alfonso made sure Greg was right behind. Now that they could run freely, everything seemed clearer. Even the air seemed fresher.

They raced though the meadow, and the fireflies scattered. The square edges of buildings appeared above the tree line. Alfonso glanced about to get his bearings. They were behind the main classroom complex. Dr. Moreau Junior Academy was to the left. RJ Gatling Plaza beyond that. Judgment Knoll. A half mile more, the airfield.

Sarah entered the shadows of the far tree line and waited, gasping for breath. Alfonso and Greg reached her and also paused to let their breath catch up.

"Where to, Dr. Livingstone?" Sarah whispered.

Alfonso answered, "These are the warehouses and maintenance shops behind the central campus buildings."

"If you're looking to escape, don't see how."

Maybe Lilith had betrayed them. After all they'd gone through, to get this far, only to get captured. Alfonso kept these thoughts to himself. Their little team had enough worries.

Alfonso led them to the edge of the woodline closest to the warehouses. A narrow gravel road separated them from a tall chain link fence lit by everburn flame torches. A clutter of small cinder block buildings stood inside the fence. They faced the back of Disaster Hall, the main undergraduate classroom building. Many of the windows along its four stories were illuminated, no doubt by students hard at work honing their evil genius skills.

Greg's face glistened with sweat. He wiped his forehead with a shirtsleeve and sat on a log, acting too tired to care.

Something hummed and lowered from the trees.

Alfonso and Sarah shrunk into the shadows. Greg remained sitting.

A hover chair cruised toward them, Lilith with her elbows on the armrests, boots on the footrest. She halted, slid off the chair and gave a very un-vampiric shriek. "Sarah, they found you!"

Sarah rushed toward her. "It was awful." Her voice cracked. "But I'm okay."

Alfonso stepped after Sarah. "Wait. Keep it quiet."

"Hush yourself, Franken-face," Lilith scolded. "Sarah, I'm so glad you're alive."

"That makes two of us."

Lilith brought her arms up to keep Sarah away and wrinkled her nose. "How about we wait for hugs until later?"

Sarah picked at her tangled, matted hair. "No kidding."

"Why did you lead us here?" Alfonso gestured to the fence.

Lilith climbed back into the chair and floated to the road. "I knew that if you guys escaped the Lake of Terror, you would definitely stink. Which you do. You'd never be able to sneak around reeking of swamp."

"So what did you bring?" Alfonso scraped at the greasy goo on his sleeves. "A change of clothes? Soap and water?"

"Please. I'm no laundry maid."

Alfonso picked at the grime caking his hands. "Then how are you going to get us clean?"

"*Tsk. Tsk.* Alfonso, you've been away for too long. You're going to get clean with mad science, what else?"

Lilith glided forward in the chair. "You guys make sure to stay downwind."

She led them to a gate secured with a chain and heavy padlock. Halting the hover chair, she extended her gold-tipped fingernail to the keyhole of the lock.

Spiders marched down her arm and crawled into the lock. The lock snapped open. The chain went slack and fell away. The gate creaked open. The spiders crept out of the keyhole and up her arm to disappear in her hair.

Lilith nudged the gate with the chair and floated through. Sarah, Alfonso, and Greg followed her. Lilith gestured that Greg secure the fence.

Afterwards, he pressed against Alfonso's back and whispered, "Yo, ever been here?"

"No. Because there are only two ways in. The back way through the Lake of Terror, and I never want to do that again. The front has got undergrads coming and going 24/7 and the last thing they want to see is a bunch of middle-schoolers crowding their turf. You think a grizzly-shark is dangerous?"

They cut across the lot to the first building, a neglected single-story structure. White paint flaked off the cinder block walls. Smudges of rust fanned from the gutters. All the windows were dark.

Lilith stopped the hover chair, slid off, and levitated to the concrete pad before the front door.

Sarah kicked at the cigarette butts and discarded aluminum cans littering the front. "This looks like the alley behind the 7-Eleven."

"It's where the minions come for their smoke breaks and to hang out." Lilith touched her gold-tipped finger to the dead bolt keyhole. Her spiders repeated their work and the door opened. The interior overhead fluorescent lamps flickered on.

They entered. The hover chair followed like a dog. It floated to a corner, turned, and hovered, waiting.

Alfonso looked around. There were shelves stocked haphazardly with random boxes, bottles, and scraps of equipment. A large machine that resembled a front-loading washing machine stood against the middle of the far wall.

"How are we getting clean?" He didn't see a change of clothes, a shower, or tub. No way was he going to strip out of his clothes in front of the others.

Lilith skimmed to the machine and posed beside it, voguing like a spokes model. "We're using this. An atomic expurgator."

Sarah winced. "Atomic? As in radiation?"

Lilith cranked the latch on the front door. The port opened like a round mouth. "It's just a name. This thing was made during the 50's when everything was named 'atomic.' Atomic drive-ins. Atomic coffee shops. Atomic architecture."

"What do I do?"

"You crawl in and it cleans you completely. Every stitch of cloth. Every pore and crevasse in your stinky body."

"Really?"

"You've been at the University of Doom how long?"

"Three, four hours, at least."

"And you've seen monsters, robots, and yet you ask *really?*" Lilith held the door open. "Who wants to go first?"

"Me." Sarah elbowed past Alfonso and Greg. "I feel like I've been pooped out an elephant."

She hunched over and crawled up and into the expurgator. Her grimy head peered out the portal like a monkey in a space capsule.

"One word of warning." Lilith started to close the door. "Close your eyes and mouth and pinch your nose shut. And hold your breath."

"For how long?"

"Till you're clean."

Lilith slammed the door and checked the latch. She reached into a Styrofoam cup on the machine and pulled out three quarters. She fed them into the coin slot and shoved hard.

The expurgator groaned. Sarah held her nose, eyes clenched tight, cheeks puffed out. She began to spin.

A cloud of what looked like oatmeal beat against the glass, obscuring Sarah. She thumped inside the expurgator like a shoe in a clothes dryer.

Smaller material, like sand, replaced the oats.

Greg counted out loud. "Nine. Ten. Eleven."

A dust-like material filled the expurgator.

"Fifteen. Sixteen."

A finer dust, like talc, shifted in the expurgator.

"Twenty-one. Twenty-two."

A howling erupted from the expurgator, like the screech of a fierce wind.

All the dust was sucked away.

Twenty-five.

Sarah tumbled inside, eyes still clenched, nose still pinched, her face red.

Thirty.

The expurgator went *ding!*

Sarah quit spinning and she settled against the bottom of the drum.

Lilith opened the door.

Sarah spilled out and onto the floor, huffing for breath.

She was so clean she practically glowed. Her clothes were wrinkled but spotless. Her skin freshly scrubbed and rosy pink, perfect except that her hair poofed like a dandelion tuft.

She lifted herself from the floor. She spread her arms and pointed one foot then the other to examine herself. "That was amazing. How come that's never been on the market?"

"Each cleaning actually costs fifty thousand dollars and seventy-five cents. If you had not closed your mouth and nostrils, your insides would've been scrubbed clean and dry as your socks."

"Dead, in another words?" Sarah smoothed her hoodie and jeans. She touched her hair, winced, and examined her reflection in the side of the expurgator.

"Yipes! My hair. It looks like a tumbleweed!"

"Let me help." Lilith stood close to Sarah. Spiders jumped from Lilith's head onto Sarah's shoulders. They scampered up her neck and burrowed into her hair.

"What's going on?" Sarah asked, eyes rolling upward.

"My spiders are great beauticians. They'll tend to your hair, stand by strand."

Lilith pointed to the open door of the expurgator. "Alfonso, your turn."

He climbed in. The tub was just big enough for him to curl into a ball. Rubber paddles jutted from the inside of the tub.

Sarah said, "Let me do this," and slammed the door. "Have a nice trip."

Alfonso pinched his nose, shut his eyes, and took a deep breath. Coins rattled in the coin slot, followed by a mechanical slam.

The tub began to rotate. He started to tumble and pressed his back and the bottoms of his feet against the tub wall to keep from flipping over.

The oatmeal material swirled about, scrubbing his skin and working its way into his clothes. The sand material came next and crept into his underwear and the toes of his socks. It felt like was being dragged through a bowl of warm, dry sugar.

Then came the dust, then the talc.

Air whooshed around him, hot like a summer breeze, tickling every part of him.

The air stopped and the spinning halted.

The door cranked open, and he fell out, gasping.

His skin tingled, raw, clean, absolutely funk free.

Alfonso picked himself up. He rubbed his head. His hair felt like dry straw.

He looked at Sarah. Spiders crawled the length of her hair, busily stroking their skinny legs over each strand. Already, the hair around her ears fell in lustrous curls.

Alfonso sniffed. Now that he was clean, he noticed that Greg really stank. Alfonso cocked a thumb to the expurgator. "In you go, Pig Pen."

After they were all clean, Alfonso checked his watch. 10:23PM. The honors banquet might have already ended but they still had a chance to stop Moriarty. He couldn't give up until there was no hope of saving his friends.

Sarah cracked the front door open and peeked. She shut the door. "Security-bots."

Lilith stared at the hover chair in a focused thought-control stare. The chair rotated toward the door.

Lilith flung the door open. The hover chair darted out. Two Meka-Menn were on the road outside the fence. The hover chair zoomed across the lot, sailed over the fence, and crashed into the brush. The security-bots sprinted after the chair, vaulted the fence, and plunged into the woods in a tearing and thrashing of branches.

Lilith leaned out the door and looked left and right. She slipped out, her lacey gown dragging across the ground like smoke. Sarah, Alfonso, and Greg followed her to the back of Disaster Hall.

"No way can we sneak in here," Greg whispered. "The upper classmen catch us and we'll get weapons-grade wedgies. Those hurt!"

"Over there," Lilith gestured, "to the Museum of Horrific Failures."

"And escape how exactly?" Alfonso asked.

She answered, "We get inside and you can take your pick."

"It's called the Museum of Horrific Failures for a reason."

A hover car cruised through the intersection by Gatling Plaza. Alfonso and the rest plastered themselves against the wall until the car disappeared from view. They crept along the shadow next to the wall.

"What about security cameras?" Sarah asked. The spiders were almost done with her hair and it glistened with PhotoShop perfection.

Lilith twirled a finger. "All taken care of, arachnid-style."

Alfonso guessed that every security camera and sensor along the way was cocooned with cobwebs.

Three undergrads followed a smart-cart down the ramp to the curb. Two of the undergrads were draped in rubber aprons, hands clad in heavy gloves. One of them wore the head-set controller for the cart, which was laden with cryogenic coolers feathered in vapor.

A trolley rumbled to the curb and halted. A cluster of minions sat in the back, looking haggard and beat. One of them had his head and arm wrapped in gauze. Smoke wisped from the bandages.

The undergrads climbed aboard. The smart-cart circled to the rear of the trolley.

"Wait up," someone called. Another group of undergrads trotted down the front steps to the curb. They all crowded onto the trolley.

A shout commanded the trolley to get moving. It rolled away, packed with college students and minions. The smart-cart trailed like a duckling behind its mom.

Alfonso stepped past Lilith toward the museum. No one on campus had as much practice as he did sneaking into places he wasn't supposed to go. Sarah and Greg crept after him. Lilith glided along.

At the entrance, he swung under the railing and followed a narrow path in the grass parallel to the wall. The path curved around a vent cover. He crouched beside the vent.

Greg knelt to one side.

"Screwdriver." Alfonso held out his hand. "A flat tip."

Greg reached into a cargo pocket and gave the screwdriver to Alfonso. He unscrewed the retention screws on the vent and set it on the grass. Sarah and Lilith arrived and peeked over his shoulders. The opening revealed a metal tunnel with a ten-foot drop to a shiny floor. The tunnel was barely wide enough for his shoulders.

"What about the alarms?" Greg asked.

"My spiders are working as fast as they can," Lilith replied. "It might take an hour."

Alfonso shook his head. "That's an hour we probably don't have." He swung his legs into the tunnel. "Once inside, I'll do a quick look around to find the most-promising gadget."

"Most promising gadget?" Sarah asked.

"You want to get home?" Another fretful glance at his watch. 10:30 PM.

"No point in getting there unless I'm alive."

He offered his hand to Sarah. "Trust me."

She clasped his wrist and helped him ease into the tunnel. He let go of her hand and slid down, bouncing from side to side like a potato falling through a narrow chute. Once clear of the tunnel, he flexed his knees to absorb the landing, rolled sideways and sprawled across the hard, cold floor.

Red lights strobed on. An alarm cried out.

Alfonso pushed up, nerves cringing that they were almost out of time before security found them.

Sarah landed beside him. He grabbed her wrist and pulled her away. Greg fell right where she had been.

Alfonso stared about, breathless, feeling the precious seconds of freedom being ripped away.

Dozens of exhibits crowded the museum floor. The Solid-State DNA Configurator. Prototypes of light sabers. The ACME catapult. A Sea Dart supersonic fighter floatplane resting on a dolly.

Maybe they could use the Sea Dart to escape, since every display was kept in operational condition.

But the Sea Dart could only take off from water and that meant they would have to push the jet to the Lake of Terror. Impossible even if they had the time. Besides, the jet was some fifty feet long, had a wingspan of thirty plus feet and weighed six tons.

Alfonso read the panic and despair in Sarah's eyes.

They were trapped. Armored doors slammed shut around them. Make that double-trapped.

"You got one chance." Greg tugged Alfonso by the sleeve. He led him to the Time-Space Continuum Pretzeler.

The device reached to the ceiling and looked like an upright pretzel in a pink metallic hue. Wires and cables twisted over its curved length. The twisted conduit was tall enough to crawl into.

"What does this do?" Sarah wrinkled her nose as if the idea of escaping in this contraption already stank of disaster.

"It's a matter transporter of sorts." Alfonso crouched and peered into the entry port. Inside, it looked like a plain metal tunnel curving upward.

"Of sorts?" she asked.

"When it works."

Alfonso and Greg stood by the control console, a rectangular pedestal crowded with switches, knobs, levers, lights and gauges.

Sarah tiptoed to watch over their shoulders. "You guys know how to operate this?"

Alfonso didn't answer; there was no reason to state the obvious. He flicked a switch. Pressed a button. Turned a knob.

A virtual map appeared over the console. He touched the ghostly image and played with it until Ty Cobb Middle School appeared.

Greg scrunched his eyes. "What's that?"

"The most boringest place on earth." Alfonso examined the controls. He touched a big round dial. "This is the power switch. Now the problem with matter transporters is that the delivery gets messed up. Greg, you have to keep Sarah and me centered in the matter de-atomizer during the start of the teleportation process"—he pointed to a pair of gauges—"and in the re-atomizer at the end. You let anything happen and Sarah and me will be vaporized to nothing."

"Technically, not nothing," Greg corrected. "You would be reduced to protons and electrons. A few neutrons. Mesons."

"Basically nothing," Sarah said.

"Not nothing," Greg replied. "You'd be charged particles."

She put her face close to his. "Nothing."

He retreated a step. "Okay. Nothing."

Alfonso led Sarah to the open end of the pretzeler. He got on his hands and knees and crawled inside, Sarah at his heels.

He yelled out. "Okay, Greg. Full power."

The pretzeler hummed. Sparks danced along the inside of the conduit. A tingly feeling raced along Alfonso's skin. He crawled farther into the conduit. It should've curved upward but through some illusion, it seemed to remain level.

The sparks grew brighter. It was like being inside a skyrocket that kept exploding and exploding.

CHAPTER
FORTY–FIVE

Then the sparks inside the Time-Space Continuum Pretzeler grew dimmer. The humming grew softer. The inside of the conduit became dark and tipped up, sliding Alfonso and Sarah to the opening.

He scratched at the walls but his fingernails wouldn't catch on the glass-smooth surface.

He tumbled out the end, arms and legs tangled with Sarah's.

Alfonso struggled loose, scrambled to his feet, face heated in anger and surprise.

Sarah jumped up beside him. "Greg, what's going on—"

Dr. Golem stood beside Greg, the doctor's misshapen bald head the jaundiced color of raw spoiled chicken. Lilith stood between a pair of Meka-Menn, their metal hands on her shoulders. She looked withered and defeated.

Dr. Golem's spectacles caught the light so that his lenses were opaque yellow disks. His toothy grimace was an oval of dull ivory. His gloved left hand rested on the pretzeler's control console. "So much damage." The claws of his right hand opened and closed ominously. "So much mayhem. I knew it had to be you, young Mister Frankenstein."

He raked an imperious stare across the group. "Interesting little cabal. You. Greg Kaminski. Lilith Vampira." His head swiveled mechanically to Sarah. "And you?"

The doctor's eyes drifted back to Alfonso. His gaze had the heft of depleted uranium. "She is of the *mano destre*, correct?"

"Uhh...yes sir."

Dr. Golem swept his prosthesis to encompass the university. "I can overlook the disruption you've caused, but this"—he pointed the claws at Sarah—"is a violation of Doom protocol that I cannot abide."

Alfonso felt his heart drop into a hole where his belly should've been. He swooned, feeling sick. "At least we almost got away."

Golem clicked the claws of his prosthetic. "*Please.* You never had a chance. We are geniuses"—Lilith's nighthawk swooped into the room and landed on the wrist of the doctor's artificial hand. He reached for the bird's head and gave a twist—"*evil* geniuses."

The feathered skull popped off, revealing a metallic noggin of woven wires and circuits. The two eyes glowed yellow. The beak clicked open and closed, powered by tiny servos.

"We always knew where you were." Golem replaced the robot bird's skull. "The problem was catching you."

Lilith's face chameleoned from dead white to tortured red. Her eyes went hollow with betrayal.

Alfonso put himself between Greg and the doctor. "What's my punishment?"

"For you, Mr. Frankenstein, I'm not sure." Golem raised his arm and the nighthawk fluttered away. "You see, we have the most thorough security arrangements in this and the adjacent dimensions. What would it do to our reputation as the foremost repository of mad science and evil genius if it became known that young teenagers trespassed onto our campus and ran amok?"

Golem inhaled. The air made a gooey sucking sound in his throat. "The upside to what's happened is that you've revealed grievous lapses in our security measures. So tonight's mischief will be promoted as an exercise testing campus security. Besides, how often does the Kraken show itself?" The doctor's tone turned gleeful. "We really let him have it on the kisser with the Hercules missiles, didn't we? Absolutely spectacular."

The hint of a smile distorted the doctor's lipless mouth. "Now when it comes to you and your friend," his eyes flicked to Sarah, "what happens next depends on whether you'll take the appropriate defensive measures."

"What's he talkin' 'bout?" Sarah whispered.

Alfonso knew exactly what Dr. Golem referred to. Erasing the memory of the University of Doom from Sarah's memory. Escape, which seemed impossible only seconds ago, now gaped before him.

"I will, sir." He nudged Sarah with an elbow that she also play along.

"Very well." Golem patted the pretzeler's control console. "You and your friend return home. I know you intend to foil Professor Moriarty's plans."

"It's okay to stop Moriarty? Why?"

"Because I've never liked the arrogant so-and-so."

"Then why don't you stop him?"

"Politics. Besides, you deserve the honors, young Mr. Frankenstein."

"Doesn't matter. We're too late."

The doctor chuckled and it sounded like he was gargling oil. "You forget that you're using *TIME*-space continuum disruption. You'll be there 7:30 local time. But you would've never made it without this."

He reached into a pocket of his smock and pulled out a golden lever with a ruby knob. He inserted the rod into a knob on the right side of the console and pushed.

A panel along the top of the console opened and a roulette wheel slid out.

"The pretzeler is not foolproof. That's why it's in this museum. Plenty could go wrong." Golem was looking at Sarah. "Every journey through the pretzeler is a one-way trip. You could end up in the Mesozoic era."

"Dinosaurs," Alfonso explained.

"That's cool," Sarah replied.

"We'd be stuck there."

"Not cool."

"Or you could end up in the near future," Golem said. "On the boiling surface of Mercury."

"Definitely not cool."

"Or," the doctor glanced to the map, "you could end up at Ty Cobb Middle School at seven thirty earlier this evening."

He grasped the ruby golden rod and levered it toward him. The number 10 ghosted above the console. The roulette wheel began to spin. A steel ball popped onto the wheel and bounced from slot to slot. The pretzeler hummed. Sparks shot from its entrance.

The number became a 9.

Alfonso stared at the pretzler and then at Sarah, knowing he couldn't make the decision for her and he couldn't return alone.

8.

The ball clattered across the wheel.

7.

Sarah waved at Lilith. "We'll keep in touch?"

6.

The Meka-Menn lifted their steel fingers from Lilith's shoulders and backed away a step. Her lips trembled.

5.

She raised her arm to show off the string bracelet, Sarah's gift. "We shall see." The spiders formed a line across the top of her forehead and they waved *au revoir* with their skinny little legs.

4.

Breathing deep, Alfonso stooped and entered the conduit.

3.

He checked his watch. 10:51PM. Sarah followed at his heels.

2.

They lowered to a crawl and crept forward.

1.

Just as before, the pretzeler hummed. The walls glittered. Sparks filled the conduit. The cylindrical walls seemed to unroll before them.

The sparks shot faster and faster, coming so thick they merged into a cloud of pulsating light. An ozone smell burned their nostrils.

The humming grew louder. Louder. Louder still until it shrieked like a hurricane.

Alfonso crawled blindly in the only direction to proceed. Forward.

The conduit inclined downward. Alfonso had the sensation of falling. He stiffened his arms to stop his progress. Sarah bumped from behind, and the two tumbled forward.

At one instant they were in the conduit, smothered by the shriek and the lights. The next, they were rolling over grass.

Alfonso landed, sprawled on his back. Sarah pancaked beside him.

He lay still, sucking at the air, his mind still dazzled from the spectacle of transporting through the pretzeler.

The fuzzy dots above him sharpened into stars. Streetlamps glowed at the edge of his vision. The air smelled clean. Grass tickled the back of his neck.

Sarah curled to her haunches, blinking as if just waking. Her cheeks were flush and her lips parted. With an absent wave, she brushed stems of grass from her hair and arms. The color in her cheeks faded and she closed her mouth. The realization of where she was slowly inched onto her face.

Alfonso sat up. The cartoon mascot of Ty Cobb glared from the brick wall of the school. A quick gaze around confirmed they were on a grassy strip north of the auditorium of the main building.

Alfonso looked toward a point in space just above and beyond him. He tried to imagine where the pretzeler had bent space to regurgitate them here.

Sarah came to her feet. She brushed the grass clinging to her pants. "What time is it?"

He read his watch. "10:49. Practically the exact time we had left." His chin dropped to his chest.

"But look, we're back at Ty Cobb! Safe." Her eyes bugged out in delirious astonishment. "This so unbelievable. We did it." She jumped to her feet and pumped her arms. After a moment of dancing in a circle, she knelt beside Alfonso and hugged him. Hard. Practically squeezed the breath out of him. "Alfonso, tonight was so capital F freakin' awesome. Monsters. Robots. Meeting Lilith. It was all so cool. Except for the grizzly-shark. But all ended well, didn't it?"

"Not yet. We still have to stop Moriarty. And it might be too late."

She offered her hand. "Maybe not."

Alfonso let her roll him to his feet. He had two tasks left to complete that night. Taking care of Moriarty and then Sarah.

CHAPTER
FORTY-SIX

Alfonso and Sarah ran to the chain link fence surrounding the back lot of the school. Security lamps outlined the plain squat form of the gymnasium. A white delivery truck was parked next to a van by the back doors which were propped open. The apprehension festering inside Alfonso eased for an instant, then clamped tight again. Maybe the professor was still here, and if so, there would be the ultimate evil genius show down.

He boosted Sarah to the top of the fence. Balanced there, she gave him a hand up and over. Seconds later they were on the other side and hustling to the gym. A magnetic sign was stuck to the side of the van. *Suburban Discount Caterers—for when your taste is on a budget.*

Alfonso pressed his face to a rear window. "Too dark to see what's inside."

Sarah yanked the door latch. "No duh." She opened both rear doors. A woman and a man lay sprawled over trays of food, unconscious, their white chef's coats and striped black pants smeared with meat sauce and cake frosting.

"Moriarty's been here for sure." Sarah closed the door.

Alfonso opened the back door of the delivery truck. The sides of the interior were lined with shelves, crammed with the instruments, machines, and bottles needed for reanimation. A two-liter canister of Knock-Out gas rested in a portable sprayer labeled US Army Chemical Corps.

There was a low, shambling noise from inside the gymnasium. They followed the noise through the back entrance and to a short hall stinking of sweat and musty socks. To the right, the locker rooms. The left, another turn and then the main floor.

Alfonso and Sarah crept along the wall to the left and dropped to crawl to the main floor. Carefully, they peered around the corner.

Crepe streamers hung from the lights and the basketball hoops. Rows of banquet tables lined the gymnasium floor. Adults, many of them teachers, and students were slumped at the tables, some leaning back in their folding chairs, slack-jawed; nuggets of bread, noodles, and tomato sauce slopping from their open mouths, empty eyes staring at nothing. At a middle table, Ms. Humboldt looked very undignified with her cheek plastered into a bowl of salad, a cell phone blinking by her hand. Others were facedown in plates of Mac-n-cheese, including Ms. Banard, the school secretary. Spilled punch puddled on the floor.

"Are they dead?" Sarah whispered anxiously.

"No, it's the Knock-Out gas."

The tables faced the back of the court, which was to Alfonso's right, where a row of tables rested on a podium. There was a lectern at the center of these tables, with Principal Mulligan slouched against the lectern, his head resting against a microphone, arms dangling. Men and women in dressy clothes were sprawled in a variety of embarrassing positions on the chairs behind the tables. Legs spread. Arms twisted. Mouths open. A banner behind the podium read: Welcome to the Honors and Awards Banquet! Congratulations Honor Students and Athletes!

Two military cyborgs, shiny and black, ambled up the center aisle toward the podium, moving in the strange gait of dogs walking on their hind legs. They carried students in their arms, limp as sock puppets. Reginald in a powder blue suit and matching tie, Candace in a dark green pleated skirt with a yellow blouse.

A third cyborg guarded Jerry Tremont who lay on a gurney by the podium.

Why Jerry?

Alfonso pondered the question until seeing Jerry made Moriarty's plan twist into focus, and Alfonso realized its great flaw. The professor had expected to find Alfonso here. He needed three brains and with Alfonso not here, had taken Jerry instead. Maybe there was cosmic justice in the universe.

Moriarty stood by the gurney, dressed in a black jacket over black pants, his back to Alfonso. The professor checked his watch in an impatient gesture, as if behind schedule, another clue than his scheme had not unfolded according to plan.

Beelzebub the vulture circled the gurney, pacing with wings half-raised, squawking like it was giving orders.

"Yuck," Sarah said, "there's that bird. So what's Moriarty planning?"

"He's taking them back to the university. Then take their brains. Probably use them in cyborgs."

"Why?"

"Part of his evil plan. He is an evil genius."

"Now what?"

"Gotta rescue them." Alfonso started to get up.

Sarah grasped his wrist. "Hold on. Making Jerry Tremont into a mechanical-zombie-thing might be an improvement."

Alfonso hesitated. Sarah had a point. But no. He had to save them all.

Alfonso wondered how to stop Moriarty and those cyborgs. What had he seen in the professor's lab? The three Golden Retrievers in stasis.

Of course, the dog brains were in the cyborgs. That way Moriarty had docile and obedient machines to do his bidding.

Alfonso scooted from the corner and toward the back door. "I know exactly how to stop him."

CHAPTER
FORTY-SEVEN

Alfonso and Sarah sprinted out the back of the gymnasium. They raced around the catering van and the truck and headed toward the trees in the school commons. Lights in the courtyard made the grass look yellow and the shadows inky black. When they reached the trees, he slowed to halt.

Sarah stopped beside him. "What are we doing?"

Alfonso searched and found a varmint trap behind a hedge. A large squirrel lay curled inside, asleep.

Alfonso grasped the end handle and slid the cage from behind the hedge. The squirrel woke up, lunging at the wire mesh with an angry chattering of teeth.

"Sure is mean," Sarah said.

"Then he's perfect. Help me pick this up." Alfonso grasped one end handle, Sarah the other. They jogged back to the gym, the squirrel jostling inside the cage.

"What's your plan?"

"I'm sure Moriarty used dog brains in the cyborgs. If he did, then they're going to act like dogs."

The squirrel snarled and yanked on the wire mesh until it tired and calmed down. But it still bared its teeth, tiny furry chest heaving, eyes glaring.

Once inside the gymnasium, Alfonso and Sarah halted to peek around the corner toward the main floor.

Moriarty had all three students stacked on one gurney, one cyborg pushing it, the other two walking alongside. Beelzebub rode at the front of the gurney like the figurehead on a ship.

The squirrel threw itself against the cage and rattled the metal.

One of the cyborgs stopped, turned its head toward Alfonso, and barked.

Moriarty whirled about. Beelzebub whirled about. The professor's face blanched, then turned thermometer boiling-hot red. Both nostrils flared wide and looked like the muzzles of a double-barreled shotgun. "You," he breathed through clenched teeth.

"Yeah, it's me," Alfonso replied. "Here to stop you."

Moriarty's face returned to its normal pasty white complexion. The vulture flew to his shoulder.

"Stop me? Ha!" He pointed to a gurney. "Before I leave, I'll have you strapped in place and ready to go. Cyborg take-out, as it were."

"Fat chance, buster." Sarah shouted. "You are done. Game over, creep. Adios to you."

Moriarty's grin flattened, annoyed.

Beelzebub hissed.

"Tonight you're going to get a long overdue lesson in manners." He snapped his fingers. "Sic her."

The cyborgs turned from the gurney. Advancing, they barked and growled and formed a semi-circle. Titanium fangs glistened like the oiled teeth of a chain saw.

Beelzebub launched itself from Moriarty's shoulder and flew toward the ceiling.

"Now," Alfonso whispered. He and Sarah set the varmint cage down. He released the catch and spun the cage across the floor. The squirrel tumbled out, landed spread eagle, tail twitching, fuzzy head scanning left-right.

The cyborgs halted. Their electronic eyes lit up with the same message: *SQUIRREL!*

The squirrel darted to the left. To the right. Back to the left.

The cyborgs dropped to all fours and lunged after the desperate rodent.

Moriarty screamed. "No! No!"

The squirrel dashed under a table. The cyborgs tore after it, upending the table. Plates, serving trays, and cups crashed to the floor.

Moriarty chased after the cyborgs zigzagging for the squirrel. "Heel," he jabbed a remote at them and stabbed at its buttons, "I command you to HEEL!"

The cyborgs knocked people off their chairs, and they tumbled over each other in big piles.

Beelzebub screeched and dropped from the ceiling, claws spread to attack Alfonso.

He spied a cupcake on a nearby table and hurled it at the vulture. The cupcake spattered its small leathery head, smearing cake and frosting into its eyes and mouth. Beelzebub crash-landed on the floor, where it shrieked and beat both wings against its beak.

Alfonso hopped from foot to foot. This was going better than expected. No way could that fink Moriarty pull this together.

Alfonso turned to Sarah. She was gone.

Just as panic flashed through him, she reappeared coming from the back door, a 2-liter cylinder cradled in her arms. The canister was like the others, only green instead of red and stenciled along the side with: Revive Gas.

"Time to end this party." She set the cylinder by her feet and crouched beside it to open the regulator knob. An invisible gas hissed out. She kicked the canister across the floor where it rattled against the table legs.

The cyborgs were frozen in place by the podium, Moriarty staring vacantly at them, sweating, gasping in exhaustion and panic, the remote clasped in his limp hand.

Alfonso and Sarah stood in the middle of the floor where they could admire the mess. They were surrounded by upturned tables and chairs, spilled food and punch, crumpled plates and napkins, and dozens of sleeping people.

The squirrel scurried from behind a stack of bleachers and darted for the back door, chattering like it had won a great battle.

Moriarty jerked back into the moment. He spied the canister and ran to it, scowling, picking it up, madly twisting the regulator knob.

People around him stirred.

His face collapsed in defeat. He balled his fists and clenched his eyes shut, curling forward until his head rested between his knees. He sobbed.

Alfonso crossed his arms and smiled, enjoying the professor's wallow in defeat. *Moral of this story, Moriarty? Don't mess with the Frankensteins.*

Moriarty lifted his head and stared at the gurney. His sad, swollen eyes crinkled with a thought command. The gurney tilted dump truck-style and the unconscious bodies of Candace, Reginald, and Jerry slid to the floor.

Moriarty rose to his feet and approached the gurney. He pushed it out, the three cyborgs coming back alive and shambling behind him. Beelzebub rested on the gurney, head decorated with cupcake.

"Don't forget this." Sarah picked up the gas canister and heaved it at Moriarty.

He ducked and the canister clanged against the gurney and got lodged between in its legs.

The adults and students kept stirring. Some rubbed their eyes. Others yawned.

Alfonso tugged Sarah's arm. "Let's go. I don't want to be here when everyone wakes up. No way am I explaining what happened."

Alfonso and Sarah dashed for the front entrance and kicked the double doors open to bound outside. Far to the right, beyond the school grounds, Moriarty's delivery truck tore through the intersection and receded down the street.

They sprinted across the school grounds to the street and ran and ran, for blocks and blocks, lungs burning for air. But Alfonso wouldn't stop as long as his heart pumped happiness and triumph.

They turned the corner for the alley behind Alfonso's house. Finally winded, they stopped, hands on knees, panting.

Sarah caught her breath enough to laugh. "Alfonso, this was the most awesomest time ever. Mutants. Robots. Monsters. Cyborgs. The Pretzeler. Your friends Greg Kaminski and Lilith Vampira. Everything was so amazing. I'll never forget it."

She rested a hand on his shoulder. "Course I know this is all supposed to be a secret. The University of Doom, the Lake of Terror, all of that. But we made it out alive. And we beat Moriarty." Sarah gestured with wild movements. "Wasn't the pretzeler supposed to send us back in space and time?"

"Yeah. But in this case, one out of two wasn't bad."

"I mean," her voice burned with excitement, "what if had we gone back in time? I mean more than a couple of minutes. Would I have the memory of what happened in the future? A future that couldn't exist?" She pressed her fists against her temples. "Oh man, I'm getting dizzy trying to get my head around this. Would we be folding time and space?"

"I don't know how it works," he answered. "I wasn't suppose to take transcendental krono-physics until next semester."

Sarah leaned forward and pecked his cheek. She drew away, her eyes shiny with something warmer than friendship. The spot she had kissed wasn't even moist and he knew it was simply the pressure of her lips, but the spot tickled as if touched by a magical force.

Which made what he had to do that much harder to bear.

Efficere debes quis efficere debes.

They reached his house. He crept to the alley and opened the back gate. The kitchen windows facing the backyard were illuminated. His dad was home.

Alfonso loosened the wire securing the shed door and pushed it open. With a sideways nod, he beckoned Sarah to follow.

He stepped inside the gloomy shed. It felt odd being back where they had started, almost as if they hadn't left. There was a space along the wall, where the Rocket Fish had been, now in torched pieces at the University of Doom.

Alfonso reached behind the box on the shelf and fished out the Forgettor Gun. The power readout on the back said: 09%

He had left the power on and the battery had drained. His spirit slumped in disappointment at his carelessness. The power readout showed one shot remained.

Checking his watch, the time was 11:25PM. He grasped the Time Set knob above the grip. They had started their mission at 6PM.

He rotated the knob to erase her memory back five and a half hours. Clicked the safety to OFF.

Sarah trusted him so much. They had been on a great adventure together. He knew this would probably be the most exciting thing that ever happened to her. Something profound they had both shared.

And now to wipe it all away. Duty weighed heavy on his shoulders.

Alfonso adjusted his grip of the gun. "Sarah, I need to show you something."

FORTY-EIGHT

Sarah waited just inside the threshold of the shed. The warmth in her face cooled with concern. "That didn't sound good."

He aimed the Forgetter gun at her face.

Sarah backed away. "Is that a pistol?"

"Of sorts."

"Like a weapon?"

"Of sorts." Tears clumped in his eyes. To enforce the rules of *la mano sinistre*, he had betray a friend.

"And you're going to use it on me?" Her voice cracked.

He could lie but his betrayal was already too painful. "I have to."

There was just enough light to see the strain on her face, like glass about to shatter.

He could try to explain, but there was no point. All he said was, "You'll forget what happened tonight." The Forgetter gun trembled and he gripped it with both hands to keep it still.

"No, Alfonso. Please." Her eyes bored wide open, staring. Hurt. Afraid. "I want to remember everything. I'll keep your secrets. I promi—"

He squeezed the trigger. Two thin jagged rays pulsed from the muzzle and forked into her eyes.

Her pupils opened into black tunnels, absorbing the rays. Her face went slack. The pupils shrank to points, locking in the forgetter beams where they bounced inside her brain, scrubbing every neuron of memory from when she had arrived earlier tonight and until now.

Head wobbling, her knees buckled, and she collapsed to the dirt.

Alfonso didn't want to cry, but his treachery burned. He wiped his face and looked at his friend, repeating, "I'm sorry. I'm sorry."

In a few minutes she'd wake up, oblivious to the lost memory. He didn't how to explain the lapse in time.

He lay beside Sarah. He wanted to cry, to relieve the sorrow for what he'd done, where it smoldered inside him and ate his soul.

The best mad scientists were cold and unfeeling calculating machines. Emotions—other than pride and revenge—had no place in the mind of an evil genius.

Maybe Alfonso wasn't fit to be a mad scientist.

The Forgetter Gun felt heavy and obscene in his hand. He wanted to cast it away, but he wouldn't. The gun belonged to his father; plus, someone else might find it.

The triumphs over the night's troubles evaporated before this heartbreak, the harsh duty scorching him like a hot iron branding his heart.

All Alfonso wanted was to return for good to the University of Doom. Alfonso felt so small and undeserving because he couldn't find a better solution to do what he had to.

How could he tell his father what had happened tonight? How much of his father's trust had he trampled over? Just as he had Sarah's.

She began a quiet snore. Her REM sleep floated in thoughts unmuddied by guilt and remorse.

A shadow moved across the dim light leaking from outside.

It could only be his father.

"Dad." Alfonso rolled to face the door.

A grown-up's body filled the threshold.

Only it wasn't Dr. Frankenstein.

It was Professor Moriarty.

CHAPTER
FORTY-NINE

Alfonso sat up, goose bumps bunching on his arms and neck.

Professor Moriarty propped the door open with his right hand. His left clasped a pipe wrench. His face shone larvae white in the gloom.

"Well, how convenient that I found you two little devils."

Alfonso's hand groped for the Forgetter Gun. He raised it.

Moriarty's eyes widened in alarm. His posture tensed.

Alfonso aimed and jerked the trigger. The muzzle sputtered with tiny sparks, then went out.

Moriarty's face relaxed and the surprise in his eyes gave way to anticipation and vengeance.

"You are done, my slippery weasel." Moriarty advanced, scrolling his sleeve back, his hand squeezing the wrench so tightly the sinews on his forearm stood out. He paused beside Sarah and nudged her with his shoe.

"Leave her alone." Alfonso warned.

"Or what?" Moriarty sneered. "I see you've depleted the Forgetter Gun on her. What a rule-abiding evil genius you are. For once."

Alfonso threw the gun. Moriarty parried it aside.

Alfonso crab-walked backwards to the rear of the shed.

Moriarty stepped over the snoring Sarah. He waved the wrench. "Now for a lesson in simple, basic physics. Mass"—he shook the wrench—"times acceleration"—he raised the wrench—"equals force."

Alfonso retreated under a table and bumped against the wall.

Moriarty grasped the table and flipped it aside, attacking like an enraged mutant monster.

Alfonso had nowhere to go. He started to cry out but held his voice. He wouldn't give Moriarty the satisfaction of hearing him whimper. He drew his legs under him. At best he could launch himself at the professor.

Moriarty swung at Alfonso. He ducked and grabbed the professor's wrist. He bit the edge of Moriarty's hand and sank his teeth deep into the flesh.

Moriarty dropped the wrench and muffled a cry. He latched his left hand over Alfonso's scalp, seized a handful of hair, set his left hand under Alfonso's jaw and lifted him off the ground.

Alfonso tried to yelp but the hand around his neck strangled him. He grabbed Moriarty's wrist and flailed his legs.

Moriarty pushed Alfonso against the interior wall, splinters dragging into the boy's skin.

The professor brought his face to Alfonso's. "It will be so wrong to kill you, but doing right has never been my style."

Everything shrank around Alfonso. Blood pumped into his head. The valves in his veins clicked. Blood rushing, growling in his arteries. His vision went red, then maroon, brown, and faded to black.

Alfonso's lips sputtered drool. He squeaked.

A blow thumped him against the wall. Moriarty's hands released. Alfonso crumpled to the floor. With one arm he propped himself upright and with his other hand, grasped his throat and gulped for air.

Moriarty was drawn back. The professor's eyes shone big as poached eggs.

A huge silhouette framed his. There was no mistaking the broad shoulders and muscular arms.

Alfonso's father.

He yanked Moriarty's arm back and spun him around.

The dim light reflected across Dr. Frankenstein's spectacles and the gloss of clenched teeth showed in a grimace of animal fury.

The doctor heaved Moriarty through the door. The professor staggered to the ground and struggled to get up.

Dr. Frankenstein kicked him down. He hooked an arm around Moriarty's throat and readied a fist.

"Moriarty, I can't believe that even a degenerate like you could be this stupid and cruel."

"W...wait," Moriarty sputtered. "I lost my temper. I went go too far."

"You're not talking yourself out of this one." Dr. Frankenstein punched Moriarty's jaw.

The professor cried out.

Alfonso pushed to his feet and staggered around Sarah to the door.

His father's hulking frame—the wide back, the gigantic shoulders, the thick neck—were bent over Moriarty. Dr. Frankenstein radiated a feral, murderous energy.

Alfonso wanted to see Moriarty get his due, but he didn't like seeing his father act like a wild beast.

Dr. Frankenstein hoisted Moriarty to his feet. "I won't beat you like a dog. So get on your feet so I can beat you like a man."

Dirt and blood smeared the professor's ashen face. His lips swelled like stewed prunes.

"That's enough," a woman's voice said.

Dr. Thiên Tai stood in the gate to the alley, her petite frame needle thin. A tiny Fiat coupe idled behind her, its lights off. The passenger door was open. The front and rear ends of the car were ghosted by the aura of an inviso-beam. A Meka-Mann was behind the steering wheel.

Dr. Gefährliche unfolded himself from the cramped interior of the Fiat. He stepped forward and let one, then a second Meka-Mann unfold themselves and stand upright beside him, plasma blasters drawn.

To hold so many passengers, the Fiat must have been fitted with the latest Whovian Clown Car technology.

Pacing forward, Thiên Tai ordered, "Dr. Frankenstein, let him go. We'll see that Professor Moriarty is appropriately punished."

"How do I know you haven't come here to rescue him?"

Alfonso heard the skepticism in his father's question.

Dr. Gefährliche motioned with his finger.

One of the Meka-Mann robots aimed its blaster at Moriarty's feet. A flame twisted from the gun and lapped the professor's shoes. He danced from foot to foot. "Ow. Ow."

Dr. Gefährliche snapped his finger.

The flame disappeared, leaving the odor of scorched earth and burnt shoe leather.

Moriarty dropped to his butt and beat out his burning shoelaces. He pulled off a shoe. Smoke curled from his sock. He pulled the foot close to his face and blew on his toes.

"Other than a hot foot, what other punishment can Moriarty expect?" Dr. Frankenstein asked.

"That is for the disciplinary committee to decide," Thiên Tai answered. "At the very least, banishment."

"That's what happened to me," Alfonso's father replied, angry, "and I didn't do anything as odious as what Moriarty had done to my son and me."

Alfonso stayed in the shadows, not certain what was going to happen next. Watching evil geniuses square off was like waiting for dragons to fight.

Gefährliche motioned to Moriarty.

A chest panel on the Meka-Mann to the left clicked opened. It sheathed its blaster and drew out a pair of electro-cuffs. The chest panel clicked closed.

Electro-cuffs in its claws, the security-bot approached Moriarty.

The professor let go of his foot, his big toe poking through the scorched sock. His face swiveled from Thiên Tai and Gefährliche to the omni-eyes of the Meka-Mann. The professor presented both wrists and his expression wilted in resignation.

The security-bot placed the electro-cuffs on Moriarty's forearm. The cuffs wrapped themselves around his wrists and clinked shut.

Moriarty hunched forward to his knees and levered upright. He wore his pride like a tattered flag.

Alfonso wasn't sure what to think. Moriarty deserved much worse for what he had done as the villain responsible for their humiliation and misery.

His father grabbed Moriarty by the arm and shoved him toward Thiên Tai.

The second security-bot menaced the senior Frankenstein with its blaster.

"Easy now, Dr. Frankenstein," Thiên Tai cautioned. "Let us take care of the professor."

"Where does this leave us?" Dr. Frankenstein extended his arm across Alfonso's shoulders. "Moriarty was behind the conspiracy to impugn my reputation and get me banished. The charges against me were fraudulent."

"True. But you know the university bureaucracy." Her wig was crooked and she tipped it straight. "I've taken your place as head of the Doctorate Committee, a coveted position that I'm not going to give up. Sorry."

"Hire me as an adjunct, for now."

"No can do," Gefährliche replied. "There's no budget for it. You see, your son's escapades—"

"Escapades?" Alfonso's father asked.

Gefährliche smiled at Alfonso. "I'll let him fill you in. His escapades cost a great deal of money. You see the irony, don't you? Alfonso brought you justice but not resolution."

"You're not giving us much hope."

"You know the drill. Come up with an incredible invention—"

"A new kind of revenant?" Alfonso's dad interrupted.

"Something original," Gefährliche answered. "Enough with zombies already. Then we'll see about getting you reinstated."

"With tenure?"

"One step at a time, doctor."

Alfonso and his father traded looks. *Back to square one.*

"This way, Professor Moriarty," Dr. Gefährliche said.

The security-bot pushed the professor toward the Fiat. As Moriarty hobbled to the door and bent down, the Meka-Mann grasped the back of his head to make sure the professor didn't bump it.

The security-bot turned its wide shoulders and pulled himself inside. The second Meka-Mann followed, then Dr. Gefährliche.

Dr. Thiên Tai dismissed herself with a nod and climbed into the little Fiat.

The Fiat's headlamps flicked on, dazzling the Frankensteins. They shielded their eyes. The inviso-beam spread over the car, blurring its outline, then faded and disappeared.

Alfonso blinked. So much had happened tonight and in the quiet, it seemed like he had nothing to show for what he had done.

His father grabbed Moriarty's shoe from where it lay in the weeds and pitched it into a nearby Dumpster. He turned for the shed. "What about your friend Sarah? Is she hurt?"

"No." Alfonso squinted into the shadows inside the shed until he made out the outline of the Forgetter-Gun. He picked it up and brushed off the dust. "I used this on her."

His father took the gun.

The weight of Alfonso's need to confess pressed on him like he was at the bottom of the sea and an ocean of mistakes pressed down on him. Where to start?

Alfonso looked straight into his father's eyes. He knew to stand proud, even if he wasn't, and admit to every bit of bad judgment.

But as Alfonso began with the story of the corked bats, his father's gaze lashed him with hurt and disapproval.

"I had to beat Jerry Tremont," Alfonso said, his voice quaking.

"And did you?"

Alfonso shook his head. "Everything went wrong."

"What else?"

"I found out that Moriarty was tricking you."

"Then why didn't you tell me?"

"I would've. But there wasn't time." Alfonso launched into his explanation. "See, Moriarty-had-these-cyborgs-and-he-was-using-a-video-game-Undead-Siege-which-is-majorly-awesome-and-was-nothing-but-a-way-for-him-to-find-victims-and-to-stop-the-professor-I-needed-Sarah-to-fire-up-the-Rocket-Fish-and—"

Dr. Frankenstein pressed an index finger on Alfonso's lips. "I get it, son."

Sarah moved. She rolled to her side and sat up, opening her eyes and squeezing them shut. She cleared her throat. She shook her head, peeled her eyelids open, her face blank with incomprehension.

"What's going on?" She shot a worried look at her surroundings. "What happened?"

"You were helping Alfonso," the doctor pointed to the broken shelf and the spilled contents, "and hit your head."

In reflex, she grasped the back of her skull. "Last I remember it was late afternoon. What time is it now?"

Alfonso and his dad looked at their watches simultaneously.

The doctor said, "Almost eleven thirty."

"PM," Alfonso added.

"And I've been knocked out all this time?"

"Seems that way."

"Not cool, Dr. Frankenstein." She rolled to her hands and knees, stood awkwardly, and brushed dirt from her jeans and blouse. "I could have a bad concussion."

"It wasn't his fault, Sarah. My dad just got out here."

She glowered at Alfonso. "I thought you would've known better, Mr. Science Smarty-pants. I'm out that long and it could be major brain damage. I already got enough problems."

"How do you feel?" his dad asked.

Sarah put the back of her hand to her forehead. "I actually don't feel that bad. No headache. No nausea. Seem kinda rested, actually."

"Then you're lucky," Alfonso's dad said. "Let me walk you home and I'll explain to your mom. If she decides to take you to the doctor, let me handle the bill."

"Okay, Dr. Frankenstein." Her gaze hopped about the shed. "Funny. I remember coming here cause we were planning to do something."

Alfonso lifted his hands palms up and shrugged.

"What a shame," she said with remorse. "I can't believe I passed the time zonked out. It's a Friday night. There's supposed to be excitement. Bam. Boom."

Alfonso shrugged again.

"I better get," she said.

He remembered her backpack and found it for her.

They walked together to the sidewalk, Alfonso in step with Sarah, his father trailing. The night air was cool, refreshing, like iced lemonade soothing a parched throat.

After so much ordeal in the darkness, the neighborhood looked carnival bright. A few stars managed to shine through the glow of the streetlamps.

The wail of sirens approached. Alfonso's neck stiffened and he locked his head forward to avoid giving the idea that the shrieks interested him.

Sarah stepped into the street searching for the noise.

Several blocks down the street, a line of police cars and ambulances screamed in the direction of Ty Cobb Middle School.

CHAPTER
FIFTY

Another Monday, exactly three days since Alfonso's adventure at the University of Doom.

He sat in the grass of the commons, next to Sarah. Reginald and Candace shared a concrete bench under an oak. Squirrels chattered above.

Yesterday, Alfonso had chatted one last time with Greg Kaminski before the Undead Siege connection was shut down. Greg had told him that Moriarty and his vulture had been booted off campus.

And the dogs?

For punishment, Greg had to help Dr. Umpetha HooDoo reinstall their brains and return them unharmed to their owners.

A large squirrel scampered down the tree and stared at Alfonso. Perhaps this was the same squirrel that had provoked Moriarty's cyborgs into a wild chase and ruined his scheme.

The commons was jammed with kids, all eating sack lunches because no parent trusted any food served in the school until a lot of questions were answered.

Questions only Alfonso could answer, and he was keeping very, very quiet.

Last Friday night, the police and EMTs had been dispatched to investigate the weirdness that had happened during the Honors and Awards Banquet. One moment, Principal Mulligan was droning on about yet another baseball as life metaphor, and the next, everyone woke up smeared in Mac-n-cheese and cake frosting.

"Really bizarre," Reginald said. "Candace, Jerry Tremont, and me waking up in a pile on the floor. What kind of a practical joke was that? Gives me the chills."

"You know what else is weird?" Sarah mumbled over a mouthful of sandwich. She swallowed and then sipped from a juice box. "That I also can't remember what happened that night."

The comment wasn't directed at anyone but Alfonso felt it circle around and spear him.

"How did that happen?" Reginald asked. "You weren't at the banquet."

"I was with Alfonso. We were in his shed and a bunch of stuff fell on me and I got knocked out."

Reginald squinted and tilted his head for a close look at her. "You seem okay."

"I am, I guess." Sarah pressed the toe of her cross trainer against the bottom of Alfonso's shoe. "You got anything to add to this conversation?"

Alfonso munched a meat and bean burrito his dad had made for him. He dodged the question. "No."

"So what you thinking?" Her large eyes pressed the question.

"The usual."

"Which is?"

He said, "Stuff," but he meant returning for good to the University of Doom.

ABOUT THE AUTHOR

Mario Acevedo is the author of the bestselling Felix Gomez detective-vampire series, which includes *Rescue From Planet Pleasure* from WordFire Press. He contributed to both *Nightmares Unhinged* and *Cyber World* from Hex Publishers.